War of the Wedding Wagers

Matchmaking Mischief Makers, Book 1

Beverley Oakley

ARE YOU SIGNED UP FOR DRAGONBLADE'S BLOG?

You'll get the latest news and information on exclusive giveaways, exclusive excerpts, coming releases, sales, free books, cover reveals and more.

Check out our complete list of authors, too!

No spam, no junk. That's a promise!

Sign Up Here

www.dragonbladepublishing.com

Dearest Reader;

Thank you for your support of a small press. At Dragonblade Publishing, we strive to bring you the highest quality Historical Romance from some of the best authors in the business. Without your support, there is no 'us', so we sincerely hope you adore these stories and find some new favorite authors along the way.

Happy Reading!

CEO, Dragonblade Publishing

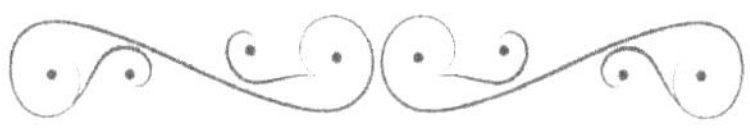

Chapter One

L ADY PENDLETON SURVEYED the ballroom activity through her lorgnette and sighed. "I must say, the debutantes this year seem far less polished than last season, when my Jane faced such worthy competition before making her brilliant match."

Lady Eugenia Townsend, who'd been gazing with rapt admiration at the young ladies in their diaphanous white muslin gowns, dancing a quadrille on the polished parquet floor, blinked. While she was rarely in agreement with the formidable Lady Pendleton, she'd learned over the years that it was pointless to offer a counter opinion.

"Doesn't Lady Nosegay look like she's just escaped the guillotine?" Lady Pendleton went on, nodding at an aged dowager in a gown of heavy burgundy brocade, adorned with outdated gold braiding. "How could her daughter let the unfortunate befuddled soul out of the house wearing such an abomination? Don't you agree, Eugenia?"

"Naturally, Lady Pendleton."

Lady Pendleton adjusted her purple toque, its ostrich feather trembling with each movement, and looked satisfied as she fanned herself with a painted ivory fan, though she said with a sniff, "It isn't wise to agree with every opinion that is aired, Eugenia. I sometimes think that is why you never married. While a man naturally wants a wife who is in agreement with him on every subject, she must also prove that she has *some* faculty for forming an opinion that is her own."

Eugenia bit her tongue as she remained seated beside her companion a little distance from the dance floor, observing the gaiety around them. Lady Pendleton neither needed nor deserved an answer to this.

"But perhaps I do you an injustice." Her old friend leaned forward to pat her hand. Even before Barbara, Lady Pendleton, was out of the schoolroom, she was acutely aware of the power she wielded. The Special Remainder allowing female succession associated with her family's title meant that, being an only daughter in the direct line of succession, she would be Lady Pendleton and whomever she married would have to take her name.

Power and status had always been important to Lady Pendleton.

"Perhaps you never met a man you wished to marry." Lady Pendleton sent Eugenia a sly smile as she leaned back in her chair. "Or perhaps you couldn't make up your mind. We were spoiled for choice during our first season. Such a long time ago, that was." She sighed. "Of course, Pendleton fell so swiftly in love with me I had barely three weeks to enjoy my debut before he'd whisked me off on our wedding tour. But I do sometimes wonder if, had I stayed longer in London that season, I might not have helped guide you in a matrimonial direction, my dear Eugenia. Alas, being such a loyal wife and mother, I was so caught up with Pendleton's political career, and the children, that for the next two decades I quite neglected my old friends. And now, here we are. My serious-minded Albert is being groomed to make an excellent viscount and my little Jane is now Lady Chance while you, my dear Eugenia… well, I don't mean to sound dampening, but life is passing you by."

Eugenia managed to look impassive, though she had to blink rapidly to keep the tears at bay. And her tongue in check.

"Well?" Lady Pendleton fixed her with a gimlet eye. "Do you not think so?"

"I am fortunate to have been well provisioned, Lady Pendleton, despite my sex precluding *me* from inheriting the viscountcy. It is rare for a woman—as in your case—to inherit both," Eugenia managed through clenched teeth, her fingers nervously smoothing the green silk of her gown. "But with my handsome fortune, why would I wish to encumber myself with a husband at my advanced age when I enjoy all the freedom I could wish for?"

Lady Pendleton leaned back as she nodded comfortably, the candlelight softening the lines of age around her eyes. "Ah yes, there we were, both the only daughters of viscounts, yet you had to see the title go to your cousin. Poor Eugenia. No title, no husband, no children when, if you'd only been born a male, you'd have had it all. But, yes, you have your freedom." She smiled as if it were now no longer of any importance to Eugenia.

The truth was that Eugenia would have willingly given up all the freedom she could have wished for if only a certain gentleman had crooked his little finger.

It had ever been thus; in her first season out, and no different now, thirty years later when Lord Thornton had reappeared last year in the London ballrooms Eugenia frequented, this time as a widower.

Lord Thornton. She closed her eyes briefly as she remembered how handsome he'd been as a young man and how distinguished he now looked.

His late wife, Alice, had been Eugenia's bosom friend.

But that was all so long ago now, and Eugenia was a fool for allowing those old feelings any license.

"Ah, Lord Thornton!" Lady Pendleton waved her fan to waylay a passing gentleman, and Eugenia's mouth was suddenly dry. In fact, it was even difficult to breathe as the man poor Alice had married (with misgivings, it might be said, when Eugenia would have walked on knives for the rest of her life to have received the same offer) appeared before them.

"What are you ladies gossiping about?" he asked with the easy familiarity of thirty years' acquaintance. "Matchmaking?"

Lady Pendleton tittered.

"Aha! And who have you paired up this evening?"

"A real gentleman would never ask such a question." Lady Pendleton gave another affected little laugh and Lord Thornton, no doubt to humor her, scanned the room, his gaze sweeping past the gilt-framed mirrors that lined the walls, then chuckled. "Aha! I spy the reclusive—some would say, mysterious—Sir Frederick emerging from the shadows with a very eye-catching golden-haired damsel in his wake."

Eugenia fanned her heated cheeks and sought vainly for inspiration when he leveled his gaze at her and suggested that, indeed, the very handsome and eligible Sir Frederick might prove an entertaining candidate for a bit of matchmaking mischief.

But it was Lady Pendleton who said, coquettishly—for she, too, was clearly not immune to Lord Thornton's chiseled features, strong jaw, and aristocratic nose—"Sir Frederick? Perhaps you are trying to deflect attention from yourself, Thornton. Might I be so bold as to wonder if you are here for the very same reasons as these young hopefuls?"

Eugenia nearly gasped out loud. *Marriage?* Could Lord Thornton really be looking for a second wife?

She was relieved by his easy laugh and answer. "Lord, no! However, I've been a widower too long and grown bored by my own society. That's why you see me here tonight—" He encompassed the room with a sweep of his arm before inclining his head at the ladies to add with his stock charm. "—Enjoying the company of the most entertaining guests at Lady Nosegay's ball."

The look he sent Eugenia caused her to bite her lip so hard that this time she did give a little gasp.

Lord Thornton fixed her with a level stare, the crystal-drop chandelier above casting a warm glow across his distinguished features. "Eugenia—?"

Yes, he called her Eugenia because Alice had insisted he Christian-name her during the agonizing dinner parties Eugenia had endured as their guest. Alice had enjoyed entertaining before the children.

"Yes, Thornton?"

His eyes, a deep, contemplative hazel flecked with gold, bored into her as she waited, breathless, for him to pose his question.

"Marriage is a serious business, would you not agree?"

"I… wouldn't know." Why had she said that? He wasn't referring to her personal experience of it.

Lady Pendleton clicked her tongue. "Eugenia hasn't an original opinion in her head. She doesn't know what she thinks, as I was observing earlier. And she certainly has no idea of who would make an ideal marriage partner. How could she since she is a spinster? Which is why I don't engage her thoughts when it comes to the matchmaking of which you've just accused us, Lord Thornton; though I would lay claim to a few successes over the years." She looked smug.

"Couples of different dispositions can make very successful marriages, I think." Eugenia stuck her chin out, quaking inwardly at Lady Pendleton's disapproving frown as a quadrille ended and couples moved across the polished floor in a swish of silk and muslin. What? For venturing an original opinion?

But Lord Thornton's interested look was sufficiently bolstering for her to go on. "The difficulty is that if one party is of a shy and retiring nature, it is a challenge for the other to find the—"

"The what, Eugenia?" Lady Pendleton snapped. "Spit it out!"

"The pearl within," Eugenia said faintly.

Perhaps her nervous humility pleased Lady Pendleton sufficiently, who said, "Why, that was very poetic, Eugenia," albeit with another of her condescending smiles.

Thornton smiled too, though not at Eugenia. His interest had returned to Sir Frederick and his young companion. "Our newly returned baronet *is* a challenge," he murmured. "I have a niece who has quite lost her heart to him. Her mama—my sister—has implored me to keep her out of his sights, even though I've reassured her that Sir Frederick will be no threat if he remains true to his proclivity for tiny, vivacious blonde damsels. My niece, Emma, you see, is chestnut-haired."

"Well, then, your sister has no need to worry."

"You would think not. However, my sister is not convinced and says she won't rest easy until Sir Frederick has made it to the altar without embroiling Emma in scandal. My observation is that, since Sir Frederick's return from the Continent, he remains interested only in bold, golden-haired young ladies with beauty and wit—of which my dear niece has neither, though she has many other redeeming qualities. However, this has not reassured my sister at all."

Eugenia gazed at Thornton's handsome profile while her mind sought desperately for a response. It was difficult to concentrate as she breathed in a waft of his bay rum cologne mingling with the sweet perfume of hothouse flowers arranged in tall Grecian urns around the ballroom. Thornton had voiced a problem. Well, a problem for his sister which manifested as irritation for himself.

Perhaps this was Eugenia's opportunity. Perhaps she could be the person who could solve Thornton's sister's concern so that she would stop vexing him, which would in turn earn Eugenia the gratitude of both… and maybe the admiration of Thornton.

These thoughts were landing so quickly with no means of outlet so that, when a tall, dark-haired young lady, soberly attired in Pomona green crossed her path, she seized her opportunity— mostly because Lady Pendleton had opened her mouth to speak.

"I maintain my belief that couples with disparate dispositions complement one another and I will prove it," Eugenia interrupted, indicating the young lady who had stopped a little distance from them to send a dispassionate look about the ballroom before she seated herself in a window embrasure half retreating behind the thick, brocade curtain.

Emboldened by Thornton's look of interest as much as by Lady Pendleton's clear disparagement, Eugenia went on, almost desperately, "If Sir Frederick has such a flamboyant, bold disposition, he needs a quiet, serious, even dull helpmate to temper his restless impulses. I propose Miss Amelia Fairchild as his ideal match."

Lord Thornton's eyebrows rose. "Surely you jest, Eugenia?"

Eugenia tried to keep her smile steady in contrast to the beating of her heart. "I do not."

"You propose that these polar opposites can be united by your devious machinations?" Thornton's voice took on a gravelly note as he leaned towards her, a collaborative look in his eye. "Are you suggesting a wager?"

Eugenia was proposing no such thing. But even if the glint in Lord Thornton's eye was due to an excess of Madeira, he was nevertheless singling Eugenia out for his especial attention. And what's more, suggesting something that, though she'd consider it outrageous under normal circumstances, had attracted his positive attention.

Why, now she thought about it, agreeing to turn it into a wager would surely facilitate further contact with the handsome viscount.

So, ignoring Lady Pendleton's scandalized look, she said, boldly, "Indeed, I am."

Even Lord Thorton looked taken aback as if he'd never imagined Eugenia would take his remark seriously. So, in case he withdrew, Eugenia thought quickly. She'd just accepted Lord Thornton's wager. What was required in a wager? Money? She had no need of money. Neither did he. No, she needed to wager something much more creative. Something Lord Thornton would find intriguing; something he might want.

But what did he want?

Then she remembered. After all, thirty years was not so long ago. She'd felt like a girl only yesterday. His visit to her father's house when she'd just reached marriageable age was imprinted on her mind. But he, five years older, had barely noticed her. No, he'd had eyes only for the painting of Persephone that graced the wall of her father's library. That painting now hung in her own drawing room.

However, she'd not forgotten how he'd admired it as he'd spoken to her father of his love of art, particularly Greek mythology.

"A wager, Lord Thornton? Why, I'll wager my Persephone if I am unsuccessful in uniting reclusive Miss Amelia Fairchild and swaggering Sir Frederick. I recall you once admired it. What will you wager?" Now she *was* being bold. The flare of surprise in his eye was gratifying and for the first time in as many years as she could remember, Eugenia felt a frisson of excitement and, yes, *need*, thrum through her body. She'd already accepted that she'd lose the beloved painting for undoubtedly Sir Frederick was as unlikely a contender for Miss Fairchild's affections as the rake was for that bluestocking's.

But what was the loss of her Persephone compared to the loss of Eugenia's heart to Thornton thirty years before? And if she could attach certain provisos to this wager, then this could be her most enjoyable season in thirty years.

That's if he even remembered what he'd wagered, she thought, her enthusiasm tempered as reality hit. Lord Thornton was, if not in his cups, then mildly inebriated. And he was an inveterate flirt—if that term could be applied to a man. The ladies loved him. He'd forget Eugenia and the wager the moment he agreed to the terms. Such a wager was nothing to him, just as Eugenia was nothing to him.

"Good lord, you inherited the Persephone? But of course. You were your father's only child. I never forgot that painting." The enthusiasm in his voice was palpable. "Why, I nearly offered for you just to get my hands on it." His eyes twinkled before he went on. "Why would you wager such an exquisite painting when you know you are bound to lose?"

Eugenia followed the look he directed towards Sir Frederick who was in a corner of the ballroom looking thunderous as he confronted the petite blonde damsel he'd just shepherded through the throng and who was bowing her head as he spoke to her. Ah yes, now she recalled who she was. Not a marital contender, but Sir Frederick's little sister, Caroline, freshly launched this season.

"Why would I wager the Persephone?" Stuck for an answer, Eugenia considered statuesque, raven-haired Miss Fairchild still seated quietly in a corner. The daughter of an old friend of hers whom she'd not seen in many years, Miss Fairchild had made her debut six years ago and had become betrothed in her first season just before her intended had gone to France to fight.

But the young man had died at Waterloo. Since then, Miss Fairchild had cut a figure of ladylike restraint and reserve, in contrast to her irrepressible brother, Edward.

"Why would I wager my Persephone?" repeated Eugenia. "Why, because I do not believe I will fail. It may not appear likely that Miss Fairchild and Sir Frederick would willingly make a match, but I intend to surprise you."

"So, as I intend to wrest from you the Persephone, there needs only for you agree to my terms—"

"Eugenia, think of your reputation! You cannot make wagers in public like this!" Lady Pendleton interjected, breaking her silence. "My dear, I have never had to speak like this to you in thirty years, but now I feel I have no choice. You do not know what you're saying!"

Eugenia considered her a moment. She'd always listened to Lady Pendleton. Taken her cue from her. Lady Pendleton had status that Eugenia would never have as a spinster, no matter that she'd inherited a fortune.

But suddenly Lady Pendleton looked like what she probably always had been: a killjoy. Or someone who couldn't bear to see Eugenia enjoy the attention of a man as handsome as Lord Thornton.

So, ignoring her friend, Eugenia asked, "You were about to propose the terms of your wager, Lord Thornton?"

His eyebrows rose a little before he smiled. "I have heard of Sir Frederick's proclivities. The gentleman is recently returned from the Continent where he was embroiled in quite a scandal with the Portuguese Consul's wife. Now I see that he is most discomposed by that little blonde chit who will no doubt be scolded by one of your arbiters of respectability for following him about like a little lamb. He will not wed Miss Amelia this year or any other, and I look forward to claiming my Persephone. In fact, so confident am I that I will soon be its proud owner that I boldly invite *you* to suggest the terms."

Eugenia was rendered speechless. He was asking what she wanted from him. How could she answer that without giving herself away?

"Come, Eugenia, there must be something that I am able to offer to match your beautiful painting. A ruby necklace? A diamond bracelet? I can afford both but I'm confident I will not have to deliver. What is your desire?"

Eugenia already had a ruby necklace and a diamond bracelet. Funds had never been in short supply.

But excitement had.

And suddenly, as Eugenia gazed about the ballroom illuminated by thousands of beeswax candles, and a dance floor filled with lovely young ladies in pale, diaphanous gowns with bright shining faces, dancing with handsome young men, she wanted to remember what it felt like to have a heart full of hope.

And if not hope, just a few moments of thrilling ecstasy to remember for the rest of her life.

"What is my heart's desire, Thornton?" she repeated as her mind spun with possibilities. Then she smiled. "If I succeed in uniting Sir Frederick with Miss Fairchild, and their marriage is agreed upon by the end of the season, why, I would like you to organize a hot-air balloon ride and to accompany me in it over the capital. You are a viscount and used to looking down on a good portion of society. But I am a spinster who spends much of her life in the country or, when in the capital, as the overlooked chaperone, relegated to a corner keeping watch over her charges. For once, I, too, would like to look down on all of society." She felt her mouth stretch as she added, "And I should *very* much enjoy your company as I crow over my success in doing what you believe I can not."

Now it was Lady Pendleton's turn to enter into the fun, though Eugenia suspected her motives were not to secure Eugenia's success when she said, "Why, I have just had the most marvelously diverting idea! I shall host a gathering at Pendleton Castle and invite Sir Frederick and Miss Fairchild and all the debutantes I can think of so that at the end of a week, we shall determine, in good faith, the winner of this wager."

She smiled at Eugenia, an undertone of malice present as she said, "Let us see how wise you were in making such a thrilling, outrageous proposal, my dear."

Eugenia inclined her head, taking a sip of her orgeat while reflecting that she'd never noticed how much Lady Pendleton's eye teeth resembled those of a young wolf.

Chapter Two

AMELIA HADN'T WANTED to come to Lady Nosegay's ball tonight. Reading a book quietly in the window embrasure of the townhouse her mother had leased for the season was her idea of an entertaining evening out; not music and dancing.

However, as her younger brother Edward had declared he wished to find himself a wife, their mama had insisted he needed a chaperone as much as any delicately reared debutante.

And a chaperone for Edward meant Amelia.

With a sigh, Amelia ignored the smile of a passing gentleman. She was not quite at the age where she could refuse to dance when it was requested, but she was certainly not going to encourage familiarity.

So far, her stony face had been sufficiently discouraging.

Just six more weeks, she reminded herself, pretending to study the weave of the heavy brocade curtains behind which she was trying to remain unobtrusive.

Six more weeks to endure all this…

She struggled to find the word to describe what it was she disliked so much and settled upon "gaiety". Gaiety and hedonism. How could people pursue pleasure when there were so many more admirable pursuits?

Like acquiring knowledge.

She sighed again and reminded herself that in six weeks, she could pursue all the knowledge she desired.

Yes, the moment Amelia turned twenty-five, she would come into the small inheritance that had been set aside for her.

Finally, she could withdraw from the marriage mart and retire to the country where her inheritance would enable her to live modestly, no longer subject to the ridiculous hopes of her deluded mama who believed that if Amelia could lose her heart once, she could lose it again.

Nor, as an independent spinster, would she be subject to the dictates of her foolish brother who had come into his majority at twenty-one and thus, as the man of the family, made the decisions that affected Amelia and their mama.

Not that Edward was unkind and dictatorial. On the contrary, he was as soft as butter, which was why he needed careful managing.

Amelia turned her head quickly to avoid the gaze of that reprobate Sir Frederick, whose reckless antics on the Continent where he'd disappeared five years before had set tongues wagging. Oh, she knew him well from her first season out and no greater contrast was there between pleasure-loving Sir Frederick and Amelia's brave and noble Thomas. Thomas had answered the call to protect his country and paid the ultimate price.

But what had Sir Frederick done other than carouse and take his pleasures as he chose?

Amelia leaned back in her chair and stared at the gilt work on the ceiling. She'd grow maudlin if she thought of Thomas, so long in the ground.

But her darling brother Edward had his future ahead of him and Amelia was pleased he was suddenly so eager to settle down to comfortable domesticity. Nevertheless, his good nature made him susceptible to the influence of others. He really needed a practical wife to counter his sentimental heart, which was why their mama had insisted Amelia keep a sisterly eye on him.

It had not been easy for Amelia to persuade Edward that she

had no wish to marry and that no man could live up to the heroism of her faithful, honorable, and beloved Thomas.

But when Edward finally understood that spinsterhood and a quiet country life would make Amelia happy, her brother had shown the extent of his tender-heartedness.

Not only had he agreed to no longer pressure Amelia to find a husband, he'd even vowed that, as he wished so greatly for his sister's happiness, he would do whatever necessary to facilitate her desires.

"If my sister wants to knit socks for one-legged returned soldiers, rather than gad about London ballrooms, she should be allowed to do it," he'd loyally declared only hours before as they'd settled themselves in the carriage that was to take them to Lady Nosegay's ball tonight.

Edward might not be the brightest star in the firmament, but he was loyal, and Amelia loved him for it.

SO, HAVING DECIDED that Edward seemed disinterested in any of the pretty debutantes here tonight, Amelia felt she could relax; especially when she saw him advancing towards her from the card room, a very pleased grin upon his face.

"I take it luck was on your side." Amelia matched his smile, for she liked to see him enjoy himself. When he found the right young lady, he'd make a doting husband, and Amelia would enjoy playing aunt to the nieces and nephews that, she hoped, would follow.

"Chance played right into my lap, sister dear." He puffed out his chest.

"I am pleased! How much did you win?"

"Patience, Amelia, my most *impatient* one. My winnings will be delivered in a few short weeks." He plucked a glass from the tray of a passing footman and handed it to his sister.

"You made a wager?"

"No need to sound so suspicious. I only make wagers when it's a sure thing."

"No wager is a sure thing, Edward." Amelia was needled by the faintest alarm. Edward looked a little too cocksure and a little too in his cups. "You haven't wagered what you can't afford to lose, have you?" Edward had little in the way of capital. Though Amelia had argued that the townhouse they'd leased for the season was larger and in a more fashionable area than they could afford, Edward and their mama maintained it was necessary to keep up appearances if he was to find the sufficiently dowered young lady with whom he wished to fall in love.

Amelia's arguments had fallen on deaf ears. Edward controlled the family finances.

"We won't be rolling up the carpets, if that's what you mean, Amelia." Edward seemed unperturbed by her concern. "And I disagree with your observation. A wager is a sure thing when, for example—" He touched the side of his nose and winked. "—a fellow overhears Sir Frederick speak of marriage to a golden-haired nymph."

Edward had made a wager on *this*? Amelia's alarm ratcheted up to monumental proportions. "Speak plainly, Edward!" she snapped. "What, exactly, are the terms of your wager? *What* have you wagered?"

Edward took a sip of his champagne, and his happy, inebriated smile broadened. Amelia followed his gaze, which narrowed in on the far corner where Sir Frederick continued in close conversation with his fair companion.

"I wagered that nothing could be more of a sure thing than Sir Frederick walking down the aisle with a tiny, golden-haired nymph before the season is ended," he said, pointing. "And, having just overheard the happy pair over yonder speak of marriage, I knew when a wager was a sure thing."

"No, Edward!"

"Yes, indeed." Edward remained unruffled by his sister's

alarm. "I told you, I overheard the happy couple speak of marriage with my very own ears. And if Sir Frederick is a happy man right now for ensuring his future, I am even happier because I've been able to secure *your* future, Amelia. That small inheritance of yours which would only allow you to live modestly? Why, I've doubled it. In a few short weeks—"

Amelia's horror culminated with an enraged gasp. "You've wagered my *inheritance?*" She began to tremble. "On the fact Sir Frederick will marry in six weeks—?"

"Exactly. *A golden-haired siren*, I believe, was the term since it was based on the description of the young lady to whom I overheard him speak of marriage."

"But Edward—"

"Calm down, sis. It's a sure bet, I tell you, and in fact I'm very sorry to hear that you think I've lost your inheritance when in fact I've ensured—"

"You haven't! And my inheritance was yours to hold in *trust* until my twenty-fifty birthday, Edward! And that's only six weeks away. Please don't tell me you've wagered it *all* on a bet you are about to *lose.*"

Edward patted her shoulder with that same fond, frighteningly inebriated smile upon his face and said, reassuringly, "I've just returned from writing it up in White's Betting Book—"

"No, Edward!"

"Indeed, I have. You see, it's like legal insider trading. I saw with my own eyes Sir Frederick disappear into a dark corner with that engaging little blonde chit—just the kind I've heard he's partial to—and when I followed them, I heard him very distinctly, speak of marriage—"

"But Edward—"

"My dear Amelia, when Sir Frederick announces his betrothal to a golden-haired maiden within days—though I've been cautious and allowed six weeks—Roger Morley will have to hand over twice the size of your inheritance. And, just so you can buy as many books as you like, and to prove how fond a brother I am,

I shall give it *all* to you. In six weeks, when Sir Frederick walks down the aisle with his diverting blonde, you will be able to retire to the country a rich woman."

"No, Edward!" Amelia clapped her hands to her mouth. "I can't believe what you're saying!" She pointed to the couple her brother had indicated. "There is Sir Frederick, but if that is the blonde young lady to whom you heard him speak of marriage, then Hell will freeze over before he weds her!"

"Amelia!" He was shocked. "It is unlike you to blaspheme and certainly not in public. How can you possibly know—"

"Because she's his *sister!*"

There was no satisfaction in seeing the dismay on her brother's face. Amelia knew Edward had acted with the best of intentions. It's what made matters worse.

"But, sis, I really thought—I mean, I was so sure I was doing you a favor—"

"Yes, Edward, I know—"

"Sir Frederick has only been back in the country a couple of months and there's been no mention of a sister."

"Yes, Edward, I know all that. Sir Frederick has been gallivanting on the Continent, no doubt up to his usual antics, for I remember what a swaggering braggart he was during my first season out, though he certainly fooled my fellow debutantes at the time." Assailed by memories, Amelia had to steady herself with a hand upon the back of a chair as she went on, "And his sister is very young to be out. Only seventeen, and still in the schoolroom several months ago. However, their mama is ailing, and Caroline is very headstrong, so it was decided to launch her early in order to secure her future to the old man's satisfaction. In fact, she's so lively and easily-led, I heard it whispered Sir Frederick was afraid she'd climb out of her bedroom window and elope with a fortune hunter, so I don't wonder you've never heard of her. And with a reputation for being so headstrong, it's little surprise her brother, Sir Frederick, has found some reason to take her to task tonight. No doubt you heard the word marriage because Sir Frederick was cautioning her on its *dangers*."

Edward's mouth dropped open. "How do you know all this, Amelia? I thought you took no interest in these things." He waved his arm about to encompass the room as his gaze narrowed and he added, suspiciously, "In fact, I thought you had no interest in anyone here tonight, and certainly not Sir Frederick."

"Lord, Edward, what do you take me for? I'd marry a goldfish before I married a swaggering lothario like Sir Frederick!"

Amelia brought her hand to her mouth a second time, for that gentleman was in fact passing them by that very moment and, at the sound of his name, he frowned. But he continued with a polite incline of his head, albeit a slight flaring of his nostrils.

Amelia's cheeks flamed. "Lord, Edward, what if he heard me?" she whispered. "But worse! What if he learns of your wager? Oh, do go and strike it out this very minute!"

Edward bit his lip. "I might succeed in getting it removed from *public* view, but the fact is that Morley ain't going to release me from it."

"So, he was the only one who saw you write up the wager?"

Edward nodded.

"Then do what you can to erase it from White's Betting Book. Or at least from making it appear publicly. As for Roger Morley, you'll have to deal with him when the time comes." Amelia's shoulders sagged. But no, she could not show her distress in public. She prided herself on her stoicism. After brave, beloved Thomas had died a hero's death, society had expected her to weep and wail like a lovelorn snowdrop. But she'd proved she was as different from her mother as it was possible to be. The battle had been hard won, but she'd fought her grief and presented to the world the face of a woman who could survive any pain or disappointment life threw at her. She'd not allowed emotion to fell her then, and she'd not do so now.

Tears and self pity were not her recourse.

But action was.

"Edward," she said, putting her hand on his shoulder and forcing him to meet her gaze. His eyes were a little bloodshot and hazy, but she knew he was attending. "Tell me exactly the terms of the wager."

"I did tell you, Amelia. That Sir Frederick would announce his betrothal and walk a vivacious, blonde vixen down the aisle before six weeks was up."

Amelia nodded. "That sounds simple enough," she said, forcing a smile. "Now we just need to make sure he does."

"Excuse me, Miss Fairchild." A delicate clearing of the throat interrupted Edward's response as Lady Townsend insinuated herself into their circle.

Amelia wouldn't have minded if it had only been the older woman whom she had met but a few times with her mama in the days when Lady Fairchild showed her face in society.

Making the situation even more uncomfortable was the gentleman at her side and to whom it appeared she wished to introduce Amelia.

Sir Frederick.

He was the last person Amelia wished to meet now that Sir Frederick's marital situation suddenly determined whether Amelia could enjoy the remainder of her life as a contented spinster in the country.

Or—God forbid!—be forced to find herself a husband if she no longer had the means to keep herself, thanks to Edward.

Another thought intruded.

Amelia's future depended upon ensuring Sir Frederick's heart was captured by a petite, vivacious blonde. Of course, Amelia must smile and be gracious if only to break the ice so she could begin, at the earliest, introducing to him all the petite, vivacious blondes she could find in the hopes that one of them would appeal to the gentleman.

"Miss Fairchild, I came to ask after your dear mama," the older woman said. "I am sad I no longer see her about, for she was a friend of mine, as she was of Sir Frederick's mama. In fact, I prevailed upon him to join me in sending you my greetings, for he tells me you have already been introduced."

"A long time ago." Amelia inclined her head, forcing a polite smile, but not succeeding so successfully in hiding her skepticism when Lady Townsend added, "Sir Frederick has been pursuing his interest in the antiquities during his five years on the Continent. Like you, my dear, he has a great love of learning and I'm sure the pair of you would have much to discuss."

Chapter Three

T HE AMUSEMENT SIR Frederick felt at seeing the normally collected Miss Fairchild positively flaming with mortification was fleeting.

Why should he expend any thought, much less interest, on a female who clearly held him in such low regard?

It was a long time ago, now, but he'd once admired Miss Fairchild for her charm and humor. He remembered the way her dark eyes had sparkled as they'd discussed Roman antiquities over lemonade at Almack's.

They'd danced a few sets together, her infectious laugh drawing envious glances from other gentlemen as they'd discussed literature and debated the merits of various classical artists.

But that was before Thomas Blackheath, with his severe black clothing and permanently furrowed brow, had proved himself a more desirable candidate.

Sir Frederick had been surprised by how quickly they'd become betrothed.

Then Blackthorn had gone to fight for King and country, leaving behind a changed Miss Fairchild, her vibrant spirit dimmed like a candle snuffed too soon.

No, Blackthorn was not a man Sir Frederick had cared for, with his dour and killjoy demeanor that masqueraded as a serious concern for his fellow creatures, his lips thinning in disapproval at the slightest hint of frivolity, as though joy itself were a sin.

He'd been a do-gooder who had killed Miss Fairchild's joyful spirit with his endless lectures on propriety and duty before he, in turn, had got himself killed at Waterloo. The last time Sir Frederick had seen Miss Fairchild laugh with genuine delight had been just before her betrothal was announced, when they'd been examining a collection of Roman coins at Lord Pembroke's soirée.

Sir Frederick smiled at the recollection. He'd kissed her that night. He remembered it well.

And then she'd pledged her troth to Blackheath.

After Blackheath's death, Miss Fairchild had never been the same, and while Frederick could have dealt with the fact she had little interest in replacing Thomas in her affections, it did rankle that she seemed to have formed such a poor opinion of Sir Frederick's character.

I'd marry a goldfish before I married a swaggering lothario like Sir Frederick...

That was a bit low, he thought; but, it was said on account of several public liaisons with women that had not reflected well on him, though Miss Fairchild clearly did not know the full picture of his exploits abroad.

Then again, few did, and that was how it had to be. Fortunately, that had not meant he had a shortage of female admirers.

Nevertheless, Miss Fairchild's declaration suggested that she was not of a forgiving nature. Clearly, encroaching spinsterhood had made her bitter.

Well, best to discover that now, for the truth was that he'd always admired Miss Fairchild. Not only did her dark, glossy curls, creamy complexion with an elegant straight nose, and intelligent blue gaze make her easy on the eye but she was not one of these desperate-to-be-noticed misses who seemed to be thrust under his nose every five minutes since it was presumed that his continued bachelorhood after five years on the Continent meant he was after an English wife.

"I remember, Miss Fairchild, your mama telling me many years ago, that you'd borrowed a book whose description of the Acropolis had greatly interested you. No doubt Sir Frederick has actually seen that ancient monument," said Lady Townsend with a pursed little smile to set off her bobbing gray ringlets.

Frederick waited, then murmured, "Indeed I have." Perhaps Miss Fairchild, being now put on the spot, was about to offer the olive branch. She surely must know he'd heard her barbed remark about him to her brother and wished to atone.

Instead, she merely inclined her head and murmured, "I wonder if Sir Frederick had time for more than a passing glance at the Acropolis or the Masters in the Louvre or the Uffizi Gallery. Certainly, his appreciation for the ladies on the Continent has become well known."

Ouch.

Sir Frederick matched her saccharine smile while his thoughts raced. Was she referring to his affair with Lady Langbourne? And yet, that was his only properly low moment in five years away. Lonely, neglected Lady Langbourne held a regular salon in Paris patronized by the greatest minds of Europe, and she had invited Sir Frederick to attend.

Frederick had been in his element. And when Lady Langbourne, a ripe and generous beauty, had singled him out for attention, Frederick had not been averse. Besides, he was not giving his heart—or anything else—to anyone who'd care long term for it.

But Miss Fairchild clearly knew a great deal about the beauties and wonders he had seen with his own eyes. He had few enough people of like mind with which to discuss them, so perhaps a few moments discoursing on the Acropolis and the statue of David—well, perhaps not David—might thaw the ice between them and improve his impression upon her.

He was about to open his mouth to give the lie to the assumption—no, the rather insulting charge she'd just insinuated—

that he'd not in fact visited these wonders when she suddenly cried, "Pray, there is Miss Mannerly and I do know she's been dying to make your acquaintance, Lady Townsend."

As the small, shapely blonde with cornflower blue eyes and rosebud lips that Miss Fairchild had just hailed, turned in their direction, Frederick was about to make his excuses when Miss Fairchild beseeched him to stay with the words, "You cannot be so unmannerly as to refuse to meet my dear friend Miss Mannerly," before asking Lady Townsend to perform the introductions.

Frederick was stupefied. He'd spent nearly the entire two weeks since he'd returned from the Continent avoiding this young woman whom he'd heard had singled him out, particularly as a would-be suitor. Her dowry was ample and her lineage exceptional, but she was as flighty as a butterfly. He didn't need to be introduced to her to know this, having observed her multiple times from a distance. And each time she'd deliberately caught his eye from afar, Frederick had made a point of disappearing to another room. Miss Mannerly was just the kind of young woman he deplored and now Miss Fairchild was ensuring they were acquainted, which would put all sorts of onerous obligations upon him.

"Sir Frederick, Miss Mannerly was saying only yesterday that she'd like nothing more than to hear all about your exploits on the Continent," Miss Fairchild said sweetly. "I'm sure you can never have enough of an audience of the kind Miss Mannerly has promised to be. Please excuse me, for I see my brother trying to attract my attention."

And then she was gone, and Sir Frederick was left with the garrulous Miss Mannerly as she talked without a pause in one long monologue about how much she would adore to see all the wondrous sights he had seen and how steeped in history she felt when she gazed at the books in her learned papa's library yet it barely could be believed that Sir Frederick had seen the sights they contained with his very own eyes.

And when Sir Frederick finally got a word in edgewise to ask reluctantly, "What would you like to see most out of all the great treasures and sights in Europe?" She was speechless.

In fact, she could not name one.

And it wasn't that she was tongue-tied with embarrassment.

Sir Frederick sighed inwardly, though he smiled with what might pass muster as indulgence as Miss Mannerly had focused a rather panicked look upon him.

Really, he thought. Of all the vacuous blondes he'd had the misfortune to meet, Miss Mannerly must be the most airheaded of all.

While there in the corner of the ballroom, Miss Fairchild was in earnest conversation with her brother.

He wondered what they were talking about. Young Edward Fairchild was not the brightest star, but he was pleasant and it was clear his sister was vastly fond of him.

Frederick thought how nice it would be if Miss Fairchild leveled just such an easy countenance upon him as they discoursed on some mutually enjoyable topic.

Chapter Four

AMELIA PACED THE generously proportioned drawing room of their too-expensive townhouse as she tried to think.

Edward and their mother looked on gravely.

"Edward!" she said, looking up suddenly. "I need you to make me a list of every even half-eligible petite blonde damsel you know and can think of. Now!"

"Really, Amelia, I hardly think Edward would be able to come up with six names off the top of his head," their mother remonstrated. She disliked it when her daughter adopted what she called her "fierce, masculine tone." "Edward is far more discerning than that. And I'm not sure he even wants to narrow his list of prospectives to simply blonde young ladies. Why would he?"

"Where's paper and pencil?" Edward responded, ignoring their mother and immediately scrawling an impressive dozen names which had Mrs. Townsend blinking in surprise.

Amelia too.

"Are there really that many eligible young ladies swanning around ballrooms... that are blonde?" Mrs. Fairchild asked. "Blonde ones? What an admirable eye for detail you do have, Edward."

"Next thing is introductions," Amelia went on, ignoring their mother. "Discounting Miss Mannerly, please tick three to begin with. Your top three picks, if you please. Naturally, that's barring any whose acquaintance you wish to further. Remember, the object of this exercise is to find Sir Frederick's perfect match."

Mrs. Townsend gave a loud exclamation of wonder before letting out a beatific sigh. "Didn't I give birth to such a thoughtful pair? You have your own futures to worry about and yet, out of the goodness of your hearts, you are trying to match make for Sir Frederick. Where did you get such an idea? Has his sister petitioned you? Perhaps she knows you are not a participant in the marriage mart, though I do wish you'd reconsider, Amelia. Are you really so set on this idea of quiet independence and living alone in some cottage by the sea? What people will think, I don't know, though you have finally made me understand there can never be another contender for your heart now that poor Thomas is gone, God rest his soul. Yet, you'd do this for Sir Frederick or rather for his sister? Ah dear, but it is not a secret that his poor ailing mama despairs of him ever finding a young lady who will keep his interest. As for her fears regarding Miss Caroline, well! That tearaway miss is destined for trouble, just mark my words. She must be kept right off that list and away from my Edward."

"I doubt if we can find a young lady to keep Sir Frederick's interest, mama," Amelia said snidely. "I should think that almost impossible. But if we can ensure he's not distracted by the next shiny new thing long enough to walk one of these young ladies down the aisle, then I can happily say our work is done."

"Miss Pickford, Miss Penny, and Miss Playford." Edward, who'd been leaning over the occasional table by the window, put down his pencil loudly.

"Ah, the three Ps," said Amelia. "Who do you suppose is the most winning out of the Miss P trio?"

"Well, Miss Penny has a pug she never stops gushing over. And Sir Frederick is sure to like animals. What say we start here?"

Amelia sent him a dubious look. "I'm not sure we can assume

Sir Frederick likes animals when he is primarily interested in himself. But perhaps he'd find common ground as long as Miss Penny is comely, blonde, and eligible. We have to start somewhere."

"And how do you propose to get them introduced, much less interested in one another?" asked Edward. "Oh, I know! Miss Penny is a friend of Sir Frederick's sister. He may know her already yet not realize the diamond dangled in front of his nose. That'll be our job."

Mrs. Fairchild gave another sigh. "Ah, Edward, you are so good to those around you and to your sister. What would Amelia do without you?"

Amelia raised her head to spear her brother with a look. "I wouldn't know where to begin, Mama," she said in a tone that had the desired effect for Edward forbore to reply and simply reddened at the not-so veiled rebuke.

Chapter Five

ANOTHER BALLROOM BUT the same crop of debutantes—more or less, plus a sprinkling of flirtatious widows.

Sir Frederick deplored these events, but with a flighty younger sister who needed an especially keen eye kept upon her at all times, it seemed, he had little choice but to throw himself into the social mill.

With their mama so ill, their father gone these past few years, and their older sister married and established in the north, Caroline had no one else to ensure she survived to adulthood without making a disastrous match. And despite his earlier success at nipping in the bud her efforts at inveigling herself into the company of that inappropriate cad, the monstrously wealthy upstart, Mr. Algernon Greene, she seemed determined to thwart her brother at every turn.

In fact, Frederick had his eye on Caroline and Mr. Greene right now and was just considering moving across the ballroom to draw Caroline away, when Lady Townsend appeared at his elbow, saying, as she followed his gaze, "What a delightfully charming sister you have. I have no doubt her season is destined to be a successful one. What a handsome young man beside her, though a little old for her, perhaps. Is that Mr. Greene?" A concerned frown creased her forehead for Caroline was not with her chaperone, Mrs. Robins, whom Frederick could see laughing with another gentleman a little distance away.

"It is indeed," he said grimly, "and I was just about to intervene—"

"As is only right. Oh, but here is Miss Fairchild. Perhaps she can offer chaperonage if that is what you are concerned about. Miss Fairchild!"

Before Frederick could stop her, Lady Townsend had hailed the dark-haired beauty over to her side. She really was a beauty, thought Frederick. Her self-composed serenity had quite forcibly struck him during her first season out when she was so different from giggling chits like Miss Penny, who was Caroline's bosom friend.

Caroline might be of a lively disposition, but at least she wasn't so cheerfully... vocal... as Miss Penny. Or as vocal as the frightful little pug the young lady carried around whenever she was visiting Caroline, and which had taken a decided disliking to Frederick. Indeed, the feeling was mutual. Frederick liked large, self-confident dogs. Not yappy lap dogs.

"Good evening, Lady Townsend." Miss Fairchild bobbed a curtsy and inclined her head, smiling a little at Frederick before turning in the direction of Lady Townsend's meaningful look.

"Your sister appears to be enjoying a lively conversation with Mr. Greene," she said, stating the obvious but obviously not understanding the gravity. Well, in Frederick's eyes.

"Mr. Greene is ten years too old for her and has not of the kind of temperament I would wish for my sister."

"He is also enormously wealthy. However, do you wish me to join them and perhaps draw her away?" Miss Fairchild suggested with beautiful acuity.

"I would like that very much," said Sir Frederick, watching her graceful form part the throng while Lady Townsend said, "Such a charming and accomplished young lady. She is as beautiful on the outside as she is on the inside. And that's from someone who has known her since she was a child. No surprising temper tantrums with that one. And so very knowledgeable."

Her admiration was cut short by the return of Miss Fairchild and a glowering Caroline who nevertheless appeared to be trying to rein in her temper as she greeted the pair of them, adding in a whisper while the other ladies exchanged several words, "It does seem a coincidence that my innocent conversations with Mr. Greene are forever being interrupted, brother. I would just like to understand your objection. Not only is Mr. Greene vastly wealthy and most charming, he is in line for a viscountcy. There! Does that change your mind, brother dear?" Angling herself a little away from Miss Fairchild as if she understood that she was being childish, she put her nose in the air.

"I know all about Mr. Greene's claims to a bogus title, and I'm surprised you've fallen for it, Caroline." Frederick tried not to let her words irritate him, but she was so young. She'd learn. He just needed to make sure she had time to grow up a little before she fell victim to someone as smooth and charming as Greene.

"Last time you sent Henry to drag me away, as I recall."

"And I'd have done the same again except Miss Fairchild was on hand. Ah, Henry, did you in fact hear us speak your name? Caroline is looking for a partner for the next dance. Perhaps you'd oblige. But first, I must introduce to you these distinguished ladies."

The tousle-haired youth, with a dusting of freckles and a cheerful expression who'd just arrived in their midst, bowed to the ladies before giving Caroline a grin. "Causing your big brother palpitations again, are you? It's that Greene fellow, isn't it? Mighty dashing, and I do admire his adorable brown curls and handsome side whiskers. Just like that Sir Walter Scott hero you were telling me about. But Caro, let me fetch you some lemonade. In fact, why don't you come with me because I've just seen..." He lowered his voice but Frederick heard very clearly that he was inviting her to covertly inspect some poor woman in a purple toque whom he'd spied and clearly wished to parody. It was ever thus with the pair of them, he thought, with something between fondness and exasperation.

With Caro giggling like a schoolgirl, Frederick could see that Lady Townsend and Miss Fairchild had also overheard so, shaking his head, Frederick explained. "The pair of them are like school children when they are together. Henry lives on the neighboring estate and they grew up together. At least I can count on Henry to some extent to keep Caro out of trouble, if only by enticing her away from fortune hunters like Greene."

"And what constitutes a fortune hunter, Sir Frederick?" Miss Fairchild asked. "Either female or male. I am curious. You see, I was under the impression Mr. Greene had quite a fortune and was in no need of an heiress."

"Mr. Greene's reputation is not all that he makes it out to be. I have heard concerning things. But, you ask me what I consider constitutes a fortune hunter?" Frederick considered her question. "Why, simply when marriage is based on pecuniary considerations *before* character."

"Pity the couple who has not a penny between them," said Miss Fairchild. "Would you suspect every young lady without a fortune behind her of less than honorable motives if she smiled at you?"

"Why, Miss Fairchild, that is an interesting question," Lady Townsend murmured, while Frederick, too, thought it rather direct. Still, it was refreshing…

"Take, for example, Miss…" she appeared to be scanning the room before she settled upon a young blonde miss looking longingly at the dance floor while the matrons on either side of her prattled away. "Miss Playford is a charming young lady without a fortune. Yet she has so many other graces and accomplishments. What is it that you are looking for in a young lady?"

"Lord, I'm not in the market for a bride!" Frederick exclaimed with such vehemence that Miss Fairchild jumped before glancing with slight concern at Lady Townsend who blushed and stammered, "But if the right one happened to come along you'd surely not be averse."

"But the right one has not come along," said Frederick regaining his good humor. "And I am not looking. Now, pray excuse me, but I have claimed Miss Barrow for this dance."

As the tall gentleman stalked through the crowd, Amelia turned to Lady Townsend with a frown. "I fear I must have misunderstood you, Lady Townsend, for I was certain you elicited my help in narrowing down the prospective matrimonial pool for Sir Frederick, who, I was led to understand, was looking for a wife."

Indeed, Lady Townsend's words had been welcome and percipient, for it supplied Amelia with just the excuse she needed to plumb the depths of Sir Frederick's interest in a manner that would not appear odd or calculating.

If Amelia could discover the character traits that appealed to Sir Frederick, it would enable her to find the right "blonde" young lady who possessed such attributes.

But how dampening to learn that the gentleman seemed almost averse to the idea of marriage.

Particularly when Amelia needed him to marry in six weeks, if she was to enjoy any kind of a future, she thought gloomily.

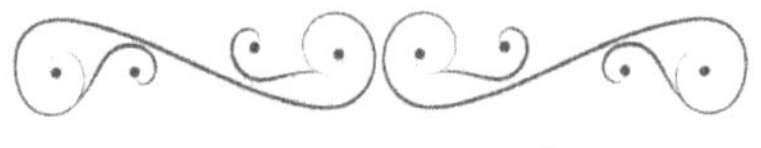

Chapter Six

"WELL, EUGENIA, IT didn't look as if your meddlesome antics achieved your aim of uniting Sir Frederick and Miss Fairchild in any meaningful way. I think you should simply give up your idea as a lost cause."

Lady Pendleton's look was smug, not sympathetic, as she went on, "Maybe I needn't go to the bother of hosting my Ghostly Gathering at Pendleton Castle so the pair can get to know one another. That, my dear, is what I'd been thinking of doing *purely* for your benefit, given our long friendship."

Eugenia smiled. She'd learned that Lady Pendleton was full of talk but rarely followed through on her grandiose plans.

It didn't matter.

By hook or by crook, Eugenia *was* going to find a way to unite Miss Fairchild and Sir Frederick.

For she had quite simply set her heart on a hot air balloon ride over London with Lord Thornton.

Lady Pendleton surveyed the company. "Such predictable dreariness," complained her friend leaning back. The dissatisfaction on her face made her look old and peevish. Eugenia touched her throat as a sudden thought occurred to her. Did she have a turkey neck like Lady Pendleton's?

"And nothing to look forward to with my daughter launched

and, predictably, having made the match of the season," her friend went on before her eyes widened. "However, there is, of course, my duty to Caroline!" Her sudden clap of the hands made Eugenia jerk forward in fright, as the young girl passed by on the arm of Mr. Greene. "Why, I do believe I shall do it, Eugenia! Yes! I shall hold that Ghostly Event, after all. A haunted castle week in the country. Pendleton may not think it a wonderful idea but he really has no say in the matter. And dear Caroline is my god-daughter. It would be such a kindness to her. Everyone will say it."

Eugenia regarded her friend thoughtfully. Poor Pendleton had never had much say in anything. Lady Pendleton had inherited the viscountcy which had been created two hundred years before with a Special Remainder for Female Inheritance.

The former viscount had had to change his name to that of his wife and allow her to make all the decisions as per the stipulations made at the time the viscountcy was created. Eugenia often wondered if he'd thought it worth the cost to his pride.

"A ghost gathering. It so happens I'm fascinated by ghosts," Eugenia lied, trying to think of any exposure to ghosts, or talks in which she'd participated. "As you say, there is only so much of such dreariness one can take." She thrust out her chin—while smoothing her neck for Lord Thornton was somewhere about—and surveyed the room once more.

There he was, she thought in sudden excitement, her eyes alighting on handsome Lord Thornton who, perhaps feeling the intensity of her gaze, turned and immediately came in their direction.

His smile was as lazy and confident as Eugenia remembered. He'd never suffered from self-doubt. "I saw Miss Fairchild and Sir Frederick briefly confer with one another as a result of your clever engineering, Eugenia," he remarked.

"Pure chance," argued Lady Pendleton. "The pair has nothing in common so trying to force them to even like each other is a lost cause. See how Sir Frederick watches over his little sister while Miss Fairchild clearly disdains society. There she is in her tucked-away corner looking like she'd rather be anywhere than here. Nothing more calculated to put off a man than disinterest."

"I don't know about that." Thornton shrugged. "Thrill of the chase and all that. I'd wager most men are more intrigued by disinterest than a female who hangs off their very word."

"In which case, Miss Fairchild and Sir Frederick are not a lost cause," said Eugenia. "My cunning plan might, in fact, unite them."

"A cunning plan, Eugenia?" repeated Thornton admiringly. "I didn't think cunning plans were your preserve. I thought you very demure and conventional."

"Perhaps I was when I was younger and forced to hide the wild spirit that my father said would be my undoing," Eugenia said bravely.

"Wild spirit? Goodness, Eugenia! I think you've said too much!" Lady Pendleton admonished her but Thornton grinned.

"So what is your cunning plan, pray tell?"

"It is actually my cunning plan," said Lady Pendleton sounding bored. "I had been thinking of holding a ghost-hunting week at the Castle. That's if the old pile hasn't fallen down since we were there last August."

Eugenia clapped her hands. "I think it a wonderful idea, Lady Pendleton, for it will serve as the arbiter as to whether you are right and my match-making will come to nothing."

Her calculated plan bore fruit. Predictably, Lady Pendleton's nostrils flared as she said, "Of course, your matchmaking will come to nothing, Eugenia. Sir Frederick and Miss Fairchild? It's not difficult to see why you never married if you think such a pairing even within the realms of possibility."

Even Lord Thornton seemed to think this a little harsh for he said, "I do see merit in an event that might relieve the *ennui* of events like this. A ghostly challenge, eh? Well, with Sir Frederick a known skeptic, and with Lady Pendleton seeing no *earthly* means that your mismatched young people will find themselves suddenly attracted to one another, perhaps the services of an obliging ghost might just do the trick."

Lady Pendleton sniffed. "You will lose your Persephone to Lord Thornton, Eugenia, and I have a mind to insist on my own reward for being proved right."

"So, are we to dress up as ghosts, Lady Pendleton?" Eugenia asked, knowing she sounded much too eager; but really, this was the most excited she'd felt in a long time.

"Dress up as a ghost?" Lady Pendleton repeated with clear disgust, her lorgnette trembling as she raised it to her eyes. "Pendleton Castle is overrun with ghosts. I don't need my guests confusing matters."

"Well, well, Lady Pendleton, I had not thought you a believer," Lord Thornton marveled, studying her with newfound interest. "And pray tell, which is the most troublesome of your ghostly cavalcade?"

"My great-great aunt Pernilla," Lady Pendleton said, absently touching the heavy gold ring that bore her family crest. "But as I am an avowed skeptic, I believe it's only because of her unusual and early demise that various family members have conflated her into some tragic heroine."

"Ooh, how exciting!" Eugenia rubbed her hands together then immediately felt childish as her friend raked her with a beetling look.

"Defying one's parents to follow one's youthful heart earned Ancestor Pernilla her just desserts," Lady Pendleton declared. "Well, now that you have pressured me into a great deal of work, Eugenia, I trust you will make yourself available tomorrow to help me draw up a guest list."

"Do we really need anyone other than Sir Frederick and Caroline? And, of course, Miss Fairchild?" asked Eugenia, who'd decided she would not have her spirits dampened by her old friend.

"Good lord, Eugenia." Lady Pendleton's fan snapped open with unnecessary force. "You don't suppose I shall go to all that trouble for only a handful of thanks. No, this will be a grand event held during the full moon, with a Ghostly Rout, a Treasure Hunt, dancing, and a feast. After all, one must maintain appearances when one holds a title."

"Bravo," said Thornton. "You will outdo yourself."

Lady Pendleton sniffed. "If I am to put myself out doing anything, there are no half measures."

"And how do you think Pendleton will like the idea of a Ghostly Rout, a Treasure Hunt, dancing, and a feast?" asked Lord Thornton. He cleared his throat. "It won't be a cheap exercise."

"Pendleton will do as he's told, like he always does."

Eugenia and Thornton glanced at each other but were silent.

Pendleton had had a fortune when he'd married, but his wife wielded the power with her title and estates, the upkeep of which relied heavily on Pendleton's funds.

"No, this Ghostly Event will be the highlight of the season," said Lady Pendleton. "I predict that Caroline will meet her match and that your instincts, my dear Eugenia—when it comes to matchmaking—are quite off the mark."

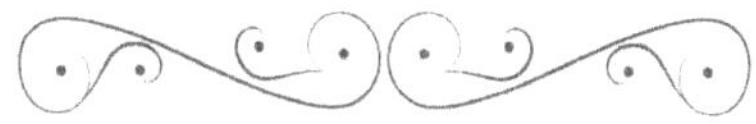

Chapter Seven

"ARE YOU SURE you're going to be warm enough, Amelia?" Mrs. Fairchild fussed, adjusting the fur trim on her daughter's traveling cloak for the third time as the horses stamped and snorted in the cool air in the shafts of the carriage. "I just fear you might catch a chill. I've heard Pendleton Castle has not been maintained as well as Lady Pendleton's other houses, so I worry that her attempts at authenticity might involve freezing, rather than frightening, her guests to death."

The fact that this was not said with an attempt at humor made Amelia smile, even as she caught the shadow of real concern in her mother's eyes.

"I'm sure Lady Townsend and some of the other guests who will surely be invited by Lady Pendleton will have reassured themselves of sufficient comfort," Amelia said as she put her foot on the carriage step.

"And I hear that handsome Sir Frederick is going to Lady Pendleton's Ghostly Affair, too," Mrs. Fairchild went on happily. "Are you sure you don't wish to further your acquaintance with that gentleman for there was a time when I did think you and he—"

She trailed off at Amelia's look, while Edward said, firmly, as he followed his sister into the carriage, "Sir Frederick's preference is for blondes. Besides, Amelia is much too serious for a man of his tastes."

"I did think him a fine young man all those years ago," Mrs. Fairchild persisted. "Why, before Thomas—"

Amelia's hand jerked away from the locket she'd been fingering. The one Thomas had given her. "You thought Sir Frederick a fine young man?" she repeated, her voice sharper than she intended. "When could you ever have thought that? When Thomas went to fight for King and country, Sir Frederick disappeared to the Continent for many years of revelry." Her voice caught slightly on the word "disappeared," remembering that last assembly before he'd left.

He'd kissed her.

It was something she'd never forget.

The tension in her voice made Edward look at her curiously, but before her wide-eyed mother could respond, the footman had slammed the door, and they were trotting down the driveway.

"Thank you for not revealing to Mama what I'd done." Edward looked downcast for only a second before he leaned forward, his eyes bright with that dangerous gleam Amelia had come to dread. "But this weekend will be a master stroke in cunning and ingenuity. And I feel sure that the consequences of my actions that have put you so out of countenance will result in great rewards. Sir Frederick will find the wife of his dreams, and your inheritance will be doubled."

Amelia smiled at him. How could she feel cross with Edward for long with his enthusiasm to not only atone but to make everything even better? Yet that familiar twist of anxiety in her stomach reminded her of how his "improvements" typically ended—with her scrambling to contain the damage.

"Well, please consult me before you embark on anything too outrageous. Two heads are better than one."

Edward chuckled as he patted the large wooden box on the seat beside him. "I didn't think you'd seen what I had specially made, but yes, it is a second head which I shall wear as part of my costume for the Masquerade Ball." His fingers drummed an excited rhythm on the box's lid.

"Who? Janus?" Amelia couldn't hide her surprise, nor the note of apprehension that crept into her voice.

"Janus indeed, and a nod to my love of Roman mythology, and fascination for the god of beginnings, transitions, and some other things I've since forgotten. The head has two faces looking in opposite directions. You will be astonished, as will all the young ladies who'll think me awfully cultured." He sat back, clearly pleased with himself.

Amelia shuddered, watching the autumn landscape blur past the carriage window. "A ghost is bad enough but a head with a face on both sides is bound to send any young lady running in the opposite direction."

"And if that opposite direction is into the arms of Sir Frederick, then isn't that clever? Oh, do compliment me on my imagination, Amelia. You think you're the imaginative one of the family." The carriage hit a rut, making Edward's box slide slightly on the seat. He quickly steadied it with a protective hand.

"Oh, not true at all. You, Edward, have often shown you have the imagination for more than the two of us."

"I do have a good imagination, don't I, sis?" Edward looked smug while inside Amelia quailed. There was a time when Edward had confided everything to his sister, when they'd shared secrets over stolen biscuits in the nursery and plotted harmless pranks together in the garden. But lately, with the wager being the worst of it, he was increasingly acting spontaneously. The fact Edward had not told her of his costume suggested he might well have other plans up his sleeves that he'd not consulted about with Amelia. She watched him from beneath her lashes as he hummed contentedly to himself, wondering what other surprises he had in store.

So much depended upon the next few days.

And one misstep could mean disaster.

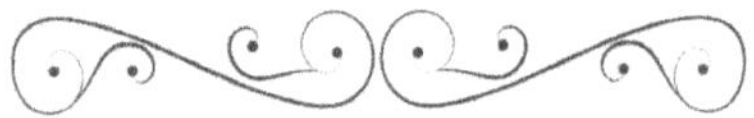

Chapter Eight

I T WAS MIDDAY when they arrived at Lady Pendleton's grand castle. The impressive stone structure loomed against the pale sky, its tower reaching up like an accusing finger. Though apparently mostly unused, today the castle stirred with new life.

Really, Amelia decided, as she stepped out of their carriage, its only resemblance to a ghost-ridden castle in some fairytale was the castle tower which, Amelia was informed by the housekeeper as she led her and Edward towards the drawing room, could be reached only by some crumbling stairs.

Lady Pendleton was already welcoming the first of the guests when they were announced, and in the middle of explaining the layout of the castle.

"But while the tower cannot be safely accessed and so will be out of bounds, there are many other hiding places and unexpected nooks and crannies that no doubt harbor all the ghosties and ghoulies we could wish for," she said, as she gestured toward the comfortable chairs. "Do sit down while the servants take your trunks to your rooms. Miss Playford and Miss Penny arrived a short while ago with their aunt and mama who are out in the garden. I believe you have already been introduced?"

Edward sent his sister a significant look as they nodded at the two young ladies, Miss Playford's golden curls bright in the sunlight streaming through the tall windows.

"It's going to be such an exciting weekend," Miss Penny said with girlish enthusiasm. "Miss Playford and I have made a wager as to who will discover the first ghost."

"But you don't really believe in ghosts, do you?" Amelia asked before she could stop herself.

"But of course! I mean, how could I not?" replied the young lady before shrugging prettily. "I dare say we'll all know whether they do or don't before we go home."

"Hopefully unscathed," Edward said with dark portent and a twinkle in his eye, causing both young ladies to titter and exchange glances.

"Though hopefully there will be some handsome gentlemen on hand to rescue us," Miss Playford added, smoothing her already immaculate skirts. "That is why my aunt decided she was prepared to travel farther than she usually does. She also says if I scream and jump onto a chair if I see a mouse, then this should get me used to anything." She glanced toward the doorway as if hoping a particular gentleman might materialize. "Do you believe in ghosts, Miss Fairchild?"

"Not in the slightest," Amelia said, straightening her spine. "Ghosts are nothing but a ridiculous concept used by charlatans to further their own ends but if you're happy for a handsome gentleman to rescue you from a mythical being that in your heart you know doesn't exist, then that's what we're here for. Nothing but a bit of fun and frivolity."

"That's not really what you're renowned for, is it, Miss Fairchild?" came a familiar voice from the doorway, and Amelia's heart gave a surprising leap as she swung round and found herself looking up into Sir Frederick's amused countenance. He filled the doorframe with his broad shoulders, and Amelia noticed with irritation how both Miss Ps immediately sat straighter, their faces brightening.

But then, that's what they were all there for. For one of them, at least, to win his heart.

"Excuse me?" Amelia responded with prickly pride as he strode across the floor. "I have as much desire for enjoyment as anyone here."

"But your book learning is more important to you than fun and frivolity. Please, my remark was meant as a compliment," he went on as he leaned an elbow on the mantelpiece and smiled at the seated young ladies.

But the way the young ladies looked at Amelia suggested that a love of book learning was a dubious attribute.

"It is true that the characters in books disappoint me less frequently than in real life," Amelia said, looking down at her fingers as they folded the fabric of her muslin skirts. While her gown was of good quality, she was not dressed as fashionably as the Miss Ps, who seemed to have coordinated their ensembles in shades of spring green and pale pink.

It was in fact Amelia's Mama who had insisted on selecting the gowns Amelia was to take with her for the weekend party, saying she feared Amelia's predilection for the sober and severe would dampen her already muted propensity for fun and frivolity. The deep blue of her current gown at least brought out her eyes, though she noticed Sir Frederick's gaze lingering on Miss Penny's more modish costume.

"Goodness, Amelia," her mother had admonished her, "you've already started to dress like a staid spinster or bluestocking as I think they call girls like you which is not a compliment. And you haven't even begun your new life in the country which I still think is a mistake you'll learn soon enough when you discover that being alone is… lonely."

Amelia had countered that with all her lovely books to keep her company, she could never feel alone.

Now she felt herself coloring at Sir Frederick's considered contemplation and grappled for the first thing she could think of. "Lady Pendleton says there is a particularly troublesome ghost who floats between the tower—which I understand is unsafe to visit—and the library. Do you have any ideas as to how it can be rendered… *untroublesome* to be helpful to our hostess?"

Lady Pendleton turned from the conversation she was having near the doorway with Lord Thornton who'd just arrived. "Indeed, if only someone *could* send the troublesome spirit away during our ghost hunting! I've never seen it, but I can't tell you the number of guests who say they have. It's the main reason I dislike coming here though Lord Pendleton enjoys his fishing and hunting here very much. Generally, I will not accompany him for I get so many complaints from guests who say they can't sleep because of its moaning and clattering."

Amelia noticed the amusement on Sir Frederick's countenance and considered this one of the few things they had in common: a skepticism for ghosts.

"My goodness, who is this ghost, Lady Pendleton?" asked Miss Playford.

Lady Pendleton lowered her voice. "It is the ghost of my great-great aunt. Some say she died after she tried to escape from the tower attempting to elope with one of the grooms, though others claim that's just a myth. There she is." She pointed to a small portrait hanging on the wall. "Now, apparently, her ghost makes a habit of wailing in the tower at all hours of the night, though I do believe it's really the wind. Never mind that Pendleton doesn't hear a thing. He's as deaf as a door post at the best of times. But you, young ladies, and my other guests, I will be most interested in what you report in the morning."

Amelia studied the portrait more closely, noting the book clutched in the subject's hands and the intelligence in her eyes. Somehow, this didn't look like a woman foolish enough to throw her life away for a mere stable hand.

"Yes, indeed. And we shall have to deal severely with this ghost, will we not, Lady Pendleton?" said Sir Frederick, moving behind Miss Playford's chair. "This ghost-hunting weekend will hardly be a success if we cannot at least ensure that the spirit of your great-great aunt is laid to rest so that you can get yours. What did you say her name was?"

"Pernilla," said Lady Pendleton, her tone dismissive. "Poor, pathetic Pernilla."

Conscious of Sir Frederick's eyes upon her, Amelia resisted making eye contact though her skin felt unaccountably warmed by his attention.

He should be conversing with the Miss Ps, she thought, rising.

"If you'll excuse me, I will rest awhile before I ready myself for the Masquerade Ball tonight," she said. "Especially if I run the risk of a sleepless night due to Pernilla's ghostly wailing," she added with a poor attempt at a joke. "Come, Edward."

But her brother just grinned at her, his appreciative gaze lingering on the young ladies and Amelia had to use all her training not to snap at him as a big sister would have any reason to do.

Chapter Nine

T HE GREAT HALL at dinner time was illuminated by dozens of candles in brass sconces, their flickering light casting dancing shadows on the ancient tapestries. The table, long enough to seat thirty guests, gleamed with polished silver and crystal, though the conversation proved as lackluster as the cold soup. Amelia found herself trapped between the vacuous Miss Penny and pompous Mr. Stanley, the latter presenting her with his perpetually hunched back as he strained to catch every word of Mr. Greene's presumably fascinating discourse on hunting dogs.

Now, after an hour in which to don their costumes, a markedly more excited atmosphere prevailed as the company reconvened in the drawing room. The air was thick with perfume and anticipation, silk rustling against silk as elaborately costumed figures moved about the space.

Edward's Janus costume drew gasps and nervous titters, the two-faced mask catching the candlelight as he moved through the crowd.

Amelia, who had hastily assembled a costume to represent a mysterious fortune-teller—all flowing dark fabric and jingling bangles—earned barely concealed smirks from the Miss Ps. They had clearly spent weeks planning their costumes: Miss Playford as a fairy nymph in gossamer and pearls, Miss Penny as an angel whose wings shed tiny feathers with every movement.

"Are you really going to read people's fortunes?" asked Miss Playford. "Mama wouldn't let me go near the fortune-teller tent at the fair when I was younger but maybe I could just ask you to read my palm." She tittered but then was clearly surprised when Amelia suddenly leaned forward and, in a mysterious tone, said, "I shall happily read your fortune, Miss Playford. Take a seat in the window embrasure and let's begin, shall we?"

For it suddenly occurred to her that Miss Playford might be as easily led as she looked, and hinting at a destiny that might include Sir Frederick could give her the impetus she needed to make Sir Frederick regard her in a favorable light.

The ancient mullioned window provided the perfect backdrop for Amelia's impromptu fortune telling, its leaded panes casting a latticed shadow across Miss Playford's eager face. From this vantage point, Amelia could observe the room's dynamics: Edward holding court in his unsettling mask, Lady Townsend and Lady Pendleton engaged in what appeared to be a forcedly pleasant conversation, their smiles not quite reaching their eyes.

And then Sir Frederick entered, his tall figure drawing every eye in the room. His costume—whatever it was meant to be—did nothing to diminish his commanding presence, and Amelia noticed with irritation how Miss Playford's breath caught audibly at the sight of him. With renewed purpose, she grasped the girl's wrist perhaps a touch too firmly, channeling her annoyance into her performance as a seer.

There was Lady Townsend in conversation with Lady Pendleton. Amelia's mama had been even more surprised to learn her daughter was on the viscountess's guest list. She'd then recounted several tales of that lady's duplicitous behavior towards Lady Townsend dating back to their youth which made Amelia wonder at Lady Townsend's motivations in remaining her friend. Birds of a feather?

And then, in the periphery of her vision, she noticed Sir Frederick's tall, well-built form as he stepped into the room. So, with renewed energy, she took Miss Playford's wrist and, perhaps a little too forcefully, yanked her hand so that it lay across the table in front of her.

"What a glittering future beckons," Amelia began, speaking over the young lady's tiny yelp of surprised pain. "What an extraordinarily wondrous marriage I see you will make."

"A wondrous marriage?" Miss Playford repeated with a wondrous expression. "For a young lady who has no dowry? Are you sure, Miss Fairchild?"

Amelia gave a decided nod. "Why, the man you will marry is in this room. Renowned as a man of good taste, high rank, and with a great many friends, he puts charm and beauty before monetary gain."

Miss Playford gasped. "He's in this room?" she whispered. "Surely not for I can't see him."

Amelia made a study of the assembled guests. Of the gentlemen, many were young, there was a good sprinkling of handsome hopefuls, on the lookout, she presumed, for a wife, but she doubted they would consider penniless Miss Playford who, although well connected, had no dowry.

Like Amelia, though at least Amelia had a small inheritance to look forward to. That is, if she could persuade Sir Frederick to make a young lady like Miss Playford his wife.

Unlike Amelia, however, Miss Playford appeared to have grandiose aspirations.

"Oh, my! But he *is* here!" Amelia said on a gasp as her gaze encompassed Sir Frederick for but a moment.

"Who is he?" squeaked Miss Playford.

Amelia shook her head, saying, "A fortune-teller cannot reveal what can only be suggested for it is up to the recipient of good news such as I have just imparted to make their own futures live up to what has been prognosticated."

"But can't you give me a clue?"

Amelia considered this then nodded. "Very well. The potential future husband of whom I speak has recently returned to

England after some years abroad and he is looking, very specifically, for a blonde, petite, and vivacious wife."

"Like me?" Miss Playford squealed again, just as a stentorian voice cut through the hubbub, summoning the guests to the center of the room for what was promised would be the most extraordinary treasure hunt that ever was to be.

Reluctantly, Amelia followed Miss Playford, who was almost skipping in her excitement, over to where Lady Pendleton stood on the opposite side of a large oak refectory table, flanked by her husband and Lady Townsend.

Lord Pendleton stood a head shorter than his wife, his faintly sweating brow gleaming in the candlelight as he anxiously tugged at his cravat. A small man, he seemed to shrink further whenever Lady Pendleton's voice rose above a certain pitch, his watery eyes darting between his wife and their guests as if seeking approval from both quarters. His fingers drummed a nervous pattern on the oak table as Lady Pendleton announced the treasure hunt, and he appeared to be perpetually on the verge of interrupting her, though he never quite gathered the courage to do so.

"Ladies and gentlemen, I am about to task you with a complicated puzzle but the winners, I promise, will be well-rewarded," said Lady Pendleton. In front of her was a long list of names, unintelligible from this distance.

"Each of you will be partnered up in order to follow a series of clues which will lead you to the treasure. After the resolution, the ghostly ball will begin." Lady Pendleton's laugh echoed slightly in the high-ceilinged room. "I just hope we have everyone back here to participate because, as you very well know, Pendleton Castle is haunted by the tragic ghost of my reckless great-great aunt whom some will say got what she deserved but who is ensuring that no one who stays here gets a good night's sleep."

Lord Pendleton cleared his throat. "But do not be alarmed," he stammered, his wife's sharp glance making him shrink visibly. "Lady Pernilla simply makes a racket. No one has been harmed by a ghost in this house." He patted his shining pate, a habit that seemed to surface whenever his wife's attention turned his way. "Now, let us begin the treasure hunt. My dear, would you do the honors?"

The Miss Ps exchanged frightened looks, their elaborate costumes trembling with what might have been genuine fear—or artful anticipation of requiring rescue. Miss Playford's wings quivered particularly dramatically, Amelia noticed with barely concealed contempt.

When Edward murmured in her ear about making a duo, his Janus mask cast bizarre double shadows on the wall behind them. "Perhaps you and I will discover the treasure—with a value so great that there'll be no need for any matchmaking on our parts."

"I hardly think it'll just fall into our laps," whispered Amelia. "I'm sure it can't be anything more than a paste necklace. There is no ghost, and there are no mysterious creatures of the night. This is all just for show—"

But her words died in her throat as Edward's sharp intake of breath preceded his whisper, "Why, did you hear your name being called, Amelia? You have been paired with Sir Frederick."

The man in question stood across the room, the firelight catching the angles of his face in a way that made him look almost otherworldly. His slight raising of brows met Amelia's momentary indignation, and something passed between them.

But it was gone in a second.

Did he even remember the camaraderie they'd shared so briefly before—

"Then of course we must invite Miss Playford into our little group," Amelia burst out, her bangles jangling with the sudden movement, "and do her the kindness of proving to her that no ghosts exist in this castle, or anywhere else for that matter."

Miss Playford stood uncertainly nearby, her fairy nymph costume catching the firelight in ways that made her appear to shimmer. She frowned in confusion until Amelia, channeling more drama than her fortune-teller costume required, raised her eyebrows meaningfully while subtly indicating Sir Frederick. Understanding dawned on the young lady's face like sunrise, and she practically floated to Amelia's side, her gauzy skirts billowing.

"Ooh, yes, please!" The eagerness in her voice was almost painful to hear.

"Well, well, Miss Fairchild, we are to solve a mystery together, are we?" Sir Frederick's approach was deliberate, measured, his costume—which Amelia supposed was that of a Byronic hero—lending him an air of dangerous elegance. He cast what seemed an almost perfunctory smile at Miss Playford before fixing Amelia with that quizzical look she remembered so well from years ago.

"We'll find the treasure first, before anyone, I'm sure! We'll search the castle from top to bottom," Miss Playford declared. The way she looked at Sir Frederick spoke volumes about castles in the air already under construction.

The room hummed with excited murmurs as Lady Pendleton continued reading names, her voice carrying over Lord Pendleton's nervous shuffling of papers. Edward dropped part of his unsettling mask to send his sister a look of such smugness that Amelia's suspicions immediately awakened. He turned to follow a pretty debutante whose chaperone looked already exhausted, giving Amelia just enough time to whisper, "Who can be behind this odd alliance? Someone has paired Sir Frederick with me and surely it's not purely coincidence?"

Edward shrugged. "Not everyone is a matchmaker, Amelia," he said. "You are too old to need a chaperone and every other young lady here is properly accompanied. No need to overthink it."

Amelia supposed he was right, though something about the arrangement nagged at her.

"Cryptic, eh, Miss Fairchild?" Sir Frederick's voice brought her back to the present moment.

"I beg your pardon?"

"The first clue," he said, nodding towards the paper she'd

been clutching rather too tightly. He leaned closer—far closer than strictly necessary, she thought—to read aloud:

"Where slumber takes hold and dreams unfold,

Seek the room where stories are told.

In the library's heart,

A secret lies,

Behind the tome where romance never dies."

His voice seemed to linger on the word "romance" in a way that made Miss Playford's cheeks flush pink.

Or was that just Amelia's imagination?

"That's not cryptic," Amelia said, smoothing her dark fortune-teller's robes with a deliberately steady hand. "That's the library, of course."

"Why, I am teamed with a capital sleuth." Sir Frederick's tone held a note of gentle mockery. "Then let us proceed to the library." He glanced around the now-dispersing crowd. "Though why is no one else going there?"

"Because," said Amelia, unable to keep a hint of schoolmistress from her voice, "every pair or trio has their own set of clues with only the final clue leading to the treasure. Did you not listen when Lady Pendleton explained the rules of the game?"

"I was too busy gazing at the beauty that surrounds us," Sir Frederick said, his voice warming as he looked at Miss Playford. The young lady blushed hotly before looking away in what seemed like clear delight.

And Amelia could barely suppress her own smile.

Why, it was astonishing how easily it was all falling into place. Miss Playford was completely smitten, or at least giving an excellent performance of being so, unable—or perhaps unwilling—to hide her admiration for Sir Frederick. And he... well, he clearly was entranced by her innocent blushes. Who wouldn't be? She was everything Amelia had never been—golden and graceful, with none of the sharp edges that Thomas had told her he'd overheard Sir Frederick criticizing—in the group amongst which he was discussing her—together with her "dull obsession with book learning."

That had been a life-changing moment, the moment Amelia realized the foolishness of trying to conform and behave as the other debutantes. She did not have their natural vivacity whereas Thomas admired above all things about her—her intelligence and gravity.

Casting aside these reflections, Amelia forced herself to concentrate on the task at hand. Somehow, she needed to mastermind some means by which Miss Playford threw herself in terror into Sir Frederick's arms—and a ghost was certain to do it—meaning Amelia's troubles would be over. The thought should have brought more satisfaction than it did.

Nevertheless, feeling very smug in the knowledge that by the end of this weekend her troubles would be over (and steadfastly ignoring the hollow feeling that accompanied that thought), Amelia allowed Sir Frederick an equally warm smile. Let him take Miss Playford under his wing and discover the charms of a golden-haired nymph who hung on his every word, who clearly idolized him, and who flattered and cajoled him with an expertise that belied her supposed innocence.

Sir Frederick was clearly the kind of gentleman who was easily susceptible to such adoration. Though as they set off toward the library, Amelia couldn't quite ignore the knowledge that his gaze dwelt on her profile, or the way he positioned himself between her and Miss Playford, or how his hand seemed to hover near her elbow at every turning. But that was surely just habit—the same protective instinct that would soon be redirected completely towards Miss Playford.

Amelia tried to shake her memories of the past. This was the way Sir Frederick had behaved towards her in the early days. Attentive and interested. Not the Sir Frederick that Thomas had refashioned for her and which had taken precedence in her memory during the years the baronet had been away.

The corridors grew darker as they moved away from the drawing room's warmth, and Amelia told herself firmly that the shiver that ran down her spine was merely from the draft that seemed to follow them. Although the way Sir Frederick's shoulder brushed against hers as they walked might have had something to do with it as well.

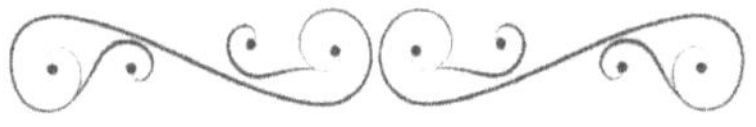

Chapter Ten

THREE MINUTES LATER, the library doors loomed before them, their carved panels gleaming dully in the light from the wall sconces. Sir Frederick reached around Amelia to grasp the handle, his arm brushing her shoulder in a way that felt far too deliberate.

But before Amelia could dwell upon it, the door creaked open to reveal a cavernous room lined with leather-bound books, their gilt spines catching what little light filtered through the tall windows.

"Oh!" Miss Playford clutched at her gauzy skirts. "It's so... so dark in here." Her voice quavered, and Amelia had to admire the artful way she shifted closer to Sir Frederick.

But instead of offering comfort, he was already striding toward one of the windows, his Byronic silhouette stark against the gathering dusk. With efficient movements, he drew back the heavy curtains, allowing more of the fading light to spill into the room. "Better, Miss Playford? Though I dare say Miss Fairchild would tell us that darkness is essential for any proper ghost hunting."

"I would say no such thing," Amelia retorted, moving towards the nearest bookshelf. "Ghosts, like most mysteries, tend to evaporate in good light and with clear thinking." She ran her fingers along the spines, trying to ignore how his low chuckle raised goosebumps on her arms.

"Clear thinking?" He moved to the shelf beside her. "From our fortune teller? I would have thought you'd be more inclined towards… mysterious possibilities tonight."

Before Amelia could respond, Miss Playford gasped. "Oh! What was that sound?"

"Merely the wind in the chimney," Amelia said firmly. "Now, what was that line again? 'Behind the tome where romance never dies'?"

"How fitting," Sir Frederick murmured, his voice pitched low enough that only Amelia could hear. "Considering our history with libraries."

She jerked her head up to look at him, but his face was unreadable in the shadows. Surely he wasn't referring to that afternoon years ago. The afternoon he'd kissed her. And she'd kissed him back.

Before Thomas had revealed Sir Frederick's true nature? Before her world had tilted on its axis?

"Miss Fairchild?" Miss Playford's voice held a note of genuine anxiety now. "Something just brushed past me!"

"Nonsense," Amelia said, more sharply than she intended. "It's merely your own costume's feathers." But she noticed how Sir Frederick had already moved to the young lady's side, offering his arm with perfect gallantry.

And she was glad of it. It reminded her just why Sir Frederick was not a man to be taken seriously—as she had once done.

"Shall we search together, Miss Playford? Though I warn you, I take my direction from our fortune teller here." His eyes met Amelia's over Miss Playford's blonde head, and for a moment she caught something in his expression that made her wonder if she'd miscalculated somehow.

But no—this was exactly what she'd planned. Sir Frederick was playing the gallant protector, just as she'd hoped. The fact that something twisted uncomfortably in her chest at the sight was irrelevant. Completely irrelevant.

A sudden gust of wind rattled the windows, making Miss Playford jump closer to Sir Frederick with a tiny shriek. "Oh! Do you think it's… her? Lady Pernilla?"

"Don't be so silly," Amelia said before she could stop herself, ameliorating her sharpness with a more conciliatory, "Lady Pernilla's ghost is a figment of everyone's imagination."

"I think," Sir Frederick said slowly, "that Lady Pernilla's story might be worth investigating further. Don't you agree, Miss Fairchild? After all, some tales of love and betrayal deserve a second look."

Amelia turned back to the bookshelves, her fortune teller's bangles jangling with the sudden movement. "We're here to find a clue, not investigate old scandals," she said firmly. "Now, shall we begin our search in earnest? The romance section would be the logical place to start," she said, moving towards the far corner of the library where she'd noticed a collection of well-worn novels.

"Logical?" Sir Frederick's voice held that maddening hint of amusement again. "I wouldn't have thought logic had much place in matters of romance."

Distracted, Amelia halted, then reverently pulled out a leather-bound tome and read aloud, "*Principia Mathematica* by Isaac Newton." Clasping it to her bosom she whispered, "I am in heaven!" as she gazed at the lofty ceiling.

She opened her eyes to see Sir Frederick regarding her with amusement which quickly turned to horror as Miss Playford pulled out a title and began to read, "*Fanny Hill: Memoirs of a Woman of Pleasure* by John Cleland. Have you read this—"

"No, and nor should you!" Sir Frederick said, snatching it from her hands.

"But we're looking for a romance, aren't we?" Miss Playford looked confused. "Wouldn't this be—?"

"No, I think not, Miss Playford, and I think you should direct your search to another bookshelf," he suggested, for now she'd pulled out a title which Amelia could see clearly was *Justine* by the

Marquise de Sade.

"Nor that title, Miss Playford!" Amelia said, taking it out of Miss Playford's hands. She caught Sir Frederick's quizzical look, blushing hotly as he murmured, "And why do you think a novel with such an innocuous title should be kept away from Miss Playford? Surely *you* are not acquainted with the works of the Marquise de Sade?"

"Who is the Marquise de Sade?" asked Miss Playford who appeared to have missed the nuances swirling about her. "I do love reading romances but my Aunt Pike says I should broaden my horizons and read other literature if I am to improve myself."

Amelia struggled to reply, for Sir Frederick was clearly waiting for her to supply Miss Playford with an answer. Finally, she said, calmly, "I do not think reading the Marquise de Sade would improve yourself. In fact, I think you should put his name out of your mind and not mention to your aunt that such a book was ever in your hands."

Immediately she realized she'd spoken the very words that would incline Miss Playford to do the opposite. She replaced the tome, feeling almost burned by the explicit sexual content of the book. The truth was that she'd inadvertently stumbled upon the volume in the library of a friend of her mama's and what she'd read would stay with her forever.

Fortunately, she was saved from saying anything further for Miss Playford suddenly gave a whoop of triumph as she whipped out the *Mysteries of Udolpho* by Mrs. Ann Radcliffe.

"I loved this romance!" she cried, and Amelia was relieved that she could concur and launch into a spirited critique of the book set in a similarly mysterious and ghostly setting.

"And this must be the next clue!" Miss Playford said as she pulled out a yellowing sheet of paper and began to read:

> "My dearest William, How my heart aches with each
> passing moment we are apart. The sun seems dimmer,
> the air less sweet, and even the horses in the stable lack

their usual luster without your presence. I know my father forbids our love—"

Amelia, who'd been staring at the letter, trying to make sense of how it could be the second clue, glanced up to see Sir Frederick frowning at her.

Gently he took the letter from Miss Playford. "This is not the clue," he said at last.

Amelia looked over his shoulder and gasped. "Look at the signature. It says Pernilla."

"The ghost?" exclaimed Miss Playford.

"Oh, my goodness," said Amelia. She bit her lip, torn between wanting to know what it said but knowing such a desire reflected badly on her. She was relieved when Miss Playford said brightly, "Perhaps reading it would help us discover why she's a ghost."

"Excellent idea," said Sir Frederick to Amelia's surprise. "Would you care to do the honors?"

In a sweet, lilting voice, Miss Playford continued:

"I know my father forbids our love, claiming it an impossibility due to the circumstances of our birth. But surely, my darling, love knows no such boundaries. Your gentle hands, so skilled with the horses, have captured my heart with equal mastery. Your kind eyes and noble spirit reveal a truer nobility than any title could bestow. They speak of my impending marriage to Baron Weatherby as if it were a fate already sealed. But I cannot—I will not—accept a life without you.

Each night, I dream of a world where we are free to love openly, where the only judgment passed upon us is the strength of our devotion. I watch from the tower window, hoping to catch a glimpse of you in the stables below. Sometimes, I fancy I can hear your voice carried on the wind, calling out to me.

My love, if only I had wings, I would fly into your

arms and never leave. Promise me you'll find a way for us to be together. I fear my spirit cannot bear this separation much longer. Without you, this gilded cage of privilege feels more a prison with each passing day.

Forever yours, with a love that defies all bounds,
Pernilla."

She stopped reading and Amelia found she had no words. Embarrassed, she turned her head away so that Sir Frederick would not witness her foolishness, quickly blinking away the tears and clearing her voice before she forced a smile.

To her surprise, she saw that Sir Frederick was frowning as he took both the book and the letter from Miss Playford who said softly, "That's really sad. That letter is from Lady Pendleton's great-great aunt Pernilla. The ghost. Do you…" She hesitated. "Do you think we should give it to Lady Pendleton?"

Sir Frederick shook his head. "Let us keep it our secret for the meantime. I don't think Lady Pendleton is going to be very receptive to more details of her ancestor's scandalous love affair being publicly aired."

"Nor do I think it would make her more kindly disposed towards her erring forebear," said Amelia. "Poor ghostly Pernilla was in love with her father's groom."

"Lady Pendleton and the family don't want to be reminded of this," said Sir Frederick. "Such a union would have scandalized society."

"So sad if she was in love with him," said Miss Playford on a sigh. "He must have been very handsome."

"Well, handsome looks wouldn't have kept a roof over her head." Sir Frederick sounded less charitable as he folded the letter and placed it back in the book. "No doubt she was a foolish child interested only in his manly physique and her head was easily turned. That is no basis for a marriage."

"I suppose if he had had money it wouldn't have mattered who he was, where he came from, or how well-connected he was," said Amelia. "Even if it was new money, I'm sure the family would have relented in the end." She knew her tone was combative as she moved along the row of romance novels, as she continued the search for the next clue.

"If he was her intellectual equal, I dare say there would not have been the same resistance," said Sir Frederick. "A lowly groom and a nobleman's daughter? That really is a bridge too far."

"Are you saying that money isn't *everything*?" Amelia couldn't help asking, as she pulled out a copy of *Pride & Prejudice*. If he was to ally himself with Miss Playford it would be helpful if she could have him answer outright in the affirmative.

"Of course it isn't," he said, taking the volume from Amelia's hands and saying with a short laugh, "My sister enjoyed this so greatly she insisted I read it."

"What did you think?" asked Amelia and was surprised when he gave an unaffected laugh. "I thought the author was a genius for all that I was highly skeptical when I reluctantly read the first page with Caroline breathing over my shoulder in case I should wriggle out of it."

"You read it to the end?" asked Miss Playford incredulously.

"Indeed, I did. And I'm sure I learned a great deal about human nature, and the minds and motivations of young ladies, that I did not know before."

"Like what?" asked Amelia.

"Well, now, you are a fiercer and less forgiving Miss Lizzie Bennett with your fine eyes and exacting manner—"

"And who am I?" Miss Playford interrupted before Amelia could object to what she felt was a grave injustice. A fiercer Miss Lizzie Bennett? Why, Amelia was light-hearted and full of fun when people only took the time to know her.

"You, Miss Playford? Why, you remind me of Miss Lydia!"

Miss Playford bit her lip and frowned. "Miss Lydia?" she asked dubiously while Amelia's heart sank though it was early days. He'd soon see Miss Playford as more than a giggling, pleasure-loving miss who made foolish choices until rescued by a noble gentleman. But perhaps that was what he really meant, she thought with a surge of hope. Perhaps Sir Frederick saw himself as being the fine gentleman who'd take the young girl under his wing, and then marry her, before she could do herself, her family, and most definitely, her reputation, any harm.

"Oh, Sir Frederick, you are too funny!" Amelia interjected with a forced laugh. "Miss Playford is much prettier and cleverer than I ever imagined Lydia who was so fortunate to make such a grand and unexpected marriage," she added with a pointed look at Miss Playford whose brow immediately cleared.

"So much cleverer!" Miss Playford suddenly cried as she snatched the book from Sir Frederick's hands crying, "For there is the clue! I can see it's not a love letter from Lady Pernilla so it must be a clue."

"Clever girl! It is indeed clue number two," said Sir Frederick glancing at the small piece of paper. "What does it say?"

Miss Playford beamed as she smoothed the paper and began to read.

> "Voice carry, though whispered low,
> In a circular path, round and round they go.
> Find the spot where the secrets are heard.
> And look for a stone that seems absurd."

All three shook their heads at the cryptic words.

"Where do voices carry?" asked Amelia. "Sir Frederick, you know this castle better than we do. I suppose it could refer to the castle tower though isn't that out of bounds?"

"Yes, it's been crumbling and untended for years. We definitely are not to try and climb those stairs. But…" He thought a moment and then said, "There's a gallery. A… whispering gallery—"

"That must be it!" said Miss Playford happily. "Oh, you are so clever, Sir Frederick. How lucky that we have you in our team. I wonder how the others are faring? We shall win this treasure, I'm sure. And then we shall all be very rich and can marry…" She trailed off, dropping her head as she blushed.

"And can marry whom we like?" Sir Frederick supplied, smiling. "Indeed, that is a recipe for success for I hold to what I said earlier. A marriage based on money is a recipe for unhappiness. Besides, I doubt the treasure at the end of our treasure hunt will be anything more than a token."

"Of course," said Miss Playford who looked crestfallen as she followed Amelia and Sir Frederick to the whispering gallery. "But it would help to have just a little bit of it," Amelia heard her say under her breath, and couldn't help concurring. It was all very well for men like Sir Frederick who had no cares in the world and could do as they wished. If he didn't want to marry, he could simply idle his life away, breaking hearts just for fun. Poor Miss Playford looked like she was about to cry, she realized as she glanced over her shoulder, and suddenly Amelia felt very guilty for getting the girl's hopes up. If Sir Frederick really did prefer young ladies with a bit of intelligence, then Miss Playford was not going to be his ideal mate and never would be.

But then, she remembered how many times she'd misinterpreted the words of gentlemen. Gentlemen who *pretended* that's what they wanted when in truth a pretty face and a pleasing, obsequious manner was really all that appealed.

That's what Sir Frederick had hinted he had wanted, all those years ago in the library when they'd pored over books, just like tonight.

And then Thomas had told Amelia what he'd overheard: Sir Frederick laughing over the serious bluestocking Miss Amelia, who thought she might actually catch a husband when all she was interested in was pretending she was cleverer than she was.

No, Amelia must not be taken in. If she was forming a slightly more positive opinion of Sir Frederick as their acquaintanceship increased, then it was because he was only putting on the kind of false front he knew would earn him her regard for the duration of the house party.

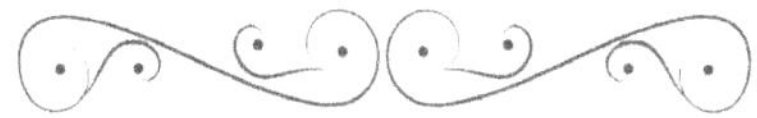

Chapter Eleven

S IR FREDERICK LED the way with an unexpected sense of lightness and discovery before he suddenly remembered that his sister was somewhere in this drafty castle and so was Mr. Greene. He'd heard her name paired with her chaperone, which was only right, and with a rather unappealing and insipid young baronet's son, but a couple of moments of reflection reminded him of how very enterprising Caroline was.

He certainly wouldn't put it past her to smilingly glide away with young Mr. Pipkins and then pull off some daring swap. Which meant that he really should make a point of learning exactly where Caroline was. He'd just stepped towards the railing of the gallery so he could look down upon the various groupings that scurried about in search of clues, when salvation came to him.

"Henry!" he called down to the ginger-haired lad who was fortuitously passing below. "Just one quick moment of your time, if you please?"

With an apologetic glance at the pretty milkmaid and her chaperone whom he was accompanying, Henry bounded up the stairs. "How can I be of assistance, Sir Frederick? Is it Caro? It is, isn't it?"

"It's always Caro. I'm anxious every time she has an opportunity to slip under our guard and make off with Mr. Greene," Sir Frederick said, lowering his voice as he heard Miss Fairchild and Miss Playford discussing the fine tapestry hung in the whispering gallery just behind him. "He's a fortune hunter, interested only in her money and he'll use any lure. Have you seen who she's with this evening?"

"Last I saw, she was safely with her chaperone and Mr. Pipkins."

"But she'll want to replace Mr. Pipkins at the first opportunity. You know that as well as I do. Lord, you probably have an even greater appreciation of the breadth of her ingenuity having had to keep pace with her throughout your childhood."

"Oh, she's ingenious, there's no doubt about that," Henry said admiringly, as he gazed after Caroline. "Remember when she convinced the vicar she'd seen an angel in the churchyard? It was just her white nightgown that she'd artfully placed in that old oak tree, but she had half the village believing her."

Sir Frederick noticed how Henry's eyes softened at the memory. "You've always encouraged her flights of fancy."

Henry's usual cheerful expression suddenly darkened. "Did you know Greene's been filling her head with tales of Paris? All glamour and fashion and fancy titles. But our Caroline's worth ten of those fashionable misses who only care about their next new bonnet."

"*Our* Caroline?" Sir Frederick raised an eyebrow.

Henry flushed. "Well, we practically grew up in each other's pockets, didn't we? Someone needs to remind her that true worth isn't measured by how many diamonds a gentleman can offer." He straightened his shoulders. "I'll keep an eye on her, Sir Frederick. She may not listen to me like she used to when we'd climb trees and hunt for fairy rings, but I won't let her throw herself away on a fortune hunter."

Sir Frederick studied the young man thoughtfully. Henry's boyish features had matured since Sir Frederick had last seen him, though that irrepressible grin still appeared frequently. But there was something new in his manner when he spoke of Caroline—a protective warmth that went beyond mere childhood friendship.

"I trust you'll be subtle," Sir Frederick said. "Caroline doesn't respond well to being managed."

Henry's laugh held a note of fond exasperation. "Don't I know it! Remember when she decided she wanted to learn sword-fighting and wouldn't take no for an answer? I still have the scar from where she jabbed me with a broken fence post." His expression grew serious. "But I'd rather have a hundred such scars than see her hurt by someone like Greene."

His smile was quickly replaced by another frown when he saw that Sir Frederick did not regard Caroline's antics in the same way he did. Gravely, he added, "But I'm sure her infatuation with Mr. Greene is a passing phase."

"I've no doubt it is, but if she misbehaves, she will have a lifetime to live with the consequences."

Sir Frederick felt a flicker of hope that the grimness of his tone had the desired effect for Henry swallowed and said, "I hadn't thought of that. No, well, she'd better behave then, hadn't she? Or it'll be Mr. Greene who carries her off after all. No, I hadn't thought of that at all for I knew her fancy for him would be fleeting. He really isn't the kind of gentleman who would make her happy for very long."

Sir Frederick patted him on the shoulder. "So, since you understand how headstrong she can be, I would be enormously grateful if you could please ensure that she's behaving as she ought to. I do not want this ghostly week to finish in tears. Or with her heading towards the altar with Mr. Greene."

With Henry's promise ringing in his ears, Sir Frederick turned back to the ladies, ready to throw himself back into solving the puzzle. If the truth be told, it was a rare and pleasant diversion to be with two such charming young ladies. Though Miss Playford was young, she was really rather sweet.

"What do you suppose we should be looking for, Sir Frederick?" the young lady asked from near a large carved wooden screen which she'd been caressing as if it might yield a clue. She sighed. "We've looked behind all the pictures and tapestries and can't find anything."

"But have you looked *in* the walls?"

They turned at the sonorous tones of Lady Townsend who'd appeared at the end of the gallery.

Sir Frederick smiled. "Very cryptic, though it would appear you know more than the rest of us, Lady Townsend."

"It is true that Lady Pendleton recruited me to assist." She nodded at the cold stone walls. "Not all clues will be so easy to find so we need to hurry if we are to have everyone at the ball in an hour."

Sir Frederick wondered if her assistance had included suggesting the groupings. Had she decided upon who would be paired up? And if so, could he prevail upon her to ensure Mr. Greene be kept as far away from Caro as possible. He glanced at the two young ladies who had turned their treasure-seeking efforts to feeling for loose stones, catching Lady Townsend's smile as he returned his attention to her.

"My, my, but I am impressed by your companions' ability to dig for clues," she said. "On the dance floor a young lady must be a model of decorum, but she may reveal hidden depths when tasked with something as important as finding hidden treasure."

"I'm sure the knowledge of such an unknown but potentially glittering reward unleashes something very different." Sir Frederick smiled. "Though that said, my sister Caroline takes no trouble to hide her rebellious nature whether on the dance floor or not. If you are wandering the castle to help the guests find what they must, I wonder if you'd do me the great favor of ensuring my sister is kept away from fortune hunters. There is one in particular to whom she is very keen to lose her head."

"I presume you speak of Mr. Greene," replied Lady Townsend to Sir Frederick's horror.

"She is so transparent?" he asked.

"As is he. Indeed, Lady Pendleton observed it, and I immediately understood her concern and now yours. You have my word, Sir Frederick, that I will do what I can to keep contact between them to a minimum."

"And have you seen either of them this evening?"

"Young Mr. Henry was squiring her about last time I checked. Poor Mr. Pipkin looked very downcast. Ah, but there's no accounting for the beating of a tender young heart. Love is spawned in the unlikeliest of places. But I will leave you as it clearly won't be too long before your next clue is found," Lady Townsend added, just as Miss Fairchild cried, "I've found it! Look! Look!"

Sir Frederick grinned at her unfettered enthusiasm but when she glanced up and caught his eye she sobered and said with more gravitas, "We found this behind a loose stone. Most definitely a clue. I shall read it:

'A lady in white, with eyes that follow,

Her gaze holds a secret in rooms hollow.

Count the doors from left to right,

The third one leads to your next sight.' "

"Yes, but what does it mean?" asked Miss Playford. "It makes no sense at all."

"Not unless you think about it. Eyes that follow? What could that refer to?" he replied.

"A gentleman who admires a lady will follow her with his eyes." She glanced at Sir Frederick who hoped his smile was bland in answer to the hope in hers. Goodness, he thought, he must not allow Miss Playford to think for a moment that his eyes followed her.

As for Miss Fairchild, he realized with a start that his eyes followed her quite a lot. Well, he was trying to understand her, when he'd clearly misunderstood her all those years ago.

She seemed so cold and self-contained and yet on several occasions she'd succumbed to the girlish enjoyment of the moment. It was a refreshing reminder of the old days before she'd inexplicably gone cold on him.

Now she said, "But what else follows you with their eyes? Why, a painting, of course! Have you never felt it before? The sense that when you're in a room with huge paintings on the wall, they are watching you. I thought that when we passed the antechamber that led here. There was a painting of—" She broke off suddenly then added, "Of a woman in white! You remember that, don't you? Come, follow me! I think I've discovered our next clue already."

They retraced their footsteps and were soon standing before a large portrait of a beautiful young woman with long golden hair falling over one shoulder, large, cornflower blue eyes gazing out from the frame with a wistful expression, her gown of the fashion from one hundred years earlier.

Miss Playford bent forward to read the inscription before gasping. "Why, this is Lady Pernilla! See how beautiful she is?"

There was no disputing this. Sir Frederick thought how much she reminded him of Caroline with her impish smile and her manner: languid but hinting at a spirit ready to be unleashed the moment she no longer had to remain still.

"No wonder she had admirers," remarked Miss Fairchild.

"A groom was her admirer. Of course she could never have married a groom," said Sir Frederick.

"No, but I am sorry for her if she lost her heart to him. Perhaps he was the only one who was kind to her. You remember in her letter that she referenced the unwelcome marriage her father was pressing upon her," said Sir Frederick. "Perhaps she threw herself at the groom in protest. That must surely have been the reason for her to have preferred him to the other gentlemen in the district. She wouldn't have chosen to be penniless if she could have found someone respectable who was worthy of her heart."

"Well, I'm not sure I agree with your speculation, Sir Frederick," said Miss Fairchild who was running her hands behind the back of the painting, withdrawing, with a smile of satisfaction what was clearly their next clue: a folded piece of paper which she began to read:

"Keys of ivory
Strings of gold
Lift the lid to find what's next
A clue to guide your future steps."

"Well, that's easy," declared Miss Playford. "The next clue is in the fortepiano, of course. I was playing it when I first got here. A very pretty instrument though quite old and not as fine as the one I play on at home. That is, when my Aunt Pike allows me to play it," she added.

"I'm sure we would love to hear you play something when we find the next clue," said Miss Fairchild, glancing at Sir Frederick with a smile.

"And what about you, Miss Fairchild? Do you play?" asked Sir Frederick, suddenly curious. "You seem learned in a great many areas. I'm sure you can play a pretty tune to amuse us."

"I'm not sure I wish to attempt to amuse anyone, Sir Frederick, and certainly not with my dubious musical abilities," Miss Fairchild replied with a sudden return to her previous cool demeanor. He wondered what he'd said to vex her but then Miss Playford was clapping her hands and leading the way out of the dimly lit antechamber saying, "I think we should hurry if we want to be the ones to win this great treasure. We must get there first!"

But as he found himself shoulder to shoulder with Miss Fairchild as they followed the other fair child through the corridor, positively skipping in her excitement, Miss Fairchild relaxed sufficiently to say, "There is something charming about extreme youthfulness. I'd pegged Miss Playford as far less ebullient." With a frown, she added, "Though, come to think of it, that was only when she was in company with her aunt."

"She's charming," Sir Frederick agreed. "A charming child," he added, thinking how much more appealing was Miss Fairchild's intelligence.

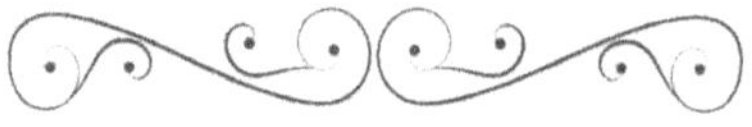

Chapter Twelve

AMELIA KEPT MISS Playford in sight while she followed at a more demure pace. The castle's tapestries, paintings, coats of armor, heraldry, and other treasures were a source of great interest and she found that Sir Frederick had much to say on the artifacts and works of art they passed.

"You are so cultured, Sir Frederick," Miss Playford marveled. "What astonishing sights you have seen. Oh, I wish I could go on a Grand Tour like you have."

Amelia said nothing but raised an eyebrow as she let Miss Playford prattle on. She knew Sir Frederick had misbehaved. Thomas had recounted many tales of his indiscretions. Her upright betrothed had even blushed when he'd touched on the fact that women were involved.

No wonder Sir Frederick couldn't meet Amelia's focused look as Miss Playford expounded on his extraordinary knowledge.

And nor could she help observing, "For most young men, the Grand Tour is a euphemism for behaving with the reckless abandon they could not get away with on home soil. I am sure you must be quite an aberration, Sir Frederick."

It was a timely reminder not to get too comfortable with the gentleman for while her Thomas had gone to fight for King and country, Sir Frederick had been wining, dining, and womanizing.

And now he seemed no longer ashamed. "Ah, Miss Fairchild, how hard must I work to gain your high regard?" he asked, obviously with an attempt at humor for he could not be serious.

"I'm not sure that gaining my high regard is worth any trouble at all," she said. "Soon these events that my mother insists I attend, mostly to chaperone my wayward brother, will be in the past."

He looked sly. "Surely you must be secretly betrothed, Miss Fairchild, for I cannot believe you wish to eschew the possibility of finding future happiness."

"You know I am not, Sir Frederick," Amelia said. "On my twenty-fifth birthday I come into a small inheritance that will allow me to retire quietly to the country."

"Alone?"

"I will have a companion, I dare say. Since my mother insists."

"She will not live with you?"

"For some of the time, of course. But she and I are not disposed to live companionably under the same roof all of the time and when I have the funds to put some separation between us—fond as I am of her company—it will be relief to retire from the revels she is so insistent I endure."

"Like this?" Sir Frederick swept his arm about the castle. They were in a gloomy corridor lit up with sconces, and had, during the past five minutes, crossed paths with several other knots of party-goers, all looking intent upon finding the ultimate prize. "I must admit to enjoying myself rather more than I had expected. I'm sorry the feeling isn't mutual."

Amelia felt bad. The truth was, she'd let herself go for a moment and had in fact felt lighter of being than she had for a long time. The challenge of interpreting clues while conversing with a man who was, she had to admit, rather unexpectedly more lighthearted and entertaining than she'd remembered, was more enjoyable than she'd expected.

"I didn't mean that," she said. "Merely that I shall enjoy reading my books and not feeling as if I am being exhibited whenever I set foot in a public place as an unmarried young woman who must surely be looking for a husband."

"And you are sure you are not?"

"I most assuredly am not!" Amelia said with more force than she'd meant for Miss Playford swung round as they reached the larger, lighter music room and asked, frowning, "Are you all right, Miss Fairchild?"

"Miss Fairchild was just explaining to me that she is not looking for a husband and intends to retire soon to the country."

"Oh." The shock in Miss Playford's expression would have been amusing if Amelia didn't feel so exposed and surprisingly put on the spot for her declaration. "Not ever? You don't ever want to get married? I thought only ugly spinsters thought like that. At least, the only people I've ever heard saying they don't want to get married are the ones who'd never get a marriage offer to begin with. But you're beautiful, Miss Fairchild, so I am surprised." She smiled. "But that's all right. No one should be forced to marry if they don't wish it." Her smile faltered as she added, "Like poor Lady Pernilla. Her father should not have tried to force her to marry someone she didn't want to marry! Though of course the groom would not have been at all suitable, either."

Amelia shrugged. "Maybe she was in love with the groom. The poor fellow hasn't been given the benefit of the doubt."

"The fact that her letter remains in the book, unsent, is probably a sign that the young man couldn't read."

"Yes, she probably wrote the letters to make herself feel better," Miss Playford agreed. "Now, here's the fortepiano. I wonder if it sounds the same as the one I play."

"I'm sure only you can give us an example of whether it does or not," said Sir Frederick. "Do play us something, Miss Playford. I have been hoping all evening to hear your musical talents on display."

"You have?"

The young girl sat down with such surprised delight that

Amelia couldn't help glancing at Sir Frederick, only to find him looking amused. He smiled at her, his eyes briefly sharing a moment of complicity, as Amelia recognized her own expression of fond amusement mirrored in his.

But their amusement turned to admiration at the first lilting notes of Miss Playford's rendition of Haydn's Sonata in G Major. She really was very good.

"Enchanting, Miss Playford. I trust you'll entertain us all at some stage during the house party," said Sir Frederick.

"Oh, my Aunt Pike says I'm not good enough to play in front of other people," Miss Playford said, standing up quickly, and adding, "And we need to find the next note. I allowed my vanity to get in the way."

Her flash of guilt was a surprise to Amelia who said, "It's not vanity to show what you're good at. Besides, all young ladies are encouraged to work at their singing and dancing skills."

"Yes, but not to be vain about it," said Miss Playford, as she began a quick search beneath the lid of the fortepiano. "Which is why my aunt, who is here chaperoning me, would not countenance my standing up in front of the other guests. Oh, look! Here it is, tucked away in the corner!"

"Our Miss Playford has hidden depths," murmured Sir Frederick as Miss Playford unfolded the note and began to read:

"Outside these walls, a puzzle grows,

Where hedges high in patterns pose.

At the heart, a statue stands alone,

Bearing a message carved in stone."

But Amelia was concentrating more on Sir Frederick's veiled admiration for Miss Playford than the actual words. Perhaps all she needed to do was to ensure the couple spent more time together. Miss Playford was very young, admittedly, but very sweet, and Sir Frederick obviously liked a pretty and accomplished young lady.

Perhaps Amelia just needed to coach Miss Playford on how to flatter Sir Frederick. Perhaps that was what was missing. Sir Frederick needed to be appreciated, and he was not going to get that kind of endorsement that would feed his vanity from Amelia.

Her attention was claimed by Sir Frederick. "So, ladies, is your footwear sturdy enough for a tramp in the grass which hopefully is not wet with dew although it is all but dark?"

"The full moon bathes everything in light. Going outside would be ever so exciting!" said Miss Playford. "And I would gladly sacrifice my slippers for such an adventure for I have another pair. Would we really go outside, Sir Frederick?"

"Outside?" Amelia gasped before Sir Frederick said, "You seemed more invested in your own thoughts than in finding the treasure, Miss Fairchild, for outside we must assuredly go if we are to solve the puzzle. What was it that so claimed your attention?"

As Miss Playford sent her an enquiring look and as Amelia clearly could not speak the truth she said, "I was thinking of poor Lady Pernilla's tragic love story."

"I'd imagine she's far from the only young lady who's unable to wed the man of her heart," said Miss Playford with surprising equanimity. "So that's not really tragic, is it? Not when her story isn't special."

"Good heavens, Miss Playford, that's not very sentimental of you," remarked Sir Frederick with a surprised laugh. "I thought I witnessed a secret tear when you read her love letter."

"Yes, but I thought about it as we were making our way through the castle and tried to list the couples I could think of who'd made matches of the heart—or rather, ones that were happy—and that's when I counseled myself to take a different approach." Her more robust tone faltered a little. "You see, my aunt is forever telling me that I allow my foolish heart to rule my mind and that my vanity will feed me with unreasonable expectations. Especially since I have no dowry." Her voice faltered. "She says a lady must learn to do what those who know better tell her, and to accept it with a good and pragmatic heart." She gave a small laugh. "Sometimes I forget her strictures and it's only when I have a few minutes of reflection that I remind myself."

"So, you don't believe in the love match?" asked Sir Frederick. "You do not know any couples who are happily wed?"

Miss Playford bit her lip as she shook her head.

"What about your parents?" asked Amelia before she could help herself.

"I don't remember them very well," said Miss Playford. "And my aunt was jilted at the altar so she doesn't have a happy story."

"You've not been to many dances or assemblies in the district?"

"Only one."

"Cousins, friends, siblings?" asked Amelia, and when Miss Playford shook her head, she gasped, "Are you not lonely?"

Miss Playford frowned. "I had many friends at the Ladies' Seminary I attended for the ten years until just a few months ago when my aunt decided to launch me. But books are my greatest friends. I cannot tell you how exciting it was to discover the library here. In fact, as soon as my aunt is asleep, I shall creep downstairs and spend the whole night reading."

Amelia and Sir Frederick exchanged glances and Amelia found she was regarding Miss Playford in a very different light. She smiled. "I hope you are transported to wondrous new worlds, in that case," she said.

"Yes, for even going outside during the night is an adventure!" exclaimed Miss Playford, leading the way towards the door. "Come along! I'm sure we are ahead and are going to win!"

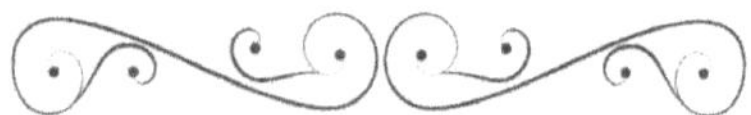

Chapter Thirteen

AMELIA WAS A little concerned by the dampness of the grass but only because her packing had left something to be desired. She really ought to have paid more attention to the possibilities of a weekend away such as this, but she'd been so caught up in matchmaking Sir Frederick with someone blonde and petite that she'd not paid too much thought to her own style and clothing choices other than the requisite costume for the ghost party they were currently undertaking.

So, she therefore lagged a little as Miss Playford strode ahead with Sir Frederick just behind her. He stopped and turned to see what was holding Amelia up and when he saw she was picking her way delicately through the grass, demanded, "Surely you've brought more than one pair of dancing slippers with you, Miss Fairchild? My apologies, I thought you'd agreed your footwear was sufficiently sturdy and not some exquisite confection of silk and satin likely to be ruined on the grass. You did not strike me as that kind of young lady."

"I don't know what kind of young lady I strike you as, Sir Frederick, but no, I do not have another pair of slippers and nor can I outlay upon another pair if these are to be ruined."

"Then allow me to rectify the problem for the last ten yards to the maze where the gravel paths are of the finest sand and represent less of a threat," he said, striding back to where she was and scooping her up into his arms.

Amelia squeaked in shock, covering her mouth so as not to attract Miss Playford's attention. "You really have no need, Sir Frederick," she whispered. "This is highly improper."

"Is it? Why? I'm serving a purely practical purpose."

Amelia was unable to reply. She'd never felt a strong manly chest against her cheek since Thomas had died, and she'd not expected she ever would.

She'd certainly not expected to feel anything other than embarrassed outrage at the experience but even more embarrassing and disconcerting was that what she felt sent thrills through her whole body.

And even more dismaying than that was her sense of loss when he put her down and strode onwards to catch up with Miss Playford.

So, he really was being only gentlemanly? It's what she should hope for, she thought, as she hurried to keep up with the other two who were navigating the maze. She really didn't want to get lost and find herself marooned in the dark.

She heard them exchange a few words and then Sir Frederick's laugh.

Good, perhaps Amelia's plan was starting to work, now that Sir Frederick was gaining a broader appreciation of Miss Playford.

And though it was foolish to feel a pang, it was only to be expected as a sort of swan song for any hopes she might entertain for a husband and family.

While she might enjoy the family, she knew she had not the temperament to play handmaiden to a demanding husband for the rest of her life. She'd seen too many examples of how easily that could go wrong. Miss Playford was correct when she said she she'd seen few examples of couples happily wed.

An owl hooted in a tree nearby and Amelia looked up to the inky sky, the golden moon bathing the world in a magical light. She heard the voices of her companions but could not see them when she turned a corner, halting her footsteps as she realized they'd gone and were out of earshot.

She really should hurry to catch up.

But rounding a corner, she realized she was at a dead end. Foolishly, she'd taken the wrong path.

It was an easy mistake but one which she must rectify quickly to avoid embarrassment.

However, after picking up her skirts and dashing the length of the path before it reached the corner of the yew hedge, she realized she was even more lost for there was yet another dead end.

"Miss Fairchild!"

She heard both Miss Playford and Sir Frederick calling for her and balled her hands into fists as she forced herself to answer, shame making her hot. She was only glad they couldn't see her embarrassment for she blushed so very violently when her pride was on a pike.

"I'm here!" she called, hearing their footsteps which sounded on the other side of the hedge. "Right here!" she called in relief for they were very close.

"Can you find your way through to where we are, or would you like to stay still and we'll find you?"

"I'm sure I can find you with little trouble," she said, not hiding the exasperation in her voice. Of course she could.

But after some minutes more, there was nothing she could do but admit defeat. Not that she intended to do so in so many words. However, when Sir Frederick said, "I think you should not move, Miss Fairchild. Miss Playford and I will rescue you."

Rescue me, thought Amelia in disgust. She'd never needed rescuing in her life, and she certainly didn't need Sir Frederick to think he was playing the gallant knight in shining armor.

Yet, she couldn't put her words into thoughts, muttering only an ungrateful "all right, I'll stay right here" before, within a few seconds, the others were rounding the corner and saying gleefully, "Here you are! And what's more, we've found the final clue. Come with us and we'll show you."

If they sensed she was vexed, they didn't show it, and when Amelia reached the statue in the very center of the maze and saw the inscription at the bottom, her annoyance at herself had dissolved and she easily congratulated them as she read:

"Though warned to stay away, you must be brave,

For in the tower, secrets the past did save.

Climb with care, watch your step,

In crumbling stone, the truth is kept."

Looking up, she asked, "Surely we are not to venture into the tower. It's unsafe."

"But I believe I know another way to access it that is not via the crumbling stairs, for assuredly they are unsafe. I believe Lady Pendleton intended for us to have this clue since she knows how familiar I am with the castle."

"First we have to get out of here," said Amelia with a sigh. "Clearly, I have not such a nose for direction as both of you and will have to meekly follow as you lead the way."

Sir Frederick laughed. He went in front and began to traverse the sandy walkways of the maze. "I can see how heartily you dislike playing the maiden meek and mild."

"Intensely," muttered Amelia which made both of the others laugh for some reason, and Miss Playford to say ingenuously, "My aunt says it's necessary sometimes for a lady to pretend she is far weaker and stupider than she is if a man is to pay her the necessary attention."

"She sounds very anxious for you to make a match this season," remarked Amelia. "I would certainly take her advice with a very large grain of salt."

"So, you have never played on a man's chivalrous instincts, Miss Fairchild?" asked Sir Frederick. "What about your fiancé? He was a very brave man. Surely you were not quite so fierce and independent all those years ago?"

Amelia gasped. How could he speak of Thomas with such lightheartedness? Even her nearest and dearest knew it was a topic that could not be broached without the greatest delicacy.

At her silence, Sir Frederick turned to look at her, raising his eyebrows as he obviously saw her expression. "My apologies if I spoke carelessly, Miss Fairchild. As it has been more than five years, I had thought it safe to think you'd accepted the past."

Again, how could Sir Frederick speak as if Thomas's death were something she could ever accept. Frostily, she said, "It's all very well for you, who did not endure the horrors of war. Thomas's sacrifice is something that of course I have to accept but there is no other man who can come close to equaling him in honor and nobility. It is one of the reasons I intend retiring to the country."

"Once you've come into your inheritance?" Miss Playford clarified. "How fortunate you are to have an inheritance. I have no dowry, but it is my aunt's hope that as my late father was a war hero, this can be overlooked. She says my connections are good and that I'm fair enough of face to warrant some attention."

Her disclosure was so artless that Amelia felt a wave of shame to have spoken earlier in such a maudlin and defensive fashion. She should have recalled that Miss Playford's father had been recognized as a war hero, fighting by the side of the great Admiral Nelson, that hero of the country, though Rear Admiral Nathaniel Playford had died some years later.

"I suppose I can understand your feelings, though," Miss Playford went on, "for my mother died of grief some months after Papa's death, which left me in the care of my aunt who really could have done without such a responsibility, she's always told me. That's why I intend to make a match this season since she doesn't want the burden of me too much longer."

"You must be discerning," Amelia cautioned, suddenly worried as she drew level with Miss Playford. "Marriage is a lifelong contract. It is not something to rush into."

"I really see no alternative," said Miss Playford. "While I am here, I will meet many potential husbands. My aunt has pointed many of them out to me already."

Amelia noticed that her glance at Sir Frederick was fleeting. Did she wonder if she had a chance with him?

Did she?

Amelia squared her shoulders. Miss Playford and Sir Frederick would make an excellent pair, she thought with even greater determination.

Sir Frederick simply didn't know it yet.

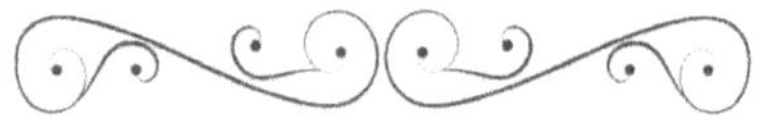

Chapter Fourteen

T HE TOWER.

Amelia glanced at Miss Playford as they set their footsteps in the direction of the tower. She'd firmly declined Sir Frederick's offer to carry her across the grass—despite the surge of feeling his words occasioned.

Now Sir Frederick was assuring them that only a couple of steps were unstable, and he knew which ones. Apparently, it was part of Lady Pendleton's ruse to keep all those away other than the few who understood its dangers—like Sir Frederick.

"Remember, she's given different clues to everyone. We'll be perfectly safe. If Sir Frederick says so," Miss Playford said comfortably as they reached the gravel path that circumnavigated the castle itself.

A few guests were gathered near the rose garden and Amelia recognized Miss Caroline's tinkling laugh. A sharp glance in that direction suggested that Sir Frederick did, too.

But when Henry's laughter joined hers, he relaxed, until another voice intruded.

Mr. Greene was there, too. Of course, Caroline was being chaperoned, and Mr. Pipkin's desultory presence was the shadow Amelia could see in the distance, but the fact that Miss Caroline had nevertheless engineered a grouping that included Mr. Greene was dismaying.

"She's very young and the novelty will wear off. Maybe even more quickly if she doesn't meet such fierce opposition to her predilection for his company," Amelia said, briefly putting her hand on his arm and feeling his tension.

"And what might you know about protecting someone you love from their worst impulses," Sir Frederick growled, barely attending to her, his focus was so squarely upon his sister who'd tucked her hand into Mr. Greene's arm for a brief moment before Henry intervened in a lighthearted manner.

"My softhearted younger brother's misguided efforts to affect the happiness of those he loves has been known to have unfortunate consequences, Sir Frederick," Amelia said stiffly, withdrawing her hand and moving forward to flank Miss Playford. If Sir Frederick could lose his manners so quickly, she thought, he would be well left alone.

In silence, the three of them traversed the path around the castle. Amelia was surprised at the number of people outside, though she supposed she shouldn't be given the balmy weather and the beautiful grounds.

A deep, masculine voice intruded on their silence.

"Sir Frederick, how goes it with you? Are you leading your ladies to victory, do you suppose?"

Amelia glanced up to see Lord Thornton bearing down upon them.

"We have only one clue remaining," said Miss Playford, happily. "I'm sure we're going to win, for we've been ever so quick to guess."

"What a clever trio, for the four other groups participating are not yet on their third clue. I'd better not hold you up then."

"Three heads are better than one, and it's been my good fortune to have been teamed with exceptionally clever young ladies," Sir Frederick said, finding his good manners at last, thought Amelia.

Not that it made her feel any more charitable towards him.

Clearly, Sir Frederick was a grumpy and gloomy fellow when not actively prodded to be otherwise. And Amelia certainly didn't intend being the person upon whom it fell to cajole him into a good temper every day. It was just as well she knew how manufactured his charming façade was, she told herself as Lord Thornton disappeared towards Caroline and her group.

And now they were at the tower. In the silence of the moonlit night, they contemplated the ancient door, half off its hinges, which otherwise served to keep everyone else away.

"I suppose it's the last clue," Amelia conceded. She was ready to finish this ghost hunt. It had occasioned many heightened feelings which had not made her comfortable and which she certainly wasn't used to.

"And it's our duty to help Lady Pendleton exorcise Lady Pernilla's ghost," said Miss Playford. "That's what she really wants, isn't it, Sir Frederick?"

Sir Frederick smiled. "I don't think Lady Pendleton really believes her ancestor's ghost rattles down the corridors at night. This is a game, Miss Playford."

Although Miss Playford looked a little crestfallen, she said nothing as Sir Frederick opened the door with some effort, telling the ladies it was only proper that he go ahead to ensure their safety.

The twisting stone staircase was in pitch blackness until Sir Frederick raised his lantern. Again, Amelia silently berated herself for her foolishness in not heeding the advice to wear sturdier footwear for the ghost hunt. Still, though she was going to ruin her dancing slippers, it wasn't as if she'd have many future occasions to wear them.

Glancing at Miss Playford and Sir Frederick chatting companionably, Amelia felt the mixed emotions and pressure occasioned by the necessary efforts in allying Sir Frederick with someone whose outward characteristics matched Miss Playford.

"Of course, if you would prefer to remain at the bottom of this flight of steps while I continue alone, do say so. This is not for the fainthearted and I'm somewhat surprised it's where we've been directed to go," said Sir Frederick.

"Of course we're going!" both young ladies said in unison, stepping up behind Sir Frederick who, leaning back, said, "And if you have any need to grip onto my hand, you need only say the word. We're not in the ballroom."

No, we're on a dark and scary staircase, thought Amelia with the faintest alarm. She did not consider herself a coward by any means, but she certainly did not like dark, enclosed spaces.

Forcing herself to breathe evenly, she took the rear, with Miss Playford and Sir Frederick in front of her. Each step took her farther into the enclosed and dark space she so hated and she could feel the sweat break out on her forehead as she steadily climbed.

"Watch the crumbling step to your right," Sir Frederick called from above, and Amelia dutifully sidestepped. "Are you ladies all right?"

"Perfectly fine," Miss Playford said brightly.

"Miss Fairchild?"

Amelia took a deep breath before forcing herself to reply to Sir Frederick's question in the affirmative. But she was embarrassed to hear the strain in her voice and, when they finally reached the top, she sagged against the wall and closed her eyes when they were on solid ground.

But almost immediately she pushed herself into the center of the circular room and turned about, taking in her surroundings with new wonder.

"It is a lady's bedchamber, clearly long-unused," she marveled, running her forefinger across the dusty-looking glass attached to a heavy wooden dressing table.

"Do you think it could be Lady Pernilla's?" asked Miss Playford, sitting down on the fourposter bed and then coughing at the cloud of dust this occasioned.

"I dare say we might find out if we search for clues," said Amelia, opening a drawer and pulling out some trinkets: small, insignificant pieces of adornment.

"Is the treasure here or is this the last clue, do you suppose? Oh! This diary belongs to Lady Pernilla!" cried Miss Playford, picking up a little book from the top of a chest of drawers.

Immediately, Amelia was at her side. She did not want to reveal her interest in Lady Pernilla's sad love story, but the truth was that she was deeply curious.

"Can I read it?" Miss Playford sent a questioning look at Amelia and then Sir Frederick, who smiled and said with a shrug, "The lady has been dead more than a hundred years. I can't see the harm."

"My aunt would say it was a terrible thing to read another's diary, but she doesn't scruple to read mine," said Miss Playford, adding with a little laugh, "But she'll never find my *secret* diary."

Amelia and Sir Frederick looked at each other, smiling as they observed the fact they'd both raised their eyebrows at the same time.

"I think you should clarify that you have nothing truly wicked to hide," said Amelia mildly. "Young ladies should be careful not to hint at things that might be misinterpreted."

Miss Playford put her hand to her mouth. "Goodness, no! I have only desires and wishes to be gone from my aunt's house. And I write all the unkindnesses of which she is guilty. It helps me greatly to write that which I cannot confide to anyone. Everyone is a spy in my aunt's house. Except Mary, the maid of all work."

"I'm sorry to hear it," Amelia said. "I cannot imagine how it must feel to be distrustful of one's nearest and dearest." She thought of her own dear brother, and of her scatterbrained mother, both of whom wanted only the best for her.

And then she thought of brave and honorable Thomas who'd given his own life for the greater good and who'd sacrificed so much for Amelia's own happiness.

"My aunt calls me *vain and venal Venetia* and says I should be grateful to the man who'll take me, but it no longer troubles me. Truly it doesn't," she added at Amelia's look. "She's said it for as long as I can remember, and now I know that that description applies much more to her. Miss Spencer, one of the teachers at my Ladies' Seminary, says I have a surprising aptitude for languages and that I could be a diplomat's wife or marry a prince and that makes me feel a great deal better." She'd been flipping through the pages of Lady Pernilla's diary as she spoke and as she closed the book she said, "Clearly this is the diary Lady Pernilla wanted everyone to find. She writes just the kind of things I write in mine. No doubt her secret diary is hidden, but I dare say we'll never find it for Lady Pernilla died a hundred years ago. Possibly in this very tower, though I do not recall if Lady Pendleton said how she died."

Amelia regarded young Miss Playford admiringly, though she said, "And I don't suppose it's of any benefit to even look. Not when time is running out to find the final clue. Now, what do you suppose we should be looking for?"

She turned to find Sir Frederick kneeling near the window, his hands gently feeling along the stonework, his eyes closed.

"Goodness, Sir Frederick, you look as if you're a spymaster conducting a deep search!" Amelia said.

"And I've found what I'm looking for, too," he said, working at a stone which he pried loose before plunging his hand into the cavity and withdrawing a small wooden box.

"Lady Pendleton must think we are cleverer than we are! And we've fooled her!" said Miss Playford, hurrying over and then sitting on the bed as Sir Frederick dusted off the top of the book and prepared to open it.

Amelia had so nearly sat on his other side before realizing the impropriety. Yet there was something rather sweet in the way Miss Playford seemed to forget she was a young lady unleashed into society rather than a schoolroom miss who was eagerly helping her older brother solve a puzzle.

Older brother? Amelia cast them both a sidelong look as she took a seat at the dressing table. No, that was the first impression that had come to mind. Miss Playford had greeted with such eagerness the possibility that Sir Frederick might look upon her as a marital contender, earlier.

"A letter! The final clue!" Miss Playford cried, but Sir Frederick shook his head and his tone was grim. "It's a letter, but I don't think Lady Pendleton knows about it or it would certainly have been burned. Miss Playford, would you care to do the honors?"

Her face lit up when he handed her the letter, and she began to read:

"My dearest Pernilla,

As I sit here in the stables, having just finished tending to your father's prized stallion, my thoughts, as always, turn to you.

The scent of hay and leather surrounds me, but in my mind, I am lost in the sweet perfume of your presence. I know that to the world, I am nothing more than a lowly groom, unworthy of your affections. Yet I dare to dream, my love, that the connection we share transcends these artificial boundaries of class and fortune.

Do you recall our conversation in the library last week? How we lost ourselves discussing Alexander Pope's beautiful poem? Your insights were so keen, your wit so sharp. In those moments, I forgot the dirt beneath my fingernails and imagined us as equals, two minds entwined in the joy of shared knowledge.

I often think of my days at Oxford, before my family's misfortunes forced me to abandon my studies. How different my life might have been had fate not intervened.

Perhaps I would have been deemed a suitable match for you then.

But I cannot bring myself to regret the path that led me to your side, even if I must admire you from afar. Your father's library has become my sanctuary. In the quiet hours of the night, I devour volume after volume, striving to better myself, to be worthy of the love I see in your eyes.

Plato, Shakespeare, Newton—their words fill my mind, but it is thoughts of you that fill my heart. I know our situation seems hopeless. A penniless scholar turned groom can offer you little in the way of comfort or status.

But I offer you my mind, my heart, and a love as deep as the oceans we've read about in your father's atlases.

Forgive me, my darling, for daring to hope. For dreaming of a world where love and intellect are the true measure of a person's worth.

Until then, I remain,
Forever yours in heart and mind,
William Greene"

Miss Playford gasped as she dropped the letter and looked at the other two.

"So, William wasn't just the lowly groom Lady Pendleton said he was? He was educated?"

"But he had no money, so of course he was unworthy of her." Amelia raised an eyebrow. In fact, she felt a little combative and wondered what Sir Frederick's response would be when she added, "The girl's father had a far more illustrious match lined up—and little matter that she didn't care for him."

Sir Frederick didn't disappoint. "If I were the girl's father, I'd certainly be concerned if a marital contender was a fortune hunter. Besides, it's not as if she could be forced to wed against her will. No one can be coerced to that degree."

Both Amelia and Miss Playford stared at him. "You are a man," Amelia said with real acid in her tone. "You exist on a privileged plane. You cannot know the degree to which a young woman can be coerced to do as her elders—her closest male relative—wishes them to do." She felt herself growing increasingly worked up, which was rather surprising, for Amelia was always mistress of her emotions—or so she thought. But the pressure was building as to what she might do if she failed in the plan required to ensure Edward didn't lose his bet. "Why do you suppose I wish to retire quietly to the country? I have a small inheritance and thank the Lord it's sufficient for me to live sparingly, but independently. I am nearly five and twenty and can retire from revels like this. Soon I will no longer be dependent upon the whims of the menfolk in my life."

He stared at her. "Your brother—?"

"Edward is the most devoted and loving of brothers. I could not wish for a better. But he is four years younger in years and a great deal younger in good sense. I am aware of his good-hearted attempts to do what is best for me but, in the eyes of the law, and with no means, yet, of my own, I am completely at the mercy of others. It is not a situation that I relish. So, if Miss Pernilla wished to marry a man who was educated but whose family fortunes had left him with no independence, I say she ought to have been able to choose for herself."

"And clearly she was not able to," Miss Playford said, taking up the argument with equal fire, "because she's a ghost!"

The fierceness of her words, and perhaps the faint ludicrousness, stopped them all in their tracks.

Even she seemed taken aback by her vehemence in saying the word "ghost" that hung in the air.

Amelia seized the initiative before Sir Frederick had a chance to respond. She might be a young lady with an independent mind, but she now wanted to play peace-maker to prove she was capable of that, too.

So she smiled and said, "Is she really? This is Lady Pendleton's Ghostly Gathering. And Lady Pernilla is a convenient prop. Can we say with certainty that the letters we've found are real?" She pointed to the letter in Miss Playford's hand. "And what of the letter in the volume of *Pride and Prejudice* in the library? Perhaps that was a clever prop, too?"

"But the painting!" Miss Playford objected. "That was a genuine painting."

"Yes, but of Miss Pernilla?" Amelia asked. "I think we should set our minds to discovering the last clue and put an end to all this. It's a game, nothing more."

Sir Frederick, who'd remained quietly standing by the door, regarding them both with surprising gravity, now said, "A game it might be, but everything you've said has more depth than a game should give rise to. Ladies, you've given me pause. I admit to feeling put in my place. Not that what you've said changes my mind with regard to the man who would run off with my sister at the first opportunity. And she, susceptible to his flattery, would need nothing more than a little persuasion."

"Yes, but your sister is only seventeen and the gentleman of whom you speak is clearly a man of dubious reputation," said Amelia. "I am of the same mind when you speak of your concerns, Sir Frederick. But I speak merely in generalities. If Lady Pernilla did indeed exist, and if the letters we've read are real, then she is in the very situation where I lament her inability to exercise the choice to follow her heart. Now." Amelia cleared her throat. "Let us read again the final clue. We were so keen to win this treasure hunt but we've allowed ourselves to be diverted by philosophical discussions."

Quietly, Miss Playford took the paper Sir Frederick handed her and read:

"A room untouched by time's swift flight,

Where a lady's ghost still walks at night.

Seek the mirror that reflects no face,

Behind its glass, find the final place."

"We should have realized what that meant," Amelia said, smiling, as she went to the dressing table and picked up the hand-held looking glass, cracked and aged. As she began to prise the glass from its backing, Sir Frederick gently took it from her. "I don't want you to hurt yourself," he said, "when I have the right tools here." Using the paper knife lying on the dressing table, they all gasped at what was revealed.

In the backing was a small cavity, and in this cavity were two gold rings. With a frown, Sir Frederick raised them to the light of his lantern, squinting as he took in the tiny engraved initials.

"What is it?" asked Miss P. "Are they Lady Pernilla's and William's rings? Surely this can't be real? Lady Pernilla was made to marry someone else."

"I think we really can't be too sure of Lady Pernilla's real story," Amelia said, stepping closer, her heart beating a little more rapidly as she directed an enquiring look at Sir Frederick. "Can you read an inscription?"

He nodded. "P and W. That's what it says. It's very clear." He hesitated, squinting at the box, then pulling back a small square of paper folded into the bottom.

With a short laugh, he read:

"Your attempts were sound,

For the treasure is found!"

The young ladies gasped. "So, is this the treasure? But these rings are heirlooms. Surely they belong to the family," said Amelia. "What do you suppose Lady Pendleton is up to with this strange treasure hunt? Or is it all make-believe?"

Sir Frederick's frown had given way to a mask of skepticism. "I think that is exactly what it is. She's made us all feel that her tragic relative is truly a ghost, and she's gone to great lengths to fabricate everything."

Miss Playford sat down heavily on the counterpane, coughing once more before she said, "Oh, she's not real? I am so disappointed." She sighed. "Well, we've found the treasure. And it is valuable, is it not?"

Sir Frederick shook his head. "Two gold rings? I think not. Still, it was a fine game."

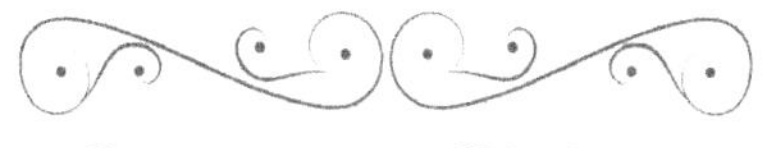

Chapter Fifteen

AFTER THE EXCITEMENT of the treasure hunt, the ball was always going to be second best.

Amelia tried to do justice to the occasion. She went to her bedchamber and changed into her best ballgown which was refurbished from the previous year. It was only the previous year that she'd begun to start to feel she might almost be ready to return to the marriage mart. She'd been admired and felt a stirring of interest in a young man whose intentions had, it transpired to her embarrassment, been more focused in toying with Amelia's affections in order to stir up the jealousy of the young lady he eventually married.

It had made Amelia feel something of a fool. She had, fortunately, not fallen in too deep, but it was a reminder that her beloved Thomas was a man apart. There would only ever be one Thomas with precious few more good men like him in the world.

So, although she might appreciate Sir Frederick's handsome jaw, his athletic physique, and his charm, she must remember that he was like most other men similarly blessed with good looks—and a great many who weren't. The interest he professed in the ladies was to further the interests of no one else but himself.

And yes, the treasure hunt had been staged. Every trio had

discovered some "treasure" relating to Miss Pernilla and her tragic love story. Every trio had been similarly duped and there was no ghostly apparition who stalked the corridors, Lady Pendleton had admitted.

"I think it was badly done of her," grumbled Miss Playford just before they went to their rooms.

"It was a game, Miss Playford. We all knew that," Amelia had said, trying to cajole her into brighter spirits so she could enjoy the ball with renewed enthusiasm.

But Sir Frederick had surprisingly agreed with the young lady. "It's no fun when someone toys with one's emotions, as Lady Pendleton is guilty of doing."

"Toying with our emotions?" repeated Amelia. "We knew it was a game."

"Did we?" His look was dark as he shook his head. "No, we entered into the spirit of it as if it were real. No one likes to feel they engaged a piece of themselves—" and he tapped the left side of his chest "—only to feel they've been played like a fool."

And his words had Amelia wondering all the way to her room and as she changed, whether Sir Frederick really had ever had his heart broken because he was, she was sure, a philanderer who had no real heart to be played with.

Not only did she know that herself from experience, but Thomas had given an excoriating assessment of him just before he'd gone into battle.

The battle from which he had never returned.

AND NOW THE dancing was in full swing and Miss Playford was in company with her friends, the other Miss Ps—all blonde, petite, vivacious, and highly suitable for Sir Frederick if Amelia could only engineer such matters.

Which she must do if her dreams were to come true...she supposed.

"Would you do me the honor of this dance? A set is just forming."

She looked up, surprised that Sir Frederick had asked. But she could not refuse. She knew him too well and it would be churlish. And she did like to dance. In fact, she'd miss dancing after she retired to the country, but not as much as she'd miss reading books and exercising her own will, which she'd have to give up if she were to wed.

She smiled, placing her hand upon the arm he offered, and together they crossed the room and took up their places.

"Miss Playford is rather charming, don't you think?" Amelia asked him.

"Far more so that I'd thought initially," he said, smiling. "There is a certain artlessness when she drops the façade of being on display that makes her a great deal more interesting than she appears now."

They both turned to glance at the young lady in the midst of her group of friends, with several chaperones a short distance away. Miss Playford was speaking in a very animated fashion, but the glances she directed towards some of the eligible young men in the room were plain to see.

"I think she's too young to get married."

This was not what Amelia wanted to hear. "She's the perfect age. She's so pliable and ready to please. Any gentleman in want of a wife would struggle to do better."

"But who wants a wife like that?" asked Sir Frederick, beginning the dance. "No, a young lady who has her own views and opinions is far more interesting. An intelligent young lady who takes the trouble to discover what she thinks first is far more appealing."

Amelia was even more surprised. Then she said, "That is not very charitable to Miss Playford who, I believe, displayed intelligence, depth, and humor."

"I thought the same until you made the remark that she appears pliable and willing-to-please," said Sir Frederick. "And, as I place a great deal of store in your opinion, Miss Fairchild, that was my answer."

Amelia felt he could have knocked her down with a feather and cautioned herself to be more careful in future. If Sir Frederick could be swayed by her opinion, then she'd have to paint a potential wife in very different terms.

"What are you looking for in a wife?" she asked.

"I'm not looking for a wife," he said simply, and Amelia blushed hotly to think he might imagine she was asking for herself.

"Just as I am not looking for a husband," she said quickly. "As soon as I—"

"Yes, yes, as soon as you get your inheritance, you're retiring to the country," he repeated with a sigh.

Amelia stared at him, open-mouthed. He seemed in low spirits suddenly, so she asked, "And what will you do as the season progresses and then the new year is upon us? Do you plan to go adventuring? Men have so many choices."

"You say that as if you were envious," he said, frowning. "Sometimes choice is not as grand as it's made out to be. Sometimes, one has no choice but to do something one really doesn't want to do."

This was such a quixotic remark and Amelia was quite dying to discover what he meant and to be furnished with a concrete example, but then it was time to change partners and she found herself looking up into the eyes of Mr. Greene who sent her a wolfish smile and asked her if she'd discovered the final fate of tragic, bogus Miss Pernilla as they had, though not everyone had been so clever.

His clear self-congratulation and the pompous way he phrased his question really irked Amelia, so she was glad there was little chance to offer more than a simple affirmation before she was required to perform a do-si-do to the side, returning a few seconds later at which point she decided to change the subject, saying, "And I couldn't help observing how greatly Miss

Caroline appeared to be enjoying herself. Her brother was part of our investigative team, and he told us all about the plans she has for her future." Amelia smiled ingenuously. She was not surprised at the stiffness of his response.

"Indeed, Miss Caroline has told me all about her future with her very own lips." He looked smug. "She happened to be in my investigative team."

Amelia nodded, smiling. "Yes, a charming young lady I thought when I met her, with much in common to discuss regarding the peculiar difficulties of our respective futures."

Mr. Greene sent her a condescending look that showed his skepticism at Amelia's comment. But as he was clearly as impatient a man as Amelia had pegged him, he finally said, with clear reluctance at having to ask, "And what do the pair of you have in common?"

Amelia responded as if she'd even forgotten her remark, saying, "Oh, just the frustration of not being able to wed before we are twenty-five, unless our future husband is prepared to wait that long for a dowry or inheritance. It is simply vexatious the number of husbands whose interest suddenly dissipates at such a revelation."

And then their partnership was at an end and suddenly Amelia found herself once again in close proximity with Sir Frederick as they waited to perform a figure with the person beside them.

There was just enough time for Sir Frederick to remark with a frown, "You look surprisingly pleased with yourself. And after such a coze with Mr. Greene, I couldn't help but notice."

"Could you not?" Amelia asked, grinning. "That is because I planted a seed that I think will make him regard your sister in a slightly different light."

"You did?"

"I said that the pair of us had been commiserating at the sudden loss of interest shown in us by eligible gentlemen upon learning we come without dowry or inheritance before we are twenty-five."

Sir Frederick's grin turned to a rueful smile. "If only that were true. In Caro's case, at least. I gather it is true for you, and I'm sorry that it has caused you angst."

"Not in the slightest. I had no desire to wed after losing my Thomas. And already I'm what most gentlemen would call 'long in the tooth'. My marriageable days are over, Sir Frederick, and do I rue the fact?" She shrugged. "I do not. But as for Caro, I hope that will give Mr. Greene pause."

"He will soon learn that you have misled him."

"Eventually. But if he withdraws interest in Caro, and she learns the truth, she'll know he was only after her money."

Amelia didn't get the chance to see his response, for suddenly she was claimed by her next partner. Nor did she see Sir Frederick for the rest of the set and it was only as she was glancing about the emptying ballroom, surprised that the time had gone so fast and she had enjoyed herself so much, that she observed Caroline by the doors to the tower room, half hidden by a large vase festooned with flowers.

At first Amelia thought the girl was admiring the floral magnificence before she realized that Caroline was weeping piteous tears, which she was trying to hide from her chaperone, who stood a few feet away, apparently quite oblivious as she gossiped with some other matrons.

"Caro, what has happened? Shall I fetch your brother?" Amelia asked, concerned, as she sidled up to the girl.

But Caro shook her head vehemently. "Don't tell Freddy!" she said. "He'll be too happy, I know. He doesn't like Mr. Greene and would do anything to part us but, oh, that has already happened, and my heart feels like it has been torn from my breast. I don't know how I'll ever be happy again."

"He's withdrawn his interest?" Amelia asked hopefully, while trying hard not to sound gleeful. "I'm so sorry. What did he say?"

Caro shrugged. "He just hinted that perhaps we were not as suited as he had thought and perhaps it would be kinder of him to allow me to lose my heart to someone else since he might be adventuring abroad shortly."

Amelia patted the girl's shoulder. "My poor Caro. I, too, know the pain of a broken heart, but believe me, the pain does ease."

To her surprise, she realized as she said these words that indeed the pain did ease. In fact, the last few hours she'd barely felt pain during any moment of reflection that included Thomas. No, she'd been thinking too much about Sir Frederick.

That is, about matching him with someone else, she reminded herself quickly, turning unconsciously to scan the room for a glimpse of him and blushing when her gaze alighted upon him across the room at exactly the moment he turned and locked eyes with her.

Immediately, he nodded to his companion to terminate their conversation and strode across the dance floor, his smile turning to one of concern as he asked his sister for the cause of her distress.

Since Amelia knew Caroline was not going to reveal the truth, she said ingenuously, "Poor Caro had formed a *tendre* for a gentleman who hinted he might be going abroad shortly when she was so certain he harbored feelings for her."

"My poor Caro," said Sir Frederick, giving his sister's shoulder a sympathetic pat while his grin over the top of the young girl's head revealed his delight.

"A good night's sleep will have you feeling far more yourself, my dear," said Sir Frederick, taking her hand and caging it on his sleeve. "I think it's time to hand you over to your chaperone. I'm sure that a good night's sleep is all you need to be feeling a great deal better about the future."

THE DANCING HAD finished by 3 a.m. and Amelia trailed off to bed thinking that she'd fall into an immediate slumber. Strangely, however, she was too wound-up to sleep. It seemed she'd only just closed her eyes when she was roused at a ridiculously early hour by insistent rapping upon her door.

"Well, sis, you solved the puzzle and won yourself some treasure, but I'm here to tell you the match-making with Sir Frederick is off to a wonderful start!" It was her brother, looking ridiculously perky for this time of the morning. He strode into the room and immediately settled himself in the single armchair, his long legs stretched out in front of him. "You voiced concerns last night that Miss Playford was too young and innocent for Sir Frederick's liking... Well, I saw him deep in conversation with Mrs. Perry. In fact, I could barely sleep for thinking of how deeply in conversation the pair of them were."

Amelia pushed her dark hair out of her eyes and blinked as she tried to clear her head. "Who is Mrs. Perry?"

"Why, only the season's most delicious and desirable widow. Tiny, golden-haired, and vivacious to boot. I don't know why I didn't consider her. Perhaps because I assumed Sir Frederick liked the young and innocent ones. But we don't all have the same taste, do we?"

"We do not," said Amelia, not sure she liked what Edward was telling her.

"Anyway, as soon as you told me that Sir Frederick likes ladies with more experience, my eye was caught by Mrs. Perry who, I will tell you now, was angling the most meaningful glances in Sir Frederick's direction of which he appeared quite oblivious until I ingeniously cried out, 'Why, Sir Frederick, I believe Mrs. Perry has dropped a pearl earring.' At least, she'd solicited help in finding it earlier—which she had, sister dear, though I heard she since had found it. Nevertheless, I went on, 'I dare say you haven't found it?' And then, suddenly, the pair were in conversation and the last I saw them, had their heads bent towards each other and were enjoying the most delightful coze. Why, I do believe I have found his perfect match. Mrs. Perry has something of a dubious reputation. She's a tremendous flirt and—"

"Not a grieving widow, then?"

"Good lord, no! It's an open secret she's been waiting for her aged husband to quit this mortal coil from the moment he shuffled her down the aisle two years ago. It's also no secret she'd been holding out for a peer, but old Mr. Perry was so fabulously rich and so very ready to die, it would have been foolish to refuse him. Now she's independently wealthy and only needs a title to secure her wildest dreams." He looked smug. "And I've neatly arranged that for her conveniently after her twelvemonth of mourning is over. Pity I don't get a fee for my efforts, though my reward will be seeing you happy." He frowned. "Though you don't look as happy as I thought you would."

"Of course I'm very happy at the prospect of marrying off Sir Frederick as required." Amelia forced a smile and tried to understand her flat and heavy mood, which she put down to lack of sleep. But the more she thought about Sir Frederick's head close to that of a captivating blonde widow, the greater the heaviness of her mood. She'd not felt that way when she'd obviously dangled Miss Playford beneath his nose as a marital contender. Or was that because she clearly did not appeal to him in any way other than a sweet and unformed child—and Amelia knew that was not what he was looking for in a wife? "You are very clever, Edward."

"I am, aren't I?" he congratulated himself. "I could see what Sir Frederick wanted. Vivacity, wickedness, a certain empty-headedness that would make him feel superior."

"Oh, you are good, Edward," Amelia murmured, thinking not of her brother's words but of Sir Frederick's kind eyes when he'd almost commiserated with her disappointment at discovering that Lady Pernilla was a fabrication.

"—Just as I know you like serious, brooding fellows with copious amounts of courage and it is a tragedy there will never be another Thomas for you because your heart is as loyal as the stone foundations beneath a cathedral and that is why I berate myself every day for being so foolish that I nearly jeopardized that which would make you happy, dear sister. But I am atoning, and I believe Mrs. Perry may be the answer to your happiness, for she is everything Sir Frederick wants in a wife—"

"Vivacity, wickedness, a certain empty-headedness that would make him feel superior," intoned Amelia, not feeling the smile she managed for her brother's benefit.

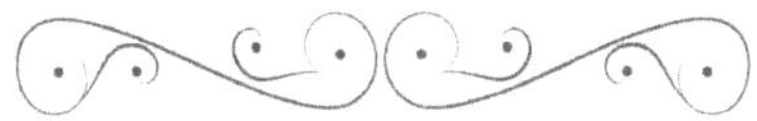

Chapter Sixteen

VIVACITY. WICKEDNESS. THE widow Perry had managed to adopt that vacuous empty-headedness designed to make him feel superior. Sir Frederick sighed. How he did despise women like that. And yet, good manners required that he first engage. And then he did what he always did: collude.

No wonder he was a draw card for vivacious, vacuous, empty-headed women, young and old.

No wonder serious women of substance like Miss Fairchild turned the other cheek when he made overtures.

Not that he'd exactly made overtures to Miss Fairchild though he had found himself, on more than one occasion, unable to keep his distance. She was so very regal and self-contained. And intelligent. So very intriguing.

She, however, clearly held him in contempt though he was encouraged that he did have the ability to make her laugh.

As for that sweet child Miss Playford, Sir Frederick made a mental note to keep a brotherly eye on not just his sister.

A short rap on the door heralded Dombey, the new valet supplied to him by Lord Pendleton.

As Frederick waited to be dressed for the morning's activities, he wondered if he could prevail upon Miss Fairchild to aid him in his endeavors. She'd done marvelously by casting Mr. Greene a lure, one that would put him off his sister. Miss Fairchild certainly understood a great deal she did not convey.

What she had no hesitation in conveying, however, was her disparagement of him.

"Your shirt, if you please, sir."

Sir Frederick raised his arms so that a fresh linen shirt could be donned.

"Are you all right, sir?"

Sir Frederick realized he'd been musing over Miss Fairchild and had neglected to either prime his new valet or don his own shirt.

Now the valet was frozen, his eyes fixated on the latticework of scars that criss-crossed Sir Frederick's back.

"A youthful injury. Long healed and nothing to concern yourself over," Sir Frederick said brusquely.

"You winced, sir."

"I did. But I am perfectly capable of putting on my own shirt every morning." He tried to keep the annoyance out of his tone. It wasn't often that he was so careless.

"The injury still pains you, sir?"

The injury was not something Sir Frederick wished to discuss but the young man went on, "Pardon my impertinence, sir, but my sister is gifted with herbal concoctions that I know have the power to ease such afflictions."

"You mean she was a witch in a less enlightened age?" Sir Frederick smiled to see the young man blush though, to his credit, he persisted. "She has treated terrible scars and injuries with an herbal balm she concocts from plants in the woods." He cleared his throat. "It might benefit you, sir, if you are still troubled by the pain."

"Oh, I feel no pain whatsoever these days," Sir Frederick said in as bluff and hearty a manner as he could manage as he again raised his arms above his head—being sure not to wince this time—so that Dombey could slip on his shirt. "Nevertheless, I thank you for your concern."

"Very good, sir," replied his valet with commendable restraint as he finished dressing Sir Frederick in silence.

But when, after a day's activities in which Sir Frederick did not participate but made all manner of excuses about how he wanted nothing more than to play billiards—when in truth it was the pain of his old injury that wouldn't stop niggling—he really did wish he'd taken Dombey up on his offer.

Well, it was too late. He'd just have to take himself off to bed for an early night and forgo the pleasure of possibly seeing Miss Fairchild for a delightful bit of conversation.

But then, he'd also escape the possibility of being ensnared by Mrs. Perry, so that was one good thing, he decided, as he nodded politely in passing, to the very young woman he'd like nothing more than to take off to a secluded corner of the drawing room.

"MISS FAIRCHILD, WOULD you like to join us for charades?"

Amelia turned to see Miss Playford signaling to her from the depths of a large chair in the drawing room as Amelia took herself off to bed.

She'd passed Sir Frederick not long before and he'd barely acknowledged her. Not long before that, she'd noticed the vivacious Mrs. Perry talking with great animation to a rear admiral, a sight which she had found unexpectedly pleasing.

So, why had her mood plunged so precipitously into the doldrums when Sir Frederick had merely nodded at her with barely a smile as he'd passed her in the great hall?

Hadn't they nearly solved a mystery together? Well, they'd been duped by their hostess, but they'd been cleverer than most of the guests. And then Amelia had concocted a clever decoy to dilute Mr. Greene's interest, so shouldn't that earn her more than a curt nod of the head after he'd appeared almost to ignore her all day?

"Another time, Miss Playford. But thank you for the offer. I hope you enjoy yourself," Amelia said in reply. And she really did. Miss Playford was with the other Miss Ps, giggling at some private joke like the very young girls they were. But Amelia did not dismiss them as vacuous, air-headed creatures like she did Mrs. Perry, who was old enough to know better.

She'd developed a much greater respect for Miss Playford's faculties since their time together.

"Amelia, Lady Pendleton is explaining the myths and truths about her ancestor, Lady Pernilla, if you'd like to hear it." Edward was with Freddy and Caroline in another darkened corner of the massive drawing room.

"Another time, Edward, but thank you," Amelia said with more coolness than she'd intended, and which she realized might offend Lady Pendleton, who clearly had not the capacity for being offended. Lady Pendleton was old and indulged and liked making her guests believe untruths for her own entertainment. Amelia felt very lukewarm towards her right now, though perhaps that was on account of her low spirits that were unaccountably due to Sir Frederick's manner.

She sighed. Didn't that just show Sir Frederick was now really showing his true colors? The convivial and collaborative episodes on the trail of discovery had been temporary and designed purely to charm the ladies while he had to suffer their company.

No, Sir Frederick had reverted to his taciturn self, and it was as if he barely knew Amelia, who was so inconsequential anyway with her tiny inheritance!

And then that thought nearly felled her with despair because maybe she wouldn't even have that since it looked as if grumpy Sir Frederick had no thoughts for anyone other than himself.

Pausing as she crossed the large, stately room, she heard Lady Pendleton's hushed voice. "Pernilla was renowned for her beauty, as you will have seen in the painting in the Long Gallery. Sometimes I wonder if it is a blessing to die young when you are remembered mostly for your beauty."

Despite her skepticism and contempt for Lady Pendleton's tactics, Amelia slowed her footsteps and then halted by a tall column.

"I wouldn't want to die old and miss out on everything that's before me," said one of the Miss Ps brightly to her friends.

Her views were shared by the other Miss Ps, one of whom said, with a shiver, "No, not at all. Who'd want to be bent and wrinkly so that all the men would look the other way and say harsh things behind one's back?"

Amelia noticed that the girls were within hearing of old Lady Townsend, who'd just caught her eye and who now signaled to Amelia to sit down, which she did, for she felt a little embarrassment at the way the girls were speaking within hearing of someone clearly in the category they were so denigrating.

The older lady was alone, reading a book, but she looked up with a smile as Amelia took a seat opposite her. "And did you learn much about the history of Pendleton Castle during your Ghost Hunt?" Lady Townsend asked.

"I became more curious about Lady Pernilla," replied Amelia. "We found some letters, you know."

"Oh, my dear Miss Fairchild, you know how Lady Pendleton plays fast and loose with the truth. I thought you knew she concocted those letters herself and put them where you would find them so you could create your own versions of the story. It was all in the spirit of entertainment."

"Some letters were real," Amelia replied. "And I think Lady Pendleton would be interested to know that Lady Pernilla's lover, William, was not just a lowly groom—"

"And does Sir Frederick believe that, too?"

Amelia frowned. What had Sir Frederick truly thought? she wondered.

"Did you discuss it with him?" asked Lady Townsend. "He's such an agreeable gentleman, I'm sure you both learned much about each other, as well as about Lady Pernilla." Leaning forward, she added, "We missed you at charades this afternoon."

Amelia shuddered. "I do not like to bring attention to myself."

"Ah, my dear! Don't be guilty of what too many earnest young ladies are," Lady Townsend warned. "We are all so self-conscious of how we project our inner selves until those dried up feelings become the extent of who we are."

The unrestrained giggling of the three Miss Ps cut short her words and Amelia smiled. "Not all young ladies are at such risk," she remarked.

"But the serious ones are." Lady Townsend looked a little sad. "The serious ones are at risk of never revealing their inner selves and what is in their hearts. As a result, happiness passes them by and they may spend decades regretting their inaction."

"I think our three vivacious young ladies are at no risk."

"Perhaps. You'd know better than I being so much closer in age in a different era and having spent time with Miss Playford yesterday. I thought she seemed quite taken with Sir Frederick, but he regards her in a brotherly light. He is a very charming gentleman, don't you think?"

Amelia shifted uncomfortably. "A touch taciturn," she said, and Lady Townsend's eyebrows rose.

"Why, I thought he looked at you with singular regard. You're obviously a very clever young woman. I think he was greatly impressed by your abilities in untangling the clues of Lady Pendleton's diverting little game."

"It was only diverting when we truly thought Lady Pernilla's tragic story was true." Indignation rose in Amelia's chest. "I am not entertained by make-believe."

"I've already explained what happened to the real Lady Pernilla," said Lady Townsend. "So what if our hostess embellished some of the facts? Remember, the best stories are based on truth."

It was these last words that ran circles around Amelia's head as she lay in bed, unable to sleep, later that night.

The best stories are based on truth.

When the clock chimed 3 a.m., Amelia bolted upright. Maybe she'd dozed, though she'd felt she'd done nothing but toss and turn since she crawled under the covers after she'd left the conversation with Lady Townsend, pleading a headache as an excuse to miss dinner.

What if Lady Pendleton had found one of Pernilla's letters and then concocted the rest?

What if Lady Pendleton had seen the letter from Pernilla that gave the impression that William was nothing more than a lowly groom? After all, the corresponding letter from William that had given the lie to that was within the pages of *Pride and Prejudice* which had not been part of the real trail of clues.

If that were the case, thought Amelia, she needed to go down to the library right now and leaf through all those romance books—for that was where Pernilla had secreted her letters perhaps being the only truly secret hiding place if the other members of the household did not read romance books.

Wrapping a shawl about her and slipping her feet into a pair of embroidered slippers, Amelia hurried down the passage, along the gallery, down a flight of stairs, and successfully navigated her way to the library with the help of the candle sconces upon the walls and her own candle stick.

Perhaps some of the guests had voiced fears about ghosts and requested that the castle not be in complete darkness.

Sweeping into the library, Amelia made her way directly to where *Pride and Prejudice* was shelved, whereupon she began to carefully go through all the pages once again. But of course, that book had been thoroughly perused, so she pulled out *Mansfield Park*, and again searched through each leaf until a thought hit her.

Lady Pernilla had died many decades before these books had been published. This was where Lady Pendleton had planted the fake clue.

So what books would have been in the library when Pernilla lived in the castle?

Carefully, she ran her fingers along the spines of some of the other books they'd pulled out; books which she recalled Sir Frederick had seen fit to snatch quite quickly from Miss Playford's hands, implying, without saying, that they were not books for ladies' eyes.

An uncharacteristic surge of prurient interest made her scan the titles once more. There was *Tales by a Lady of Pleasure*. That was not a title for ladies' eyes but it was here, in her hands, and perhaps it's where another of Pernilla's or William's letters could be found.

At least, that's how she justified opening the book.

But, no, this was not why she was here! She was here to discover if Pernilla had written more letters and Pernilla certainly would not have opened the pages of such a work.

But as Amelia flipped open a page—a page which no lady should read, she realized after a quick perusal—there was a letter. The handwriting was familiar, the paper the same cream and the penmanship showing an elegant looping of the lower letters as in the initial letter from Pernilla: clearly an original.

Once again, innocent Pernilla was spilling out her heart. This letter pre-dated the other and showed a girl whose heart had been captured during a ball at the local Assembly Hall. William had attended and from reading, Amelia gathered that his family, once wealthy, were suffering great financial hardship, but a generous aunt had funded him the cost of his entry ticket and vouched for him.

With his family well known in the area, the inference was that he had the respectability of a centuries-old name to confer upon a bride who would hopefully bring with her a sizeable dowry.

Pernilla had such a dowry, but clearly her father had set his sights on a bridegroom considerably more illustrious than poor recently impoverished William.

Amelia read the tender sentiments in the letter with a sense of sadness before she realized that William would never have received it.

And yet, he clearly had received messages from Pernilla conveying the state of her heart. Unless, of course, the letter they'd found in the tower had been forged by Lady Pendleton in another of her grandiose acts of theatre.

Thoughtfully, Amelia closed the book and put it back on the shelf, first removing the letter.

Now she needed to discover if William had in fact written any letters to Pernilla or if the romance was a figment of Pernilla's mind or not reciprocated. She couldn't set any store by the letter Lady Pendleton had clearly written.

Perhaps Amelia could spot the forgery. She had three letters supposedly in Pernilla's hand.

Holding aloft the candle, she studied the looped handwriting, deciding with satisfaction that there was a difference. Lady Pendleton had used a more contemporary style of executing certain letters. It was a good forgery, but it proved that the others were indeed real.

A little spurt of excitement propelled her more thoroughly into her task. If Pernilla and her lover were real, there really might be good reason to continue her quest for more correspondence.

Now where to look?

Perhaps close to the delightful novels of Jane Austen. She liked the fact Sir Frederick was familiar with some of them. Who would have thought it?

Who would have thought he'd be so kind to Miss Playford, and not in a romantic sense.

But he was a philanderer and, being with Amelia, he'd have realized it would not do to appear to play fast and loose with the young lady's affections.

Although the page she opened did not contain a letter, the tender sentiments of the fictional characters upon a page of *Evelina* by Frances Burney compelled her to read.

"I could not speak; but my heart was too full to serve me as interpreter. Lord Orville, at length, broke the silence. 'I fear,' said he, in a faltering voice, 'I fear that I have offended you;—I have been too precipitate,—too presumptuous;—forgive me, my Evelina, while I own my error, and—' He stopped; but when I turned to him my eyes full of tears, his own instantly overflowed, while he exclaimed, 'Oh, my Evelina! most lovely of women—forgive my impetuous feelings! Your virtues, your innocence have conquered, and I dare no longer struggle against my passion!'"

Amelia put her hand to her heart and drew in a trembling breath.

How foolish for her to be affected. Romance was for mindless misses and this was a flowery, unrealistic romance designed to toy with innocent hearts who were too innocent to know that real, long-lasting love was rare.

Quickly flicking through the pages, Amelia moved onto the volume beside it and was nearly at the end when she gasped.

Another letter. Oh, dear Lord, this time from William!

Withdrawing the delicate paper, she replaced the book on the shelf and held the letter to the light.

"My dear Pernilla,

Tonight was the most wonderful of my life. Not only to have danced twice with you at the Assembly ball but to then have been satisfied that my feelings were reciprocated has made my pleasure all the more complete.

I know your father looks unkindly upon me as a suitor, I nevertheless wonder if I could be so bold as to request a few moments to discuss those subjects which are so close to the hearts of both of us.

Perhaps at the stables, for it is where my father sometimes seeks advice on his horse from one of your father's grooms. It would not be too unlikely that such a 'coincidence' could occur at 10 o' clock tomorrow morning."

Amelia considered the letter thoughtfully, then placed it in her pocket. She was about to pick up the book beside it when her eye was drawn to a title that elicited a fragment of memory: Sir Frederick's shock when Miss Playford had opened the same book.

Feeling a twinge of wicked guilt, Amelia withdrew the volume and contemplated it thoughtfully. *Juliette* by the Marquis de Sade. She'd not heard of this writer, but he was clearly one that was not considered "respectable".

What did a not quite "respectable"' book contain? Should she read it?

Hesitating, she leaned against the bookshelf and opened the book more fully.

Well, there was no one here to stop her. No one would ever know.

She had just begun to read when she became aware of the sound of someone in the room before a low, masculine voice intruded.

"I really don't think that is suitable reading for a young lady."

"Sir Frederick!" Shocked that she'd been here all this time without realizing that the baronet sat in a deep armchair just a few feet from her, Amelia nearly dropped the book before she said, with some indignation, "And who are you to tell me what I should or shouldn't read?"

"I wouldn't dream of stopping you if you should decide to ignore my advice." He smiled. "I am just suggesting that the power of the written word is immense and what is read cannot be unread."

Amelia frowned down at the book in her hand and then at Sir Frederick. "You have read this?" she asked.

"Actually, I have not," he replied. "I have not read anything of the Marquis de Sade given his reputation as a libertine and sadist."

"A sadist?' Amelia frowned further. "I've not heard the term."

Sir Frederick, who had risen from his armchair, closed his eyes briefly as if he was in pain, then said, "Nor should you. Libertine is sufficient. In fact, I would suggest you don't even mention the man's name, for he is reviled here and across the world for his heinous acts."

"Oh!" Amelia closed the book as if stung, then placed it carefully back on the shelf. "Strange, that it is so...accessible," she remarked.

"Indeed. But I imagine the library of this remote castle is not often consulted. Now, what have you found for I heard you utter an exclamation a short time ago?"

"You've been spying on me all this time?" Amelia didn't hide her indignation.

"To be honest, I was sleeping until you woke me with your cry of surprise. After that, I thought it perhaps more seemly for me to wait until you'd finished your midnight perusals and so be none the wiser as to my presence here."

"But then you felt the need to protect me from my worst impulses."

"Curiosity? No, curiosity is a wonderful impulse."

"For both men and women?" Amelia was testing him. Surely he didn't think that? Most men didn't.

"Absolutely. But I wanted to protect you from reading what you might regret reading as I certainly have no desire to read the words of a man as depraved as the Marquis de Sade."

Amelia bit her lip then said suddenly, "I found a letter from William to Lady Pernilla!" She pulled it out of her pocket and flourished it before him, but his enthusiasm didn't match hers. In fact, disappointingly, he just smiled as if he were indulging her and said, "You know that Lady Pendleton made it all up."

"Lady Pernilla is real! We've seen her portrait, and she died here. And some of the letters are real. Lady Pendleton did admit that."

"She admitted that she found a letter, yes, and that she based the treasure hunt around it, forging all the other letters."

"I've had another look at all the letters we found, and I believe that more than one of them is real."

"So, you're here in the library in the middle of the night because you're investigating the matter?"

Amelia didn't like his slightly condescending manner. "I couldn't sleep, so I thought I would follow a sense I had that there was more to this being real. And now that I have three that are definitely real, I can show Lady Pendleton that Lady Pernilla was being courted by a young man called William who was not a lowly groom but whose family was simply not sufficiently monied for her father to accept his in place of a suitor whom he forced upon her." She stopped. "Are you all right, Sir Frederick? Perhaps you should sit down?"

For there seemed to be a pained look on his face and he'd closed his eyes briefly, as if he were wincing.

In all likelihood, he'd probably imbibed too much brandy with the gentlemen after the ladies had gone to bed and had fallen asleep in the library, though he was wearing a banyan, of course, she noted on reflection.

He eased himself back into the armchair and stretched his leg out in front of him, as if it were the cause of his pain.

So she asked, "Have you hurt your leg, or is it just your head?"

"My head? Why should my head hurt?"

"From the brandy, I assume."

"You assume I'm the worse for drink?"

"No need to take umbrage," Amelia responded quickly. "Most men do when the ladies retire. And you seem in some discomfort."

"My head is perfectly clear but you are right, my leg is hurting like the devil."

"An injury?" asked Amelia. "I'm sorry to hear it, Sir Frederick. And my apologies for being presumptuous." She really did feel embarrassed now, for he'd clearly not liked her insinuation. "Were you injured on the Continent? What's the nature of your injury? Would you like me to go to the kitchens for some soothing broth or…ointment if there's a kitchen maid I can rouse. I'm sure something can be found to relieve your discomfort."

"That is very kind of you, Miss Fairchild." He smiled. "No, there's nothing I have found that can ease the pain when it decides to pay me a visit. Like everything, it will pass."

"That's a trifle morbid. Have you, in fact, sought anything to alleviate it? Or do you just suffer through it?" she asked, suddenly suspicious. It would be just like a man to complain but do nothing to actually fix the problem. Though, admittedly, he hadn't complained.

"There is nothing that can ease the pain when it comes upon me. Sleeping upright with the leg suspended like this does help a little. Now, you go back to bed, Miss Fairchild. I hope you sleep well, having discovered another clue in Lady Pendleton's entertaining little game."

Amelia opened her mouth to respond with indignation and further corroboration of her belief that there was more to Lady Pendleton's little game but decided against it. Sir Frederick's eyes were closed once more, though the tightness around his mouth indicated that he was silently battling a demon or two.

Well, maybe he deserved whatever sword strike he took while dueling over some no-doubt married lady on the Continent during his carouses over there. Isn't that how most young noblemen received their injuries?

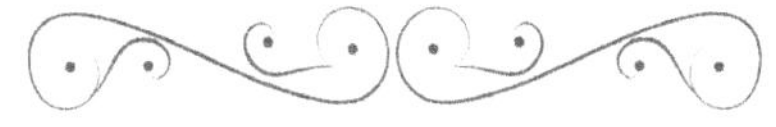

Chapter Seventeen

AN EARLY MORNING spent reading in the Castle Pendleton library was, to Lady Townsend, the ultimate in pleasure.

Alas, living alone, but for the servants, she did not often have company with whom to discuss her latest chosen reading material. What better way of spending a few hours was there than losing herself in a tragic, heartfelt romance? Sadly, neither her somewhat dour companion, Russell—who'd remained at home—nor Digby, the butler with whom she enjoyed a lively bit of banter on occasion, were readers. Not of romances, at any rate.

So, as she settled herself in a deep wingback chair, partially screened by a towering bookshelf, she hoped that luck would favor her and some unsuspecting fellow romance-lover would be waylaid by the offerings of the magnificent Pendleton library and Eugenia could while away an enjoyable few minutes exchanging book recommendations.

She'd chosen a vantage point that afforded her an excellent view of the room while remaining largely unobserved herself. A useful vantage point for one who had spent decades watching the human comedy play out in drawing rooms and ballrooms across London. But despite her enjoyment of company, she was also discerning.

For example, if garrulous Mrs. Gravey stumbled through

those doors, Eugenia knew she'd not get away for days.

She had just settled in with a volume of poetry—though her thoughts kept straying to Lord Thornton's sardonic smile at breakfast—when the library door burst open with rather more vigor than the usual sedate entrance of a houseguest seeking reading material.

Mr. Greene stood in the doorway, glancing furtively about before striding to the shelves. His usual languid grace was absent as he began pulling out books, scanning their contents, and shoving them back with growing frustration.

Surprised, then curious, Lady Townsend remained very still. Really, it was most instructive how a man's true nature revealed itself when he thought himself unobserved.

The sound of feminine laughter in the corridor made Mr. Greene freeze. Quick as a snake, he snatched up a random volume and arranged himself in an attitude of scholarly absorption just as Caroline appeared in the doorway.

"Mr. Greene!" The girl's face lit up in a way that made Lady Townsend's heart sink. "I didn't expect to find you here."

"Ah, Miss Caroline." His voice resumed its usual smooth charm. "I confess, you've caught me indulging my particular passion."

"Poetry?" Caroline asked, noting the book in his hands.

"Family histories, actually." He replaced the volume—which Lady Townsend noted was actually a treatise on good behavior—and moved closer to the girl. "I find myself fascinated by the great houses of England, their histories, their...stories of hopes and opportunities."

The way he lingered over that last word caught Lady Townsend's attention. As did the calculating gleam in his eye that Caroline, poor dear, completely missed. What was the man hinting at?

"Oh! Then you must let me show you some of Lady Pendleton's family records." Caroline's enthusiasm was palpable. "I am her god-daughter, you know, and am considered quite family.

We have the most romantic stories."

"Including, of course, ghosts, perhaps?"

"But of course! The ghost of Lady Pendleton's great-great aunt Pernilla being one."

"Indeed, poor woman! Yes, I still know little about her. Apparently, all the clues were quite made up." A frown appeared between his eyes. "Perhaps you could tell me more."

"Poor great-great aunt Pernilla." Caroline lowered her voice dramatically. "She died tragically young, as you know, after falling in love with someone her father forbade her to marry."

"So I learned during the treasure hunt." Mr. Greene moved closer still, his voice dropping to match Caroline's conspiratorial tone. "And…forgive me if this seems forward…but I fancy I see something of her in you. I know you're Lady Pendleton's goddaughter, but is there more of a family connection?"

"In me?" Caroline's hand flew to her throat.

"The same spirit, perhaps. The same…yearning for romance?" His fingers brushed her wrist. "They say history often repeats itself. Though hopefully with happier endings."

Eugenia's fingers tightened on her book. The man was good, she had to give him that, she thought, as her protective instincts rose to the fore. Every word, every gesture, perfectly calculated to appeal to a romantic young girl's sensibilities.

"I could help you research, if you'd like," Caroline offered shyly. "I know where all the old family papers are kept."

"My dear Miss Caroline, nothing would give me greater pleasure."

The way the girl preened under his attention reminded Eugenia painfully of herself at that age, desperate to be seen as interesting rather than merely decorative. Though in her case, the gentleman in question had been considerably more worthy. Her gaze drifted to the window where she could just see Lord Thornton crossing the lawn with Sir Frederick.

Speaking of worthy gentlemen… she was certain this scene could be turned to some advantage. Sir Frederick's protective instincts towards his sister, combined with Miss Fairchild's clear-sighted intelligence, were sure to create just the sort of shared purpose that could draw them closer together.

And if that happened to help Eugenia win her wager with Lord Thornton…well, that would simply be an added pleasure.

But Mr. Greene's peculiar interest in Pernilla's story struck her as worthy of note. Though exactly why, she couldn't yet say.

Rising silently from her chair, Eugenia slipped out through the library's side door, leaving Caroline still hanging on Mr. Greene's every word as he expounded on his deep appreciation for family traditions. The girl would learn soon enough that not every smooth-tongued gentleman's interests were what they seemed.

Though perhaps, Eugenia mused as she made her way toward the drawing room, that was a lesson better learned through observation than experience. And if the observation happened to involve Caroline's brother and a certain clear-sighted young lady working together to protect Caroline's interests…well, that would be quite ideal.

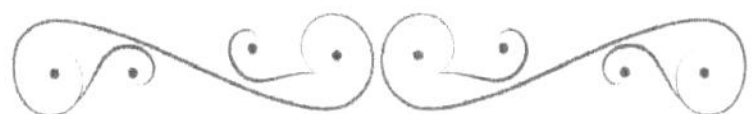

Chapter Eighteen

A DECENT NIGHT'S sleep would have had Sir Frederick riding at dawn but at least he managed to catch sufficient to appear for breakfast at what he considered a respectable hour.

Not that there were many in the dining room when he seated himself for morning chocolate and the smoked haddock and eggs that were on offer. In fact, it appeared most of the ladies had chosen to while away the morning on whatever it was ladies did in the morning.

If his sister was anything to go by, there was a great deal of time spent on dressing and checking one's appearance, perhaps writing a letter or two, and then more time at the dressing table. Caroline had always been a good girl but since Mr. Greene had been on the scene, she'd been impossible. And he knew that Mr. Greene was the cause of her altered disposition. His ridiculous compliments and excessive attention had quite gone to her head.

Fortunately, Miss Fairchild's very judicious words had poured water on the flames. Perhaps Caroline would rally sufficiently in the next day or two so that she'd countenance some of the other charming and much more suitable potential suitors.

Hopefully, Mr. Greene had not decided upon a different tack to win whatever it was he was after.

"Are you amongst those piqued to learn that Lady Pendleton's little ghost game was just that: a game?"

Sir Frederick glanced up to see that Lord Thornton had just addressed him from the other side of the dining table.

"Miss Fairchild is determined that it isn't." Sir Frederick was aware that he was smiling. Strange, for he wasn't usually inclined to talk in the mornings but the thoughts of Miss Fairchild that had come immediately to mind seemed to have lightened his spirits.

"Indeed, you were in the sleuthing trio together with Miss Playford."

"That's right." Sir Frederick was surprised that Lord Thornton had paid sufficient attention to remember the details, for he'd been roaming the castle that evening, assisting their hostess in her little game. "Miss Fairchild proved herself quite adept at recognizing each clue."

"And Miss Playford?"

"Oh, she was much quicker than I'd have given her credit, though it was Miss Fairchild's deep mind that brought us the results and the final prize."

"Indeed."

"She's quite the bluestocking, isn't she?"

"A bluestocking?" Sir Frederick considered the matter. She was obviously intelligent and enjoyed reading. Indeed, he'd once attached to her that moniker. But did that really make her a bluestocking which, really, was not a particularly flattering term for a lady? He shrugged. "Miss Fairchild is a young lady of surprising depth who enjoys discussing a range of affairs."

He felt it only right to champion her in view of Lord Thornton's perceived slight.

Lord Thornton nodded as he attacked his food. "Yes, and not too hard on the eye, though she's no longer in the first flush of youth. Miss Playford and her entourage are a lively lot. Perhaps one of those young ladies would suit, once you're more thoroughly acquainted. I can't imagine Miss Fairchild is in the running. She's not exactly the type you usually favor."

Sir Frederick paused, teacup in midair, and stared. What was

Thornton on about? He glanced about him, but they were, right now, the only ones in the room. The little he knew about his companion did not seem to accord to the way he was speaking to Sir Frederick now. Besides, what would he know about the type of young lady Sir Frederick favored? So he said stiffly as he returned his attention to his breakfast, "I have not narrowed my pursuit of potential wife to any particular type of young lady and Miss Fairchild is as suitable as any other."

"Yes, but I wonder if she'd be content with the life of a baronet's wife, given her scholarly pursuits."

Good lord! Sir Frederick didn't say those words, but he drew himself up and said, "It's quite a stretch from admiring a lady's mind to making her an offer of marriage. Not something I'm planning on doing in the near future, at any rate." Nevertheless, he added, for he also did not wish to make it sound like he was too quick to dismiss Miss Fairchild, "She is, however, a surprising young lady whom I'd not thought I would admire so greatly."

There. He'd said it. He'd championed fair Miss Fairchild when Lord Thornton looked as if he were denigrating ladies with intellectual leanings.

With intellectual leanings?

Yes, that summed her up, though she was so much more than that.

Finishing his breakfast, he rose. "The groom will have my horse ready now, so I'll bid you good day."

THE SUN WAS high in the sky by the time Amelia opened sleep-laden eyes. Hearing the chime of the clock announcing an hour that only the worst of lie-abeds would, with any self-respect, sleep until, she leapt out of bed, washed and dressed, and was about to dash out of the room to present herself for breakfast.

But a strange compulsion called her back to her dressing

table. She sat down and, for the first time in a very long while, studied her reflection. It was usual that a quick brush of her hair, which was then twisted into a serviceable knot on top of her head sufficed. She understood the need for a fashionable appearance and had perfected this style a year or so before, refining it so that it could be effected with speed and efficiency.

Now, with her elbows on the table, she frowned at her appearance before unpinning her hair so that it hung past her shoulders. How could she bind it so that she didn't appear so…spinsterish?

And her gown?

It wasn't shabby. In fact, it was of a very fine fabric, but the style was assuredly outdated. Not that it mattered when she would soon be living in the country.

Except, would she?

She hitched in a breath and contemplated her uncertain future with a beating heart as she considered the feelings Sir Frederick had evoked last night in the library.

And this was the man she was trying to marry off to another in order for her to achieve her so-called dream future?

He was charming and handsome, and he'd proved excellent company. At the memory of some of their exchanges, her heart gave a little flutter. Could it even be that he harbored some modicum of admiration for her?

She recalled the amused lift of his eyebrows in the library last night, his concern at other times.

After repinning her hair, teasing out a few tendrils of her naturally wavy hair which, she thought, looked rather fetching, she chose a more flattering spencer, and then made her way downstairs. The murmurs of a couple on the landing below caused her to stop and lean over the bannisters.

The feather of a fashionable bonnet was swaying with the emphasis of what its wearer was saying, while Sir Frederick nodded, his smile indicating he was attending with great interest.

A girlish giggle suggested it was one of the Miss Ps who was making the most of this opportunity to so impress the baronet, but when she tipped her head to the side, Amelia realized with a jolt that it was in fact Mrs. Perry.

And the widow was making fun of someone.

"I can understand the desire to come to such an entertainment as Lady Pendleton's, but if one's most modish attire was from the age of the woolly mammoth, surely it's worse to be on display as an object of ridicule. Of course, ladies notice these things."

Amelia froze. She glanced at the spencer into which she'd just buttoned herself, thinking the line was flattering and little matter that it was three years old. It was not shabby, so who would notice?

Clearly Mrs. Perry did.

Mrs. Perry who was now saying, "And I hear she can't wait to retire to the country? So why accept an invitation that would deny someone else the opportunity to take up Lady Pendleton's offer clearly designed to facilitate the meeting and mingling of those serious about making a match—"

Amelia froze. Mrs. Perry was talking about her? Her heart began to thunder while shame burned her from within. Was everyone talking about how shabby and sad Amelia was?

Did Sir Frederick think it but simply humored her as he was humoring Mrs. Perry?

Except that it looked as if he were doing more than that for when Amelia next glanced at him, Mrs. Perry's little hand was hooked in the crook of his arm and he was escorting her from the room.

Amelia felt her mouth hang open. Were the two of them laughing at her behind her back? Or was it only Mrs. Perry—though Sir Frederick had said not a thing to champion Amelia.

Slowly, she continued down to the next level. A knot of guests was at the far end of the gallery on the floor below her and when a voice called out from somewhere, they dispersed, Mr. Greene bringing up the rear. Amelia thought they'd all gone until she saw that one figure remained.

Miss Caroline.

She stopped, curiosity replacing her earlier shame for Caroline was reading a note?

Yes, she was sure of it, for she was bent over something, devouring the words that someone, just now, had clearly given her.

Mr. Greene? It was surely him.

Amelia didn't know what to do. Should she seek out Sir Frederick and inform him? Or was that too peremptory, considering Amelia was acting only on suspicions? Anyone in that group could have handed Caroline the note she was reading.

Frowning, Amelia continued to fix her gaze on the young girl as she decided what to do. And then, before her eyes, she saw Caroline take out a pencil from her pocket, write something on the note, and then, with a furtive glance about her, slip it into a crack in the wall between two stones.

The sound of another voice intruded. It was Caroline's chaperone, calling her, and immediately the girl resumed her ingenuous manner, smiling as she straightened, and calling out that she was on her way.

Amelia bit her lip, waited for Caroline to disappear, and then slowly and purposefully made her way to where Caroline's note was so artfully hidden.

"Miss Fairchild! Would you care to take a turn about the rose bushes?"

At the bottom of the stairs, with her destination only a few yards away, Amelia was waylaid by Lady Townsend who hooked her arm into Amelia's with great familiarity and said, before Amelia even had a chance to respond, "Tell me, my dear, have you seen Sir Frederick this morning?"

Amelia sent a furtive glance over her shoulder at the resting place of Caro's letter while Lady Townsend steered her away. Helplessly, she said, "Alas, I was up late this morning. Why do you ask?"

"I thought you might have gone riding together, having heard your brother expounding upon your superior riding skills in company last night."

"He's gone riding? Why, I'm surprised he had the fortitude."

Amelia realized the error of her words when, looking interested, Lady Townsend asked, "And what, pray, ails Sir Frederick when he appeared perfectly hale and hearty last night?"

"His leg. I saw him in the library when I went to find a book last night and he said he couldn't sleep for the pain of an old injury."

"So you two are becoming well acquainted, it would appear. He is a most charming gentleman, do you not think?"

Amelia chose her words carefully. She'd thought him a lot more charming before she witnessed the scene just now between him and Mrs. Perry. "He knows how to charm the ladies, that is true." Had those words sounded somehow acerbic? Amelia hoped not, but Lady Townsend's expression made her question herself.

The older woman certainly seemed interested in pursuing the topic. "Sir Frederick spent many years abroad and has not been back in England terribly long. Perhaps you should challenge him on the cause of his injury if you think it was caused by youthful folly."

The fact that Lady Townsend so correctly interpreted Amelia's tone made Amelia blush.

"I've no wish to pry, and he barely mentioned it. Only to reject my offer of a soothing balm I put great store in. No, our discussion centered upon Lady Pernilla's letters. I found one in one of the books, you see."

Lady Townsend angled a look at her. "My dear, I helped Lady Pendleton place some of those letters where they would be found. She's made no secret of the fact the story was make-believe."

"I know that's what was said, but I have in fact found letters that are surely genuine, given their age and...and other evidence," Amelia stammered. She knew they were.

"Is that so?" Lady Townsend said, as if she had absolutely no belief in Amelia's assertion. "Now, aren't these roses beautiful? Did you know that Sir Frederick's mother was uncommonly fond of roses and, in fact, something of an artist in rendering their likeness? Her rose garden is renowned in Hampshire."

Sir Frederick. Again. Amelia slanted a suspicious glance at Lady Townsend. She seemed excessively attached to the baronet. Could she harbor some strange *tendre*?

"Very fine roses," murmured Amelia, wondering why Lady Townsend had sought out her company when they barely knew one another.

"So you were in the library last night with Sir Frederick? I've noticed Sir Frederick seems quite interested in your historical pursuits. It's refreshing to see a gentleman who appreciates a lady's intellect."

"I'm not sure that is exactly the case," replied Amelia, once again thinking of Sir Frederick's apparent admiration for Mrs. Perry and his collusion in her unkindness towards Amelia by his failure to champion her. Another pang accompanied this thought, even deeper this time.

"You're not sure he appreciates a lady's intellect or you're not sure he appreciates yours?" Lady Townsend asked with surprising acuity as they turned their steps towards the castle.

"Both," said Amelia with a sigh. She wanted to get back to the alcove where she was sure she'd find a note from Mr. Greene to Miss Caroline. One that Caroline had answered.

But before she could manage such a thing, her company had been claimed by Miss Playford and then it was luncheon and then Edward wanted to go with her on a ride, insisting in the company of others that she'd promised. Which she had.

So, though dressed in her riding habit, she met Edward to offer her excuses, telling him she was much too exhausted to go riding. And finally, this was how she claimed a moment, without being shadowed, where she could safely retrieve the note without being discovered.

Adjusting her riding hat, which had once been modish and which she'd once thought highly flattering but which now felt dowdy because it was two seasons old, Amelia hurried down the stairs and made her way to where she'd seen Caroline hide her note.

Making sure she was unobserved, she checked each loose stone in the vicinity until finally, she discovered a gray brick that moved. Carefully she prised it out of the wall, finding behind it a small cavity. And it was inside this that Amelia realized was a hiding space for, as she extended her fingers, she felt the dull edge of a thick piece of paper. Pulling it out in triumph, and unfolding it, she squinted at the lettering. Mr. Greene could not be complimented on his handwriting. Nevertheless, his thick, even penmanship filled the page.

> *"Dearest,*
>
> *We don't have much time. If you wish to be with me forever then we must act. You say your chaperone has not left your side? That the best time to get away is when you dress before the dinner hour? Then meet me near the park gates when you can get away. There is a woodsman's hut that will be deserted. I shall be there with a chaise and four."*

Amelia gasped. Miss Caroline was eloping? Tonight? She stared at the letter in shock. Sir Frederick must be told.

But where was he? He'd gone riding this morning, so he must now be somewhere about the grounds.

Picking up her skirts, she hurried towards a group of ladies in company with Lord Thornton. Ladies Townsend and Pendleton were too ladylike to raise their eyebrows when she quizzed them over Sir Frederick's whereabouts, but time was of the essence. She could not let good manners get in the way of preventing Caro from making the biggest mistake of her life.

Sir Frederick had to be alerted at the very earliest so he could waylay his wayward sister.

"Sir Frederick is out riding," said Lady Pendleton.

"But he went riding this morning. Surely you are mistaken," Amelia said before she could stop herself. She knew her urgency did not reflect well on her.

"He had planned to go riding this morning but decided to rest an old injury a little longer," said Lord Thornton. He looked at her curiously. "Is there something you wish to tell him? I can send a message with my groom."

Amelia swallowed down her embarrassment and her panic. "That is quite all right, thank you," she said, managing a self-contained nod. "It's nothing that can't wait."

The moment she was out of sight of the group, she picked up her skirts once again and tore down the hill towards the stables.

"I need a mount," she told the lad working there. "I'm not particular."

The stable boy looked at her dubiously. "We have Missy. She's a spirited roan. I wouldn't recommend her unless you're an excellent rider."

Amelia considered herself a competent rider, but now was not the time for semantics. "Yes, Missy will do fine."

"And who will be accompanying you, miss?"

Amelia bit her lip. "Do you know which direction Sir Frederick and his group went? I am to join them."

"Sir Frederick went riding on his own, miss."

"He is alone? Oh, well, he was meeting his sister and me. Which way did he go?" There was no time to be more artful than that. All Amelia could hope for was that she'd spy his figure on the horizon from the gentle hill towards which the stable boy had pointed after he'd given her a leg up.

Soon she was galloping over the fields, hoping that she wasn't on a misguided goose chase and wondering, as she gasped for air and battled to control the badly named Missy, if she'd been a little too peremptory.

She should simply have waited until Sir Frederick had returned. There would have been time for him to have intercepted his wayward sister before she'd even made her way to the entrance gates. Of course, that would have been best.

It was a full fifteen minutes later—by which time Amelia was considering turning her mount for home—when she saw a single white horse cropping the grass by a copse of trees near the river.

Could it be Sir Frederick's?

Urging Missy forward, she arrived just as Sir Frederick emerged from the undergrowth.

"Miss Fairchild!" he exclaimed, "You look as if you've led the charge, yet you're alone? Let me help you down so you can catch your breath."

The nature of her mission should have had her rejecting his offer, but the sight of his hands, outstretched to help her to the ground, were suddenly too much to resist.

And even as she slid to the grass, and felt the warm pressure of his large, capable hands upon her sides as he gently steadied her, she knew she'd made a terrible mistake.

For she had allowed her heart to rule her head.

Surely that was why she didn't immediately tell him that time was of the essence and he must return to the castle to find his sister.

When Amelia's breath had steadied a little, it was with surprise that she realized his hand was still on her shoulder.

As if he, too, had only just realized it, he withdrew it then, frowning, said, "Something has happened. It's not like you to dash hell for leather, alone, on horseback, all this distance."

"Oh, it's exactly like me," she said, ruefully, only realizing how freely she'd spoken when he raised his eyebrows.

Dropping her gaze, she said with a smile, "The self-containment has been a lifetime in the making. It was a necessary counter to being far too naturally prone to exuberance."

"Exuberance, Miss Fairchild? You?"

Amelia laughed at his wry look and half smile then said, thoughtfully—though of course she should have been breathlessly warning him about his sister—"I was betrothed to a very serious-minded man who made me understand that life is not a game." Why had she said that? Sir Frederick wasn't interested in either her exuberance—or lack of—or her past. He needed to hear of Caroline and Mr. Greene's plans.

But, as their plans depended on darkness, and right now the sun was high in the sky, Amelia, blushing, opened her mouth to go on when he said, "I remember Thomas Blackheath. Indeed, he was a very noble gentleman who gave his life to this country. I'm sorry for your loss." Frowning, he added, "But he has been gone more than five years."

"Yes, and I knew I would never find his equal," Amelia said, remembering she had to call out all her defenses for the way Sir Frederick was looking at her was making her insides curdle. How could she find such a man attractive after Thomas? This charming libertine who knew how to look at a woman, and how to say all the right things, was the antithesis of her Thomas.

"You knew? Or you resolved?" asked Sir Frederick. "Naturally, you will never find his equal unless you go looking. Which, I gather, you are also resolved not to do."

Amelia blinked. There was almost censure in his words. Instead of responding, she asked, "How *well* did you know Thomas?"

"Enough to know he was a very…serious man."

"And noble."

Sir Frederick shrugged. "He died for his country. What could be more noble than that?"

And yet there was something about his tone that made Amelia question his words. She found, now, that she didn't want to talk about Thomas.

Of course, she should change the conversation and tell him about Caroline and what had brought her here.

But he was clearly still pondering what Thomas and Amelia meant to each other, for he said, "I did wonder at the time what Miss Amelia Fairchild and Mr. Thomas Blackheath had in common. The fellow was not known for his sense of humor." He must have seen Amelia's expression, for he added, quickly, "But he was an excellent soldier, and he would no doubt have been as assiduous a husband as he was a servant to the crown. Unlike many of the men you've since encountered, Miss Fairchild, otherwise a young woman of your beauty and intellect would have married long before now."

She knew she was wrong to let it happen. She should have been stronger than that, but obviously the vanity that Thomas had helped her vanquish was more integral to her pleasure-loving nature than she'd supposed. For the compliment found fertile ground.

And not only that, she found the roiling in the pit of her stomach intensifying as she gazed up at Sir Frederick.

"Beauty," she repeated in a whisper, only aware she'd spoken when he chuckled and she put her hand to her mouth.

"Most ladies parade their beauty like butterflies, but you try to hide yours, Miss Fairchild. I wonder why that is."

Amelia ran the tip of her tongue over her suddenly dry lips. "It's…not something I think very much about," she whispered.

"Since you are not looking for a husband," he finished for her, as if he were stating this as fact.

He'd taken a step closer, and she didn't step back. She stared up at him, her feet planted squarely on the ground, for if he wanted to close the distance between them, then she would not object.

She wasn't going to throw herself into his arms, but if he wanted—

Before she'd finished the thought, he'd lowered his head to look her in the eye. His dark, piercing gaze seemed to penetrate her heart and without realizing it, she'd closed her own eyes, tilting her face and slightly parting her lips.

The touch of his mouth, gentle upon hers, stirred new life into her. Sighing softly, she stepped fully into his embrace, and as his arms tightened about her, she felt her legs become boneless and her heart begin to sing.

Glorious. That's what it felt like to be kissed.

To be kissed by Sir Frederick for the pressure of lips, gentle at first, more demanding as his ardor increased, matched her all the way.

She twined her arms about his neck and pushed her body against his, needing to be closer when, in fact, they were as close as was possible.

Under the circumstances.

She would not think of that. She'd not even know what "that" was until long after Thomas had died and she'd spent more time in the company of young married friends who'd sometimes forgotten she was not one of "them" when they spoke of the agonies and ecstasies of the marriage bed.

As if sensing her increasing need, he stepped her backwards until she was against a large elm, and having the support behind her gave her the strength to draw his head down and press her mouth even more deeply against his so that for a moment she was emboldened to take charge. To let him know how deeply she reveled in this—

And then she remembered herself. Dropping her arms, with a gasp, still breathless, she ducked out of his embrace, saying with shame at her wantonness, "I don't know what came over me, Sir Frederick. Please forget this ever happened."

He regarded her with interest, his smile sardonic. "You might be able to, but I don't think I can."

"But you must! Oh, Sir Frederick, you must think I came here chasing after you when nothing could be further from the truth." She pulled Caroline's note out of her pocket. "I found this. It's from Mr. Greene and he's asking her to meet him near the park gates tonight. It can only mean one thing—"

"Pray, calm yourself, Miss Fairchild," Sir Frederick said, putting a comforting hand on her shoulder as if he wanted to maintain their earlier contact when Amelia knew this was much too dangerous.

She stepped away. "My words the other night clearly did not have the desired effect, alas. Caroline and Mr. Greene plan to elope tonight and you must speak to her and stop her."

Sir Frederick sent her a long look. "You are kind for taking such an interest in my sister."

"How could I do otherwise when I see how youthful folly could lead her into a lifetime of unhappiness?"

Smiling, Sir Frederick indicated Missy, making a cup with his hands to indicate he'd now help her to remount. "Let us talk about this on the return. For you see, I wonder if I am too harsh with Caroline. Perhaps I am denying her what would truly be in her interest if I thwarted a match between the pair. Not an elopement, of course. She might never recover from the scandal of that. But," he went on, when he'd ensured Amelia was securely in the saddle, and he was mounting his own horse, "who am I to say that Greene and she wouldn't be a fair match?"

Amelia barely knew what to say, she was so surprised at his turnaround. "But he is a…a fortune hunter. And he is so much older, trading on your sister's youth and innocence. Such a man could never be trusted."

Sir Frederick raised his head to gaze at a passing flock of starlings. "How do you know that, Miss Fairchild?"

His question took her aback. "Why, he has all the hallmarks of a rake. And surely that is why you objected before."

Sir Frederick shrugged. "I have given the matter some thought, I must admit. In fact, furthering my acquaintance with a certain…young lady…has made me reconsider my long-held belief about first impressions. We are all fallible. We make mistakes, we take what is on offer. We think we know better when it comes to other people's choices. That's only human."

Amelia felt herself burning from the top of her head to the tips of her toes. Was he referring to the fact she'd thrown herself at him? And he was excusing his alacrity in taking what was on offer, realizing how wrong was his initial assessment of her?

She swallowed, dismissing these thoughts to return to the question at hand. "But Caroline is barely out of the schoolroom. And Mr. Greene is so much older. His intentions aren't… pure."

"But he's a suitable enough match," said Sir Frederick. "He comes from a respectable family. He's in line for a baronetcy—tenuous, I'll admit, but he's made no bones about the fact that if his sickly cousin dies, he will make Caroline Lady Greene. And if Caro truly cares for him, should I be cruel enough to thwart her desires?"

"If you want her happiness for years to come, then yes!" Amelia said before she could stop herself.

"Bravo." Sir Frederick dropped the reins and gave a couple of desultory claps while his eyes danced. "Do you realize how delightful it is to bait you, Miss Fairchild? Forgive me, it is not gentlemanly, I know, but you are such a charming mix of earnest good intention and wildfire I really do not know what to make of you. Why, back there, by the tree—"

"Oh, but that was so wrong! I… I've never done that before! I behaved just as you said before…about offering what no man could refuse and now I am so mortified I cannot believe we are riding back and having this conversation as if it never happened."

"Is that what you're thinking? Why, I'm reliving it in delightful detail. It happened, Miss Fairchild, and surely your enthusiasm would lead me to think you'd not be averse to it happening again."

"Oh, no!" She shook her head with perhaps a little too much vehemence. "Please, Sir Frederick. I have a reputation to uphold. Please promise you'll never mention it to anyone."

He shrugged. "Of course not."

"And so you're going to see your sister immediately? Whatever else she does, she cannot elope with Mr. Greene tonight."

Sir Frederick inclined his head. "She cannot. And nor will she marry him. He is not the husband for her, she will soon come to realize." He glanced at Amelia. "Though sometimes one doesn't realize the apparent truth until we have made our beds. I wonder if you and your Thomas Blackheath would have been as well partnered as you might have supposed. I would wager not."

"Why, that's a terrible thing to say! To speak ill of the dead.

Of a man who sacrificed his life for his country."

"Just as you were prepared to sacrifice your exuberance because he preferred a wife of maidenly restraint." Sir Frederick grinned. "Admit it, Miss Fairchild. Do not be coy and tell me that you've never felt a hint of relief that you weren't forced to become a Puritan."

Amelia didn't answer. He'd hit a nerve for it was true that last year, when she'd felt a frisson of interest in a charming young man who had offered no encouragement but been simply the most delightful company as he'd confided in her his hopes in winning the fair debutante he'd subsequently married, Amelia had been struck by how very differently he'd wooed his sweetheart: with playful affection, abundant admiration, and lots of laughter. Yes, she'd been struck by how very different his approach was to Thomas's. And, in truth, his charm had been infectious, evoking a great more warmth on Amelia's part than when Thomas had earnestly entreated her to become his wife so that they might please God with their devotion and toil.

Even Edward had scoffed at him at the time—though of course he'd dared do no such thing after Thomas's untimely demise.

"There is a great deal of difference between a good man like Thomas and a rake," she said, not looking at him.

Sir Frederick digested this. Then he asked, "Who is the rake? Mr. Greene? Or me?"

Amelia shrugged. "You have a winning way with the ladies."

"Are you accusing me of charming you unwillingly?"

"Of course not!

But Amelia couldn't look at him as she said it. She was reliving the sensations she'd felt when he kissed her and how everything he'd said this afternoon had resonated in a way that made her question all her assumptions about him.

And about marriage.

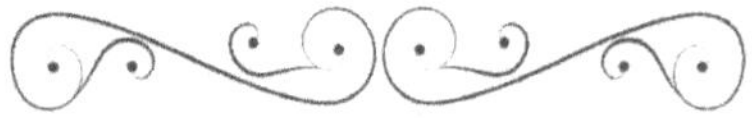

Chapter Nineteen

E UGENIA SIGHED.

As ever, Lady Pendleton was expounding on the state of the world and humanity as if she knew it all and Eugenia knew nothing. As if being a spinster put her in a category that meant she was beyond all feeling.

As if she did not know what it was to feel joy, or to grieve, or to love.

To be fair, Eugenia had almost forgotten what it had felt to love. For so long she'd existed in a state where she'd accepted that to have been overlooked must of course be her fault.

She was too plain. Too dull. Too—

Not too poor, though. In fact, as Lady Pendleton was now talking about the lavish breakfast she'd hosted for her darling eldest daughter's betrothal, Eugenia brought to mind of the fact that it had, in fact, been she, Eugenia, who had funded it on account of Elizabeth being her god-daughter.

And then, there were all the other occasions where Eugenia's generosity and good nature had been prevailed upon for all manner of expenditure for which Lady P had claimed credit.

It was as if the scales were being lifted from her eyes. Lady Pendleton wasn't more attractive than Eugenia. Maybe she never had been. She certainly wasn't cleverer. But she was more cunning. She was more calculating, more manipulative.

And she was certainly more conscienceless.

So when her friend leaned across to say to another friend, as if Eugenia were not even there, "I was talking to darling Sir Frederick this morning about his charming sister who has so entranced Mr. Greene," Eugenia said in an agreeable manner, "Not that it will do Mr. Greene any good since Sir Frederick doesn't approve."

The two ladies' heads spun round as if she'd uttered a blasphemy and, predictably, Lady Pendleton snapped, "What would you know about it, Eugenia?"

Eugenia shrugged, not looking at them as she continued with her needlework. "Sir Frederick doesn't approve, that's all I'm saying. Thornton was telling me—"

"And what was Thornton telling you, Eugenia, my dear?"

A moment before, Eugenia had felt quite superior, but now her heart was hammering like the piston engines Thornton had described to her at dinner that were driving the new weaving mills. For it was Thornton himself, dressed in a coat of navy superfine, looking just as dashing as he ever had, and much more handsome with his salt and pepper sideburns.

Eugenia glanced at the door to make sure Mr. Greene wasn't lurking in the corridor and said, "Merely that Sir Frederick is not keen on a match between Mr. Greene and his sister, Miss Caroline."

"Ah, well, I don't know anything more than that," said Thornton, taking a seat. "I'm not surprised you ladies are gossiping about such a topic, however. Isn't that what has made us arch enemies, Eugenia?" However, his grin was so disarming, Eugenia could only feel a surge of pride and satisfaction with how Lady Pendleton now regarded her.

"Pray explain yourself," said Lady Pendleton.

"I'm referring to our wager. The very reason we are all here. The very reason I am to win my Persephone." He winked at Eugenia, which occasioned a fierce fluttering in the region of her heart.

"We all knew Eugenia would never win that wager. This party is just a lovely excuse and the means to prove the impossibility of such a union—"

"Why, look! There they are!" Eugenia interrupted with a cry, standing so she could obtain a clearer look over the sloping garden. "Miss Fairchild and Sir Frederick are walking back from the stables. They've been riding. And...and they're alone!" Turning with a satisfied smile, she added, "See how engrossed they are in conversation, Thornton. Ha! My matchmaking instincts were correct."

The radiant, satisfied look she leveled upon Thornton was met with a raised brow.

"Don't be too hasty, my dear," replied Thornton. "A single conversation doesn't make a match. No, my contention stands. Miss Fairchild and Sir Frederick are such fundamentally different people, they will never make a match."

"Opposites attract, Thornton. Their differences could be what draws them together."

"Or drives them apart. I wager it won't take much to expose how unsuited they truly are."

Lady Townsend fanned herself. "I don't think you will get your Persephone, Lord Thornton. No, I think you should start planning our balloon ride over London." A smile tugged at her mouth and a warm, molten feeling invaded her insides as he gave her a slow, considering smile, then responded, "No, Eugenia, I intend to take possession of your Persephone." He pursed his lips consideringly, then turned to their hostess. "What, say, you suggest a game of charades this evening?"

"Charades?" queried Eugenia.

He nodded. "It would reveal their true natures in a social setting." Thornton gave a small chuckle. "Think about it. Sir Frederick, with his natural charm and ease in society, will likely excel. Miss Fairchild, on the other hand, with her more serious disposition, might struggle with such frivolity. It will highlight their differences perfectly."

"Or it could show how they complement each other. Amelia's quick wit might surprise you, and Sir Frederick might appreciate her intelligence."

"Really," grumbled Lady Pendleton, who never liked being relegated to the background in any conversation, "I don't know why it's of any interest whether Miss Fairchild and Sir Frederick do or don't make a match. At nearly five-and-twenty, she's virtually a spinster. No gentleman has found her sufficiently lively or attractive to even make her an offer. And that's hardly a surprise, for she gives no one any encouragement. It's well known that she's like her plain and dull parent and wants nothing more than to rusticate in the country which is what I hear she plans on doing upon her next birthday when she'll come into her inheritance, small though that is."

"And she certainly won't impress or entrance Sir Frederick who likes his women lively and quick-witted and, it would appear, small and golden-haired if his past predilection is anything to go by," said Thornton. "But, by all means, there's little else to do when we're in a house filled with preening young bloods, and pretty little show-offs. Sir Frederick is far more likely to spring a surprise upon us all by announcing his betrothal to Miss Playford, if you ask me. He's a dark horse, that one. But, let's put it to the test. Let me suggest a game of charades to our esteemed host, Lady Pendleton," he said, leaning towards her with a smile. "I'd love to be proved right about our mismatched couple. Lady Pendleton certainly knows how to up the stakes of a game, just as she did when she wove such a wonderful fabrication about her ancestor, Miss Pernilla."

"But there was truth in that story," Lady Pendleton pointed out. "Those are the best lies; the ones that begin in truth."

Eugenia did not like the way her little prune-shaped mouth turned up, as if it were a virtue to tell a good lie.

"Do you not feel a degree of pity for poor Lady Pernilla who died of a broken heart?" she asked.

"Oh, she didn't die of a broken heart!" snapped Lady Pendleton. "No one dies of a broken heart."

"But she did die young," said Eugenia. "And she did fall in love with a most unsuitable and hopeless match, you said."

"Yes, a stable boy, of all things! That was the letter I found, and around which I based everything else." Lady Pendleton sighed. "No, of course she couldn't marry him but yes, it is always sad when someone dies before they can enjoy the comforts of marriage and know that the children they have brought into the world will be their legacy."

Eugenia frowned. Was this a veiled reference to Eugenia's inadequacy? Of course it was.

"But yes, charades this evening would be delightful!" Lady Pendleton said, clapping her hands.

And Eugenia bowed her head before looking at Thornton and saying, "Very well. But don't be too disappointed when you lose our wager, my dear Thornton. You might find you have underestimated me."

SIR FREDERICK WAS about to round the corridor corner when, glancing behind him, he saw that Miss Fairchild, like him, was on her way to the drawing room. As she was alone, he stopped and waited.

"Caroline evinced complete astonishment at my suggestion that I had discovered her elopement plans," he said. "She denies everything. In fact, she was so angry, she demanded I examine the state of her packing so that I could be disabused of the idea that she had any intention of eloping with Mr. Greene—or anyone— tonight, or any other night." He looked closely at Miss Fairchild for signs of embarrassment. Could she have made the story up as an excuse to speak to him alone?

Strangely, the thought made him smile as he waited for her answer.

Miss Fairchild blushed hotly. "But the note—"

He shrugged as he offered her his arm to lead her into the drawing room where he'd heard the company would assemble for a game of charades. He was not particularly fond of the game, but if Miss Fairchild made her appearance—and his hope had proved correct—he was sure he'd perform tolerably if required.

"No matter," he reassured her, for she looked quite dumbfounded. "A confusion, that's all. Perhaps misinterpreted or meant for someone else. Let us speak of it no more."

"But you're not afraid of Mr. Greene and your sister—?"

"I shall keep a close eye on the fellow. In a few days' time we'll be home and his roguish smile will no longer be a temptation to poor, impressionable Caroline."

He only realized Miss Fairchild was still dwelling on his words when he glanced down to see her frowning before she said, "Do you think his roguish smile is really the danger? Could it not be that she is starved for anything diverting to do other than respond to his compliments? Your sister is lively, but she's intelligent. I think she longs for something worthy to occupy her talents and that clever mind of hers. Mr. Greene's roguish smile would not be such a diversion if she only had something meaningful to occupy her."

"My sister is hardly a bluestocking," Sir Frederick responded with a laugh, but Miss Fairchild regarded him severely.

"You use the term slightingly, Sir Frederick. I am considered a bluestocking, did you know?"

"Yes, yes, but you and my sister are worlds apart. Caroline is a delightful scatterbrain while you are a delightful enigma." He only realized he was licking his lips when he registered her look of outrage.

"Sir Frederick, you agreed never to refer to… what happened earlier today."

"What happened earlier today?" he asked, wickedly. "Pray, refresh my memory, Miss Fairchild, for I regret I have completely forgotten but wish to be reminded, so I am in no danger of referring to whatever it is that should not be referred to, again."

"There are people coming," Miss Fairchild hissed, raising her head proudly and looking straight ahead.

Sir Frederick registered her alarm with amusement as he realized that he was the cause of Miss Fairchild's discomposure.

He released her at the threshold to the drawing room and she immediately glided over to Lady Wentworth's side, taking up her fan and beginning a lively chatter that Sir Frederick decided, after a shrewd look, was nothing more than a ruse. Yes, Miss Fairchild was definitely highly discomposed, and he was the reason.

It shouldn't have delighted him so much, but there it was. The young woman he'd thought so distant and haughty had veins filled with quicksilver…and a mouth as soft as a rose petal.

Yes, he couldn't wait to plunder those beautiful lips all over again.

He'd just have to find another way to breach her defenses, for she was not going to fall into his arms after a bracing ride again, he realized. She'd been frightened by her susceptibility to him and she planned to withdraw completely and ensure that no future opportunity exposed her to such risk.

Well, Sir Frederick could be far more creative than she gave him credit, he thought with a little thrill of anticipation before Lord Pendleton claimed his attention.

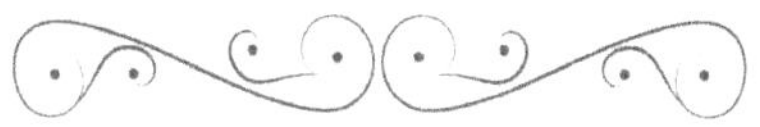

Chapter Twenty

"CHARADES?" REPEATED AMELIA. "I'm really not very good at playacting," she went on. "I think I should excuse myself."

"My dear, don't set a bad example for the more shy young ladies here. The young ones who are so eager in their hearts to step up in front of the company to have a bit of fun don't have your confidence." Lady Townsend patted Amelia's arm and indicated the Miss Ps in the corner who, Amelia thought, hardly answered to her example. They were the most boisterous debutantes she could remember having met. "And it's not because you're shy and lacking in confidence that you demur, is it? So, do say you'll enter into the spirit of Lady Pendleton's entertainment this evening? It would be such a gracious thing to do."

How could Amelia respond to such a call upon her good nature, much less obligations, as a guest without anything other than a reluctant nod and a forced smile? Oh, but she did hate charades with all that silly pretense and play-acting. Play-acting which was really barely respectable but at which she was deplorable. She knew she was.

"Well, that is wonderful, Miss Fairchild," said Lady Townsend. "Lady Pendleton will approach those who have agreed and let them know the word or phrase that they will mime for the rest of us to guess. I shall do my part, too, so you're in good company."

The older woman gave a shiver of something Amelia couldn't quite identify. Surely it couldn't be anticipation for all Amelia felt was dull dread.

A few minutes later, a tap on the shoulder heralded the call to action.

"Heartbreak."

"Heartbreak?" Amelia stared uncomprehendingly at Lady Pendleton, who was already moving forward towards the Miss Ps who were in a group that included Caroline, a little distance away.

"Your word," Lady Pendleton said over her shoulder as if she were an imbecile.

Amelia closed her eyes. She was going to have to stand in front of everyone and act out such a word? She felt sick.

Normally so confident, she was also used to being allowed to stay in the background and not be called upon to offer anything in the way of opinion or entertainment. Yes, she played the piano, as most well brought up young ladies did, but whenever she was invited to perform, she demurred to any of the more eager young ladies wishing to draw attention to their talents.

"You're looking a little pale, Miss Fairchild. And alone."

Sir Frederick was hovering nearby, not exactly at her side but looking very ready to bear her company with the merest encouragement.

With an effort, Amelia schooled her features into polite disinterest. She had to remember that courting Sir Frederick made him unavailable to anyone else. Anyone with the credentials that effectively earned Amelia the reprieve from society she so craved.

So while it would have been very pleasant to have whiled away a little time with Sir Frederick who looked all too ready to join her and, perhaps, bolster her confidence, she instead inclined her head and replied, "Lady Pendleton has just told me the word I am to enact in charades and it has confirmed my detestation of the game. But I have promised, so I will take myself off now and prepare myself."

"Perhaps I can assist?"

Amelia shook her head. "No, no, but I thank you all the same. You can encourage me by trying to guess at my deplorable efforts to mime the word Lady Pendleton has given me."

Sir Frederick chuckled. "Clearly it is not a word that fills you with the confidence to enact."

Amelia rolled her eyes. "I truly think she gave it to me to vex me because I was so reluctant to enter into what she considers fun and games."

"You don't enjoy this kind of society, Miss Fairchild?" He indicated the room with a sweep of his arms. The young Miss Ps were still giggling in the corner. Clearly, they were having a most enjoyable time. Lady Pendleton held court in another corner while Ladies Townsend and Pendleton, and Lord Thornton, suddenly burst into laughter.

Amelia swiveled slowly, pressing her lips together before she agreed reluctantly, "Everyone else seems to be enjoying themselves, I grant you that."

"Except you? Why is that, Miss Fairchild? You do not strike me as being a killjoy sour puss." His lips curved up, and he added with clear reference to earlier, "Why, you entered into the sport of a delightful afternoon's riding with great spirit and, indeed, as if you were enjoying yourself very much."

"Sir Frederick! I beg you!" Amelia exclaimed, mortified. "I don't know what came over me except that you are clearly very practiced at making ladies like me forget themselves and surely we are both of an age to accept that life has to be more serious than that when it comes to matters of such importance."

She knew she'd let her words run away from her when she saw his faint frown and the way he stilled before he responded. "Matters of such importance being...?" he prompted.

Amelia felt trapped. She didn't want to put it into words.

Why, it was ungentlemanly of him to make her. But it appeared he really did want her answer.

Crossly she said, "Hearts are not to be trifled with. And now I have this foolish word 'heartbreak' that Lady Pendleton has given me to mime. There! I've told you the word. Now, if you have an ounce of gentlemanliness and want to atone for this afternoon, you can stand in the crowd and pretend I've done such a fine job at acting it out that you've guessed it." It was a relief to get all that out in the open and Amelia finished on a laugh as she saw his features relax.

Then his smile softened and, briefly, he touched her forearm. "I consider myself a gentleman at all times, Miss Fairchild. Even during our ride—or rather, on the ground and by the trees—for I did honestly believe I had enough encouragement that my actions were still those of a gentleman. Having honor and decency does not preclude indulging in a little innocent enjoyment from time to time. Does it?"

Amelia wasn't sure if she felt entirely at peace with his answer. For a start, the unexpected tingling she felt at his touch had been exceedingly distracting, so that it was difficult to attend to his next words. But then his talk of indulging in a little innocent enjoyment when there was sufficient encouragement made some of it drain away. Did he really just consider their encounter as a one-off little piece of enjoyment?

And there was the contradiction in her heart. Sir Frederick most definitely made her go a little weak at the knees, but he was a man with a healthy reputation for dalliances. It probably massaged his ego that he'd managed to kiss the standoffish Miss Fairchild. Perhaps he'd set it up as a challenge. Perhaps she was no different a conquest than Mrs. Perry.

The thought made her stiffen as she remembered Mrs. Perry laughing at Amelia behind her back. But Sir Frederick hadn't actually endorsed her opinions. And then he'd kissed Amelia.

Her feelings about him were all very confusing, but, of course, after this house party, she'd probably not see him again.

So, forcing all these conflicting thoughts into abeyance, she said, "I suppose we are all different, so find enjoyment in different ways. I find mine in books mostly." There, that should make it clear where she stood.

He nodded. "So, you prefer to read about Miss Elizabeth Bennett and Darcy kissing rather than actually… kissing?"

Heat flooded Amelia's entire body at the words and images and recollections they conjured. She'd enjoyed kissing him immensely, but she could never tell him that the physical experience was far superior to reading about Miss Elizabeth and Darcy's romantic dalliances in *Pride and Prejudice*.

"Come now, everyone!" Lady Pendleton's imperious summons saved Amelia from answering and with a weak smile she took a seat in the audience, as directed, while the three Miss Ps went up towards the dais, clearly first on the program this evening.

Miss Playford stepped up first, miming the act of carrying something on her arm as she sauntered across the stage, shading her eyes as if she were looking for something in the distance.

"You're outside in the countryside!" someone shouted from the audience and with a bright smile, Miss Playford nodded before she turned to beckon to her two friends who jauntily crossed the stage before they appeared to consult over a matter, nodding as Miss Penny mimed the act of shaking out something before they gracefully sat upon the ground.

"You're in the countryside sitting on a blanket!" someone else cried out, as the Miss Ps, ignoring the various suggestions, pretended to pluck things from a basket, savoring various pretend dishes in great harmony.

"A picnic in the countryside!" someone shouted, and the girls laughed in agreement before, in a final act of comedy, Miss Playford pointed a finger at a pretend object, gave a little shriek, which was echoed by the other young ladies who immediately put everything back in the pretend basket, folded up the picnic blanket, and exited the stage.

"A picnic in the countryside invaded by ants!" cried Mr. Greene, and Caroline turned to look at him over her shoulder while the audience laughed at her high-spirited response: a large, theatrical wink.

Amelia glanced at Sir Frederick, who was seated beside her. His laughter had been truncated by his sister's final flirtatious act and Amelia tapped him on the thigh to whisper, "It's the spirit of the evening that's important. Don't judge your sister so harshly or by other standards. I've already been proved wrong and really don't know where I got the idea that Caroline was about to do something so spectacularly foolish, and now I'm ashamed of myself. But please allow her a little of the latitude you seem to grant everyone else, including yourself."

Immediately, he relaxed and smiled across at her. "Your wise counsel does you credit, Miss Fairchild, and I shall heed it. I'm far too much the overbearing big brother at times, and it's good to have you remind me of it. Now, I hear your name being called. Go forth and astound us with your acting skills. I have every confidence that you'll be far better than you imagine."

But Amelia wasn't.

She felt wooden as she stepped onto the dais and suddenly, to her horror, struck dumb by the sea of faces before her. Why, it was ridiculous. She'd played to a company larger than this…admittedly angled away from them and with a large floral arrangement on the pianoforte, screening her as per her request.

And she'd stood at her father's side in her earlier years and read poetry. Yes, serious, important words by learned men. And she'd been applauded and politely complimented by the serious, learned men her father cultivated.

Unlike her mama, Mr. Fairchild had had a reputation for being a man of exceedingly moderate temperament. Amelia had always striven to be compared with him rather than her darling pea goose of a mama whom Edward most definitely took after.

But now she had to enact a ridiculous word and the sight of all these houseguests who had been talking and laughing and having so much fun earlier but who'd now gone silent and were watching her, judging her, made her throat dry and her courage drain away.

She tried to suck in a breath, but her airways were constricted. She felt her panic grow and the earth seemed to fall away. This was not at all the way she wanted to portray herself, but it was as if she were an insect trapped in aspic and incapable of movement… Except for the clasped hands at her breast.

Mortification. She'd never felt it so greatly.

"Heart! Something about a heart, Miss Fairchild."

A murmur went about the room, the activity on account of Sir Frederick's words suddenly galvanizing Amelia into movement. Air filled her lungs, and she felt vitality seep through her veins.

Directing a grateful look at him, she tightened her clasped hands at her breast and nodded while she tried to shake her brain into similar activity and even remember the word.

Heartbreak.

Yes, Sir Frederick had named the first part, and now she must mime the second. She must pretend to break something. It would be easy. She'd just pluck an imaginary vase from the air and toss it to the ground and then everyone would know she'd broken it and her agony on stage would be over in a heartbeat as Sir Frederick would gallantly shout "Heartbreak."

Feeling a little more confident, she tossed her imaginary vase to the ground, leaping back to avoid the imaginary shards of glass, turning and more than ready to agree when her charade was guessed.

"Angry heart!" someone shouted, and she shook her head, seeking out Sir Frederick with a rather desperate look. However, he did not oblige and, after several more attempts down this avenue, Amelia gave up.

Heartbreak. How could she mimic heartbreak? How had she felt when her heart had been broken? When she'd heard the terrible news proclaiming Thomas's death.

Oh, that needed no acting skills whatsoever. She was on the spot and desperate, and she knew just how it felt to be heartbroken.

And she just wanted to get off this stage and slink away.

With an unfocused look of shock at the audience, Amelia closed her eyes. Then, covering her face with her hands, she fell to the ground with a wail of despair.

Heartbreak. It was a charade. She was acting, or at least trying to act, when she knew she couldn't.

But she knew what heartbreak was like. She knew that feeling of aching loss when the knowledge that she'd never know happiness again was surely worse than drowning as she succumbed to the physical manifestations of grief: weeping so hard she could barely draw breath, curled up in a ball on the ground, reaching out, her hands fisted because no hand was ever going to reach for hers again.

She'd lost her only chance for a blessed future with a good and noble man and her heart was truly broken.

It was only after a few seconds that she realized where she was and what she was doing and that she was making a public spectacle of herself.

And how long had she ignored the cries from the audience of "Heartbreak!"?

Sheepishly, she rose to her feet, wiping away what she hoped everyone thought were pretend tears, nodding that the word had been guessed, not making eye contact as she made her way back to her seat.

"Upon my honor, Miss Fairchild, you are an astonishing actress," Sir Frederick murmured as the next act prepared themselves. "Once again, you decry your abilities, which are so superior to those of the rest of us."

"Do stop your compliments, which will surely go to my head, Sir Frederick," Amelia said, feeling the most extraordinary mix of relief, embarrassment—and catharsis. She couldn't have said why, but it was as if an enormous weight had been lifted from her shoulders. "And I am not an actress, I'm a fraud. I was struck frozen up there until you set matters in motion."

"Yes, one word from me and you threw yourself to the ground and began to weep like your world was coming to an end."

Amelia swallowed, for Sir Frederick's words were lighthearted and he had no idea that they were so deadly accurate. Perhaps he understood, for his eyes suddenly widened and he said, "You were remembering what you felt when your betrothed died, am I not right?"

Looking down at her clasped hands, Amelia nodded.

"Lucky Thomas. To have been loved so deeply by a woman with as much honor as you, Miss Fairchild."

"His worthiness was what made me mourn him. I have as much or as little honor as the average woman in this room, I dare say. But Thomas was a king among men. His like will not enter my life again."

"I think you attribute too much to him, at the risk of inciting your ire. Thomas was a good man, but he would not have made you happy. He would not have made you laugh, and you need to laugh, Miss Fairchild. Happiness is just below the surface, for you, but would he have tapped into it as much as you would have needed him to in order to strike the right balance between his gravity and your vivacity?"

"You don't know what you're saying!" Amelia burst out. "Why, you hardly knew Thomas."

"I did know him, perhaps better than you think I did. And I'm sorry if my words offended you," Sir Frederick said. "Ah, now what do we have here?" he ended diplomatically as two other young guests stepped on stage. He patted Amelia's arm and offered her a smile. "I'm sorry for your heartbreak and for not coming to your rescue when you'd asked me to. The truth is, I wanted so very much to learn what heartbreak was for you and how you would manifest it under such circumstances, and in doing so I put you through a very great ordeal that I would not have had you re-live had I known what real pain it occasioned you. I therefore offer you my humblest apologies."

And as Amelia looked at him, she thought she really did believe him.

"Now for cards!" Lady Pendleton announced with a commanding clap of her hands that made several guests start. "The tables are arranged for whist, and I trust everyone knows their Hoyle," she added with a meaningful look at some of the younger guests, her ostrich feather quivering. "Let us form tables for whist. The evening is still young."

Amelia would have preferred to withdraw, feeling drained after her emotional display, but movement caught her eye. Sir Frederick had half-risen from his chair, clearly intending to secure her for his table, when Lady Townsend materialized at Amelia's elbow with the timing of a general deploying troops.

"You'll join our table, won't you, my dear?" The older woman's tone brooked no argument. "Lord Thornton has specifically requested your company."

Amelia caught Sir Frederick's slight frown as she allowed herself to be led away. Was he disappointed not to secure her for his own table? But no, that was fanciful thinking, she told herself as she took her place opposite Lord Thornton.

Lady Townsend directed Amelia to a seat that afforded an excellent view of both the room and Sir Frederick's frustrated expression as he was cornered by Mrs. Perry for her table. The card tables were arranged in an elegant horseshoe pattern, the better to allow Lady Pendleton to survey her domain from her position at the head table. From her vantage point, Amelia could easily observe the adjacent table where Mr. Greene sat with young Albert Pendleton and Henry, the former gentleman's expression watchful, the latter looking uncommonly serious as he shuffled the deck. The fourth at their table was Colonel Blackwood, a gentleman of military bearing whose florid complexion suggested a fondness for port.

"Your bid, Miss Fairchild," Lord Thornton prompted. His

eyes, Amelia noticed, kept straying to Lady Townsend's elegant hands as she arranged her cards. "Though I warn you, your partner takes her whist very seriously."

"As well one should," Lady Townsend responded with a sparkle in her eye that made her look years younger. "A good partnership at cards, like so many things in life, requires both strategy and understanding."

Amelia forced her attention back to her own cards, though she couldn't help noticing how Lord Thornton's expression softened at Lady Townsend's words. Her hand was respectable—two aces and a promising run of hearts—but her concentration kept wandering to Sir Frederick's table, where Mrs. Perry's tinkling laugh seemed to pierce the general murmur of conversation with unnecessary frequency.

They played several hands, Lady Townsend proving to be an excellent partner who could read Amelia's leads with almost uncanny accuracy. But as the evening wore on, it became increasingly difficult to concentrate. The tension from the next table was palpable, the stakes clearly rising with each hand. Albert, Lady Pendleton's son, handled his cards with the same quiet competence he seemed to bring to everything, while Henry's attempts at lighthearted commentary grew increasingly forced. Even from her position, Amelia could see that Mr. Greene's pile of chips had dwindled alarmingly, with Colonel Blackwood's voice growing increasingly strident.

"Your play, Mr. Greene," Albert said quietly as the tension mounted. Amelia noticed how the young heir's calm presence seemed to steady the table, though Colonel Blackwood's complexion grew increasingly florid with each round.

"Really, Greene, that's the third time you've reneged. A gentleman ought to know better." The Colonel's hand shook slightly as he gestured toward the trick they'd just completed.

"A mere oversight," Greene responded smoothly, though Amelia noticed his fingers drumming restlessly on the table edge. "I assure you, Colonel, I am good for it."

"Like you were good for it at White's last month?" The Colonel's tone dripped with sarcasm. "Or at Boodle's the month before?"

"Gentlemen," Albert interjected with quiet authority, "perhaps we should call it an evening."

But the Colonel was not to be silenced. "When a man's vowels are being passed around half the clubs in London—"

"I said, that's enough." Albert's tone, while still quiet, held steel. He placed his cards face down with deliberate care.

Henry, who had been watching the exchange with growing concern, suddenly brightened. "I say, did anyone see Caroline's performance in the charades? Wasn't she capital?"

Amelia, who had been watching the mounting tension at their table, noticed how Henry's hand moved unconsciously toward Caroline at the next table, as if to shield her from what was unfolding.

"Oh yes, Henry, do tell us again how I made everyone laugh!" Caroline called over, her smile brightening. "Though you're one to talk. Your impression of a lovesick swain was quite something. What was it you said? 'Oh, my beloved is like a summer's day, except when she's being as stubborn as a mule!'"

Several people laughed, and Henry's ears turned pink. "I was referring to my horse, of course."

"Of course you were." Caroline's eyes danced with mischief.

"Children, please," Colonel Blackwood interrupted testily. "Some of us are trying to concentrate."

Amelia noticed how quickly Henry's attention snapped back to Mr. Greene, his protective instincts clearly warring with his natural good humor. Caroline might be too dazzled by Mr. Greene's worldly charm to see the predatory gleam in his eye, but she suspected Henry saw it. Sir Frederick said he'd grown up with Caroline. Obviously, their shared childhood adventures and mishaps came quickly to mind. It seemed he, too, was concerned by her infatuation with a man who could never appreciate her true worth.

"Your play, Mr. Greene," Albert said quietly. But what struck Amelia most was how Henry's fingers tightened on his cards when Mr. Greene sent Caroline another calculated smile.

"Do you remember," Henry said suddenly, his voice pitched for Caroline's ears though Amelia could still hear him, "that time we found what we thought was a ghost in the old dovecote?"

Caroline turned back to him, momentarily distracted from Mr. Greene. "It was just your jacket that you'd left there the day before! But we were so sure it was a ghost, we made up that whole story about star-crossed lovers meeting in secret…"

"And now here we are at a real ghost hunt," Henry said softly. "Though some mysteries aren't as romantic as they seem."

The warning in his voice was gentle but clear. Caroline's smile faltered slightly, and for a moment, Amelia saw uncertainty flicker in her eyes. But then Mr. Greene spoke again, and the moment was lost.

But something else had happened at the nearby table, which Amelia had missed.

Mr. Greene had risen, his chair scraping back with unnecessary force as he glared around the table. "I don't care for your implications, sir."

"They're not implications," Colonel Blackwood shot back. "They're facts. And I'm not the only one who's noticed certain family heirlooms appearing in certain establishments—"

The sound of cards being flung down interrupted whatever else the Colonel might have said. Amelia was startled to realize they were her own cards.

"Oh! I do beg your pardon." She forced a laugh as three pairs of eyes turned to her. "Such clumsy fingers tonight."

"Allow me," Lord Thornton said smoothly, helping her gather the scattered cards. But she noticed his sharp glance toward the other table where Albert had also risen and was speaking quietly but firmly to both Greene and the Colonel.

"Really, Miss Fairchild," Lady Townsend remarked with apparent casualness, "one would think you'd never dropped cards before. Though I dare say it's better than throwing imaginary vases."

The gentle teasing made Amelia smile, grateful for the older woman's tact in drawing attention away from the scene playing out beside them. Yet she couldn't help noticing how Greene's hands shook slightly as he collected his winnings, or how his eyes kept darting toward Caroline, who sat at another table, blissfully unaware of the undercurrents swirling about her.

"I believe I shall retire," Amelia said, rising. "The excitement of the charades has quite worn me out."

But as she made her way toward the door, she distinctly heard the Colonel mutter, "Mark my words, that young man will bring nothing but trouble. And someone ought to warn Sir Frederick about his sister…"

As she reached the door, Amelia glanced back to see Sir Frederick had also risen, his expression troubled as he watched Greene disappear through another exit. Their eyes met briefly across the room, and she knew they shared the same concern: Caroline, still laughing at her table, remained blissfully unaware of the undercurrents that threatened to pull her into their depths.

Lady Townsend's voice carried clearly as she bid Lord Thornton goodnight. "Such an interesting evening. One never knows what cards fate will deal, does one?"

Chapter Twenty-One

THANK THE LORD the evening was over, thought Amelia as she made her way to her chamber. The charades had left her emotionally drained, while the undercurrents at the card tables had stirred an unease she couldn't quite shake. The castle's corridors seemed longer and darker tonight, the shadows between the wall sconces deeper, as if the very air held secrets.

However, it was Sir Frederick's words that still played on her mind, each remembered syllable striking a chord that resonated uncomfortably with her heart's rhythm. He'd been so very kind, his words indicating real interest—or at least, what felt like real interest. The warmth in his eyes when he'd looked at her had seemed genuine enough.

But wasn't that what house parties were designed for? Casual flirtation, meaningless compliments, the need to enjoy whatever entertainment was at hand? The very architecture of these grand houses, with their convenient alcoves and discrete corners, seemed designed to facilitate such dalliances.

For the Misses P it was a different matter entirely. They were all hoping to invoke the interest of the handful of eligible gentlemen present, Sir Frederick being chief among them. The young ladies clearly didn't consider Amelia any sort of threat— which made it all the more confusing that she felt as if she could crook her little finger and he'd be at her side in an instant. He enjoyed her mature company, that was all. She mustn't mistake his interest for anything more substantial than that.

On one of the landings, she stopped and leaned over the balcony railing. The great chandelier cast its golden light over the remaining guests below, their jewels catching and reflecting the light like stars brought down to earth. There was Mr. Greene, tall and rangy, his evening clothes cut just a shade too fashionably for true elegance. Too old for Caroline, certainly, but his practiced charm was clearly turning the girl's head. Even now, the young miss stood with her friends, self-consciously twirling a blonde ringlet around her finger as she gazed at him. The longing in her expression was painful to witness. Had Amelia ever looked at anyone with such naked adoration?

Of course she had. Thomas. From the moment she'd set eyes on him at the Assembly ball and heard whispers of his reputation for nobility and heroism, she'd known that was exactly the kind of man she wished to marry. Her heart had yearned for someone she could admire, whose integrity was beyond question, whose bravery and nobility were undisputed.

All those elements were, she'd believed at the time, far superior to mere affability and the capacity for fun. Her brother had those lighter qualities in abundance, but he was not a serious fellow. And Sir Frederick? Well, she'd only just made his acquaintance—

She cut the thought off at the root. No, it seemed clear to Amelia at the time that the two sets of qualities—gravity and gaiety—could not coexist in the same person.

So she'd made her choice: nobility and heroism over charm and laughter.

And it still held true. Didn't it?

She turned away, but movement in her peripheral vision caught her attention. Sir Frederick's tall, elegant figure was unmistakable even at this distance. Despite herself, she found her gaze following him, wondering who he was seeking out. Not that it mattered to her if it was…

Oh. Mrs. Perry.

A flush of heat flooded Amelia's face, followed by a chill that had nothing to do with the drafty corridor. The widow had been brilliant during her performance as Juliet—so natural, so at ease before an audience. Everything Amelia was not. She'd garnered compliments all evening. Sir Frederick had kept his distance while Amelia was present, but now he laughed with the widow as if she were the most fascinating creature in creation.

Was this jealousy burning in her breast? Surely not.

Crossly, Amelia forced herself away from the railing. She was about to head toward her wing of the castle when something made her pause. A half-formed thought, a nagging suspicion…

Caroline had sworn she knew nothing of any plans to elope, had laughed incredulously at the very suggestion. Sir Frederick had seemed convinced by her denial. So what had Amelia really seen in that letter? The more she thought about it, the less sense it made.

Well, there was one way to be sure.

The alcove was on this level. Heart beating a little faster, she made her way along the corridor, her slippers silent on the thick carpet. The gap between sconces left this section in shadow— perfect for secret messages, she thought wryly. Her fingers found the slight protrusion in the wall, and carefully, she eased out the small brick. Yes, there was the sharp edge of a paper, though why it remained here was curious. Unless Mr. Greene knew he was being watched…

Pulling out the paper, she unfolded it in the dim light. The words seemed to swim before her eyes: "Miss Caroline, you are an enigma. I look forward to our dance this evening." Mr. Greene's bold hand. And on the reverse: "Mr. G, you are a card. I've reserved the third for you."

Nothing about park gates or urgent meetings. Nothing about elopements or secret plans.

The furrows between her eyes deepened. Had she imagined

the other letter? No, she was certain she'd seen it. The writing had been different, the paper…

Slowly, she refolded the note and replaced it, but as she did, her hand brushed another irregularity in the wall. Another loose stone, this one fitted even less snugly than the first. The mortar around it felt different too—older, more friable.

Her heart began to beat faster as she worked it free. The darkness of the cavity seemed to hold its breath as she reached in. Yes, there was definitely another letter. As she withdrew it, the paper felt different under her fingers—thicker, more substantial than modern writing paper. The ink had faded to a warm sepia, and in places…

The date. How had she missed it before? Not just day and month, but the year: 1719.

And suddenly all the pieces shifted, realigned themselves into a new pattern. The P in the letter referred to Pernilla. The similarity of the messages—was it mere coincidence that two pairs of lovers, separated by a century, had chosen the same hiding place?

Her fingers encountered something else in the cavity. Not one letter but many, a thick sheaf of them, held together by what felt like a ribbon. The musty smell of old paper and older secrets filled her nostrils as she carefully withdrew them.

A single line caught her eye.

"I cannot live without you…"

The corridor remained empty, but suddenly the shadows seemed alive with possibility. These letters could hold the key to everything—Pernilla's fate, the truth about her William, perhaps even explanations for things happening now.

Lady Pendleton had said her ancestor died young, but what if there was more to the story? What if history wasn't quite what everyone believed?

Clutching her precious cargo close, Amelia hurried through the darkened corridors to her chamber, the letters seeming to burn against her chest, eager to give up their secrets.

Chapter Twenty-Two

MRS. PERRY WAS certainly a Merry Widow. Sir Frederick found her witty asides quite entertaining, and she was easy on the eye, her golden curls artfully arranged to catch the candlelight. Of course, she was flirting quite outrageously, each laugh carefully calibrated, each gesture precisely designed to draw attention to her best features. He must be careful lest he find himself in too deep. He could see she wasn't above resorting to underhand techniques to get what she wanted—her eyes darted too often to his signet ring, her questions about his estate too pointed to be casual interest.

And another husband was definitely on her agenda. The way she'd positioned herself just so beside him, allowing her silk skirts to brush his leg, left no doubt about that.

In his peripheral vision he saw Miss Fairchild take the stairs, her midnight blue gown making her seem to float in the shadowy stairwell. He'd enjoyed trailing about the castle on their treasure hunt, watching her mind work as she decoded each clue. He'd enjoyed their kiss even more—the softness of her lips, the way she'd melted against him before propriety reasserted itself. But she'd made it clear that while she'd enjoyed it, she regretted it. As if succumbing to pleasure undermined her integrity, as if joy itself were somehow suspect.

Well, of course, Sir Frederick didn't want to be saddled with a Puritan killjoy for life; one who went into a decline through guilt every time she experienced pleasure. If she had thrown her heart at Thomas Blackheath whom she revered as the epitome of all that was noble, then she had a most skewed view of nobility. The memory of Blackheath's perpetually furrowed brow and endless lectures on duty made Frederick's teeth clench even now.

Blackheath had been a gloomy curmudgeon who had followed orders, even if they ran counter to common sense. He saw duty in black and white, with no room for the hundred shades of gray that made up real life. The man had no capacity for joy.

And if Miss Fairchild aspired to finding a husband in his mold, then both Sir Frederick and she were wasting their time with each other. No more kisses or wondering if things might go anywhere, he told himself, as he flicked another glance at her leaning over the railings. Even as he pretended greater amusement in Mrs. Perry's latest witticism than was warranted, he couldn't help noticing how the candlelight caught the elegant line of Miss Fairchild's throat.

If she looked alone and in need of company, Sir Frederick was not the man to engage her in conversation—which he greatly enjoyed, he had to admit. Their discussions ranged far beyond the usual ballroom fare of weather and who was dancing with whom. But she was not interested in finding a husband and she was not interested in him. She'd made that abundantly clear.

And he didn't want a Puritan for a wife, as he'd reminded himself just now. Though the way her eyes had sparkled during their treasure hunt had been anything but puritanical…

No. If she'd made clear that she thought him caddish, then let her think it. The pain in his leg was reminder enough of what duty had cost him; he needn't seek out more suffering in the form of a wife who would forever judge him wanting.

If she couldn't see past his exterior, then she clearly didn't have the depths he'd once thought. She was as shallow and one-dimensional as Thomas Blackheath had ever been. Though the memory of her collapsed on stage during charades, showing such raw emotion, suggested otherwise…

After another minute or so laughing at one of Mrs. Perry's on dits—something cutting about Lady Townsend's ostrich feathers—he glanced again at the upper floor to find it empty—like his heart. Or rather, emptied of the expectation that had built up there. What had he hoped for? To see her still there, lock eyes with her, and then go up and speak to her? To explain about Waterloo, about Blackheath, about all the things she didn't understand?

Suddenly, he felt very weary. Utterly, immensely weary, and he knew it was unfair to Mrs. Perry when he offered his excuses so abruptly, telling her that exhaustion had suddenly overcome him.

The bereft look on her face made him feel guilty, but suddenly there was no enjoyment in being amidst the lively company. He just wanted his bed.

But sleep didn't come easily.

And when the same, familiar, nagging pain in his leg woke him in the early hours of the morning, he knew it would be less tiresome to take himself off to the library than to spend hours tossing and turning in a fruitless attempt to achieve the respite of oblivion.

Shrugging on his banyan and slipping his feet into his slippers, he picked up his candlestick and followed several twisting corridors and flights of winding stairs to the most astonishing collection of books accumulated by generations of Lady Pendleton's family.

He would enjoy scouring the shelves and find himself something unusual and learned.

Or maybe he'd reread *Pride and Prejudice*, he thought with a smile. That would be something he'd enjoy conversing with Miss Fairchild about, he thought, pushing open the heavy studded door.

"Miss Fairchild!"

She turned, a look of surprise upon her face. He noticed she was still in her evening gown so clearly she'd not yet gone to bed. She was at the far end of the wall of books, where the romance novels were, and for one wild moment he wondered if she'd come to seek out some of the more illicit titles he'd identified—for she'd not know them otherwise, he realized.

But she hurried towards him, her expression one of concern, a letter in one hand and a novel by Mrs. Radcliffe in the other.

"Lady Pendleton is wrong, Sir Frederick," she said. "Either she's in ignorance or she's withholding the truth, but her ancestor, Lady Pernilla, was not having a dalliance with a stable boy."

"Indeed." He wasn't quite sure how to respond. He certainly didn't want to convey his true thoughts, which were to question why it should matter to her or anyone else; because he thought it was quite delightful that Miss Fairchild should care and that she should come to him.

Not that she'd actually come to him since he'd just stepped into the room.

"Let me draw you up a chair beside this one, and you can tell me all about it," he invited, making sure the chair was as close as it could get.

She didn't seem to notice. "You see, Sir Frederick, I realized that the letter that I had assumed Caroline had received from Mr. Greene was written, in fact, a hundred years earlier." She withdrew a thick piece of paper from her lap and waved it in front of his face. "It's been very well preserved, but I should have taken note before I was so quick to run to you with tales about her so-called scandalous behavior. She must hate me now!"

"Caroline is quick to forgive. You only need to explain it to her," Sir Frederick said, smiling. He liked the proximity. Miss

Fairchild was delightfully earnest. He wasn't used to that in a woman. His flirtatious banter with Mrs. Perry this evening had been wearyingly familiar. The same old playbook. Both of them knew the code and played by the rules.

Once Miss Fairchild had left, he had little choice but to succumb when Mrs. Perry had fluttered her eyelashes above her fan. And then there'd been the small talk, laden with innuendo.

What he had made sure of this evening, though, was that she could be under no illusion he was open to more than a dalliance. She'd have left her slippers in the passage outside her door if he'd given her the smallest bit of encouragement.

With Miss Fairchild playing so much on his thoughts, he was not about to do that.

And now here was Miss Fairchild, who had appeared, as if on cue, like an answer to his dreams.

"Indeed, I shall," Miss Fairchild was saying. "I shall show her the letter. In fact, all of them. Oh, Sir Frederick, it's quite tragic. There's a treasure trove here. The young people obviously used an old brick in the wall that could move as their letter box. I don't know why they are all there, but I suspect it was safer not to keep them in their respective bedchambers, don't you think? Because of the family's opposition," she clarified.

Sir Frederick nodded as he took the letters she handed him.

"Fascinating, don't you think?" she asked again.

"Fascinating," he agreed. But she was the one he found fascinating. When she was animated, her cheeks became flushed and her eyes sparkled. In the warm glow of the room, he thought he'd never seen any woman more beautiful.

He tried to equate her with the Puritan he'd taken such pains to persuade himself out of admiring earlier.

"Just read the words young William writes to her. It quite makes my heart break."

Sir Frederick nodded. Then he frowned. "I'm curious as to why you should be so affected, though, Miss Fairchild, when you are the first to decry sentimental bunkum."

Her rosebud lips parted and for He shrugged. "Or maybe he really was a man who felt deeply and everything he says was, indeed, straight from the heart."

"Oh, that's a terrible thing to say, Sir Frederick. You suggest that there could be a calculating aspect to these letters?" She waved one of them in front of him. "How could he make up something like this if he didn't feel deeply." Holding it up so she could see, she began to read,

"My dearest, most cherished Pernilla,

Though I may not possess grand estates or noble titles, I swear to you that my love and devotion will provide a life richer than any fortune could buy. Trust in me, and I will work tirelessly to ensure your every comfort and happiness. Our home may be modest, but it will overflow with laughter, warmth, and the unshakeable bond of true affection—"

She glanced up. "Lady Pendleton claims he was a stable boy and that the letters I found suggesting otherwise were false. But this letter really is more than a hundred years old. It's real. And those are not the words of a stable boy."

Sir Frederick smiled. "He may have had someone else write it. Regardless, he was not a young man the family approved of." He patted her hand. "I think it charming that you have taken up their cause, but do remember that these star-crossed lovers are long dead. Do you suppose that enlightening Lady Pendleton will soften her stony heart?"

"You think she has a stony heart, too?" Miss Fairchild dropped the letters into her lap and clasped her hands together. "I thought I was the only one, for she does pretend to be most charming. And yet, have you heard the way she speaks to Lady Townsend who, I believe, has been her friend for more than thirty years?"

Frederick felt a surge of unexpected affection for the young woman beside him. Of course, it was irregular that they should be conversing, alone, in the middle of the night. And he'd written her off earlier as unapproachable, though in truth his opinion of her wavered all over the place. But now that she'd warmed to her theme, which was really quite a sentimental one, she was quite natural and unfiltered. Dropping his guard, he told her so, adding with another fond smile, "You obviously have less of a stony heart than I had believed, Miss Fairchild."

And then he immediately recognized his mistake.

"Sentimental?" she repeated, moving away from his hand which rested over the armrest and was quite close, though not touching, as she retreated into the depths of her chair. "Thomas deplored those who were sentimental. He saw intense emotions as a distraction from spiritual devotion and rational contemplation of God's will and said it was opposed to logical thinking."

Sir Frederick nodded. "So, that is what your Thomas thought. But what do you think?"

Her eyes widened, as if his question were unusual. Then she seemed to lose herself in thought. "I think that sentimentality might be confused with kindness."

"Precisely. And kindness is a virtue. And you, Miss Fairchild, are both kind and virtuous. Not sentimental. I apologize for being guilty of confusing the two." Slowly, he extended his hand toa moment, he thought she would respond with indignation. Then she said thoughtfully, "I decry sentimentality for its own sake. And when it's used to manipulate people into thinking something is heartfelt and touching when it isn't. Like in a badly written book. Do you not think that the feelings of the heart should be pure and noble, Sir Frederick?"

It was clear she wasn't filtering her words; she was far too excited by these love letters. Sir Frederick enjoyed listening to her and watching the emotions flit across her features.

"Have you received love letters like these?" he asked and then wished he hadn't, for the question seemed to shock her and immediately she was self-conscious once more.

"Of course, Thomas wrote to me," she said stiffly, holding the letters in her lap, almost protectively.

"But did he use the language of a lover? Clearly the young William from these letters was either clever at manufacturing the kind of sentiment he knew would win over Miss Pernilla. He knew her family was deeply opposed to a match between them. He knew he was beneath her." grip hers, bringing it up to his mouth to kiss.

The room was very quiet suddenly. Only the gentle hiss and crackle of the fire could be heard over the hushed and muted whisperings of the ancient castle. In a moment of fancy that might have embarrassed him in a more rational moment, he imaged the ghosts of the long-dead lovers, Pernilla and William, watching with quiet satisfaction as he leaned over to put his arm about her shoulders to draw her closer so that he could gently touch his lips to hers.

He felt her response; a quiet exhalation of pleasure as she succumbed. She liked it. The previous kiss in the fields had been fueled by something more urgent, but this was an extension of his compliment; his recognition and appreciation of her virtue and her kindness in being invested in the happiness of others, while at the same time she seemed to decry happiness for herself.

But too quickly she broke the kiss, though he was sure he sensed it caused her effort and was not done through anything other than that same cursed emotion: the belief that she was wrong to accept pleasure.

She stood up quickly, still clutching the letters to her. "It's very late, Sir Frederick, and I must get some sleep if I'm to be a good guest in the morning, for Lady Pendleton has solicited my help with some of her entertainments."

"Very well, Miss Fairchild, if that is what you'd prefer."

"I… I'm not saying I prefer it, but I do think it would be best," she said, awkwardly. "Good night, Sir Frederick."

Chapter Twenty-Three

AMELIA HURRIED BACK to her bedchamber, clutching the letters against her chest as she berated herself for her… what?

Lapse in judgment?

All she knew was that she was proving far too susceptible to Sir Frederick's advances. She was no different to Mrs. Perry or the young ladies. Regardless of age, they all blushed and preened when he sought them out.

No doubt, Sir Frederick had come to the library when he'd been unable to sleep because he remembered he'd found Amelia there two nights earlier and he wanted a diversion. She was a little fool if she thought his interest was for any other reason than to amuse himself.

That's what Thomas had said about the dandelions who swaggered about with their puffed-out chests, and who flicked the ribbons of their phaetons pulled by horse flesh Amelia knew was well beyond the limits of most of those she knew. All they were interested in was cutting a dash and finding pleasure where they could.

Thomas had come from a respectable family. But they decried ostentation.

And as she admired the lovely gowns of the women, both

young and old, as they amused themselves about the castle gardens on such a beautiful day, it occurred to her that Thomas would have been filled with scorn.

As for herself, she suddenly wished she had a beautiful white muslin gown with a blue sash, like Miss Playford's, rather than the perfectly respectable but quite outdated gown she was wearing.

"My dear Amelia, you're all alone!" Lady Townsend beckoned her over, adding as she hooked her hand in Amelia's elbow, "And where is Sir Frederick?"

"Sir Frederick?" Amelia repeated, immediately regretting the shock and guilt in her tone for Lady Townsend angled an interested look up at her and asked, "I can't help noticing the way Sir Frederick looks at you and I wonder if you return his regard."

Caught on the spot, Amelia was, for a moment, tongue-tied. "He is a very dashing gentleman," she said, "who obviously has an eye for the ladies. I did notice his interest in the widow Perry and would not imagine that his supposed interest in me was any different."

"Come now, don't be coy, Miss Fairchild. You are just the kind of young lady Sir Frederick is looking for: serene, beautiful, intelligent, and level-headed. The widow Perry and the young Miss Ps are much too showy or flirtatious."

"I think that is exactly what Sir Frederick wants," Amelia said with perhaps too much energy as she recalled, with embarrassment, the dismay she felt when she saw Sir Frederick's flirtatious manner with the widow the previous night.

How different that was to his more serious conversation with her in the library. It only confirmed that he was adept at adjusting his manner to suit whichever young lady he wished to enjoy in a particular moment.

Amelia had discovered this just in time and made her excuses to leave the library before he refined his approach and, more importantly, lulled Amelia into doing even more unmaidenly things than kissing him.

"I've read all the letters between Pernilla and William," Amelia now said to change the subject.

"Did you, my dear?" Lady Townsend smiled. "And are you sure that half of them were not written by Lady Pendleton?"

Amelia frowned. "Do you not believe that they document the real-life love story of Lady Pendleton's great-great aunt and the man she loved? A man who was more respectable than she believes?"

"Oh, look, my dear. There is Mr. Greene in his phaeton. And Miss Caroline is with him! Don't they make quite a pair?"

Amelia jerked her head around and was surprised at such a public spectacle of favor on Caroline's part, for, since yesterday, Amelia had seen a cluster of young ladies in Mr. Greene's orbit. She really had thought the danger had been averted, but now this?

She looked about for Sir Frederick, but he was nowhere to be seen.

"Indeed, they do. But did you not think she is much too young for him?"

"Oh, one says things one does not mean. Why, if I were young again, the things I would do differently." She tapped Amelia on the forearm with her fan. "There are some young ladies like Miss Caroline and her friends who can, perhaps, be upbraided for being just a little lively; and then there are the young ladies who take life terribly seriously. I, for one, did not leap at the opportunities presented to me." She looked suddenly sad.

"You regret a missed opportunity?" Amelia asked.

"I do. Life is short and by the time one reaches my age, I regret far more what I didn't do than what I did," she said, almost under her breath.

"And that is why I have no wish to marry," Amelia said, her previous wavering at Lady Townsend's words giving way to renewed resolve. "I cannot trust a man with my happiness for that is what I'd be doing. For the rest of my life."

"You were once prepared to do such a thing," Lady Townsend said softly.

Amelia drew in a breath. "But I knew Thomas; and his character was such that I could be in no doubt that he was not toying with my affections. He was ever such a serious, stable young man."

"A serious young man could equally be a curmudgeon," Lady Townsend said. "While a lively young man could simply be exhibiting an unfettered joy in life that might just communicate itself to his partner in life in a most happy way." She shrugged. "All the more reason to explore the nature of a gentleman in any way possible. A house party like this is the perfect opportunity. Instead of the requisite series of London balls during which each party is on their best behavior, a house party is an extended period of time during which one is more likely to see the other party under a range of circumstances." She steered Amelia around the rose bushes and together they watched the phaeton disappear down the driveway.

"I wonder how Sir Frederick will react to seeing his little sister disregard his cautions," Amelia murmured.

"Won't that be informative, then?" Lady Townsend said. "Is he cold in anger? Does he have the latitude to be forgiving? He is a most interesting gentleman."

Their path took them past an elegant circular building with Grecian columns. "Ah, the rotunda," Lady Townsend remarked, her fan fluttering. "Every great house has its romantic hideaways, but this one has quite a history. When I was a girl, no properly brought up young lady would dream of being caught here unchaperoned." A meaningful smile played about her lips. "Though I dare say more than one match was sealed within those walls. The inner room is particularly... conducive to private conversations."

"Lady Townsend!" Amelia couldn't help but laugh at the older woman's suggestive tone.

"Oh, don't look so shocked, my dear. Romance needs its

secret spaces—though these days Lady Pendleton keeps it locked after an unfortunate incident involving Lord Pendleton's nephew and a particularly forward young lady." She patted Amelia's arm. "But I'm sure she'd make an exception for the right couple."

Amelia blinked as she struggled for a response. Clearly Lady Townsend had taken up Sir Frederick's cause, if she were to phrase it like that.

"You think Sir Frederick an interesting gentleman?" Amelia asked, conflicted as to whether to reprise the subject of the gentleman who was causing her such disquiet.

"But of course. The Sir Frederick we see in public is very different from his private persona. Why, the world thinks him a man of easy charm. But that is a gift, is it not, if there are hidden depths? What do you think, Amelia? Are there hidden depths?"

Amelia blinked. "I… I do not know him well enough to say." What was Lady Townsend suggesting? Had she witnessed Amelia and Sir Frederick kissing? Was her question a sly one? Did anyone else at the house party know the extent of Amelia's connection with Sir Frederick?

She felt sick. If word got out, it would reduce Sir Frederick's chances with the likely candidates that could secure Amelia the future she so desired. She'd been a fool to be so loose with him when giving him up to someone else was her ticket to freedom.

"Well, then, time will tell," Lady Townsend said comfortably. "There are still another three days under Lady Pendleton's roof. I'm sure we'll see the way Sir Frederick reacts to this and a great many other things."

A LITTLE LATER that afternoon, as Eugenia sat with her elderly friends in the summerhouse, she recounted the conversation.

"Lady Amelia is in love with Sir Frederick but she is not comfortable with her feelings," she said, smoothing her skirts with fingers that trembled slightly at Thornton's sudden interested look. "As for Sir Frederick, he is certainly more interested in the young lady than any of the other young ladies here."

Lady Pendleton raised her eyebrows. "My dear Eugenia, you are not very cunning to be revealing the state of the opposition in front of Thornton if you wish to win this wager. But then, you never could play poker."

"Speaking of which," Thornton interjected, his voice carrying a warmth that made Eugenia's heart flutter, "I seem to recall a certain evening at Almack's where your inability to bluff cost you a dance with Lord Rutherford."

"You remember that?" Eugenia met his eyes before quickly looking away. "It was so long ago."

"I remember everything about those days," he said softly.

Eugenia gave a light shrug of her shoulders, trying to hide how his words affected her. "I was not clever at poker, no. Not like my papa was. He knew how to keep his cards close to his chest. That didn't make him happy, though. He was forever cautioning me to be on my guard for fortune-hunters. As a result, I saw danger in every smile." She glanced at Thornton. "But now that I'm older, I think that satisfaction and happiness are not bound up in money, as my papa believed—"

"You think that Miss Fairchild believes happiness is bound up in money? I don't think so, Eugenia." Lady Pendleton's sharp voice cut through the moment. "Miss Fairchild isn't interested in anything other than retiring quietly to the country. Why, look at her outmoded costumes. And Sir Frederick? Why, he's much too the ladies' man for the likes of her. Really, I don't know what argument you are trying to convince us of."

"Merely that I do wish to win my wager, but not by being secretive and hoping to score by being anything other than completely honest." Eugenia lifted her chin, meeting Thornton's intense gaze.

"Such refreshing candor," he murmured. "Though it makes me wonder what other secrets that honest heart of yours might hold."

Thornton clapped his hands, but his eyes never left Eugenia's face. "Well, my dear, I wish for that Persephone at any cost. Your honesty is endearing, but I do not intend to reveal my cards as you do. Sir Frederick and Miss Fairchild will not make a match." He moved closer, his voice dropping. "You say you've intercepted some longing looks? Why, this is all a game." He extended his arms wide, and Eugenia caught the scent of his bay rum cologne. "I won't deny you intercepted a look, despite my contention the pair are mismatched. I've no doubt that, regardless of what might happen here, the moment they are apart, they'll spare not a thought." His smile held a challenge that made her pulse quicken. "No, my dear Eugenia, I am confident that the Persephone is mine."

"We shall see," Eugenia managed, though her voice wasn't quite steady.

THE AFTERNOON LIGHT was fading as Eugenia left the house, her conversation with Thornton still echoing in her mind. The sound of youthful laughter drew her attention to a pair of figures near the rose garden.

Caroline sat on the stone bench while Henry stood nearby, demonstrating something with expansive gestures that had her covering her mouth to stifle her giggles.

"And then," Henry was saying, his voice carrying clearly, "your brother's face when he realized you'd switched his powder for crushed chalk! I thought he'd expire on the spot."

"You helped me do it," Caroline reminded him, "and then blamed it all on the stable cat!"

"Well, someone had to protect you from his righteous fury." Henry's voice softened. "I always did, didn't I?"

Something in his tone made Caroline glance up sharply, but

Henry had already moved on, plucking a rose and presenting it to her with an exaggerated bow. "For you, my lady. Though Mr. Greene probably brings you exotic blooms from London's finest hothouses."

"This one's nicer," Caroline said quietly, taking the flower. "It reminds me of when we were children and you'd help me steal roses for Mama's birthday."

"And get caught every time because you couldn't resist taking 'just one more.'"

Watching them, Eugenia felt a familiar ache in her chest. How many times had she and Thornton shared such easy moments in their youth, before her father's warnings about fortune hunters had made her see danger in every smile?

Caroline twirled the rose between her fingers, her usual vivacity dimmed. "Sometimes I miss those days. Everything seemed simpler then."

"It can still be simple," Henry said, so quietly Eugenia almost missed it. "Not everything worth having comes wrapped in gold leaf, Caro."

But Caroline was already standing, smoothing her skirts. "I should go in. Mr. Greene promised to tell me about the opera in Paris."

Henry's face fell for just a moment before he recovered his cheerful expression. "Of course. Though I doubt his stories can match our adventures in the old dovecote."

"That was different. We were children then."

"Were we?" Henry's voice was wistful. "Sometimes I think we understood more then than we do now."

As Caroline hurried away, Eugenia saw Henry watch her go, the rose she'd left behind dangling forgotten from his fingers. His expression reminded her painfully of how Thornton had looked at her, so many years ago, when she'd chosen safety over love.

"They say youth is wasted on the young," came Thornton's voice behind her, making her start. "But perhaps it's wisdom that's wasted on the old."

Eugenia turned to find him watching her with an intensity that made her breath catch. "Are you calling me old, Lord Thornton?"

"Never." His smile held warmth and a hint of challenge. "Though I do think we were both young once, and perhaps equally foolish."

"Foolish enough to make wagers we couldn't win?" She meant it to sound light, but his expression turned serious.

"Some wagers are worth losing," he said softly, his eyes never leaving hers. "If they lead us where we need to go."

Below them in the garden, Henry was carefully placing Caroline's discarded rose in his buttonhole.

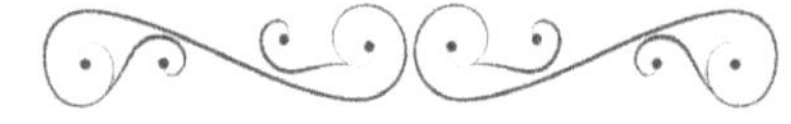

Chapter Twenty-Four

WHY COULD SHE not sleep? Amelia never had difficulty in a good night's slumber, but her time at the castle was proving most challenging.

In the far distance, she was sure she could hear a clock chime the hour. Two in the morning. Well, she'd been tossing for seemingly hours, and it was pointless to try to sleep when her brain was so restless.

Well, she certainly couldn't go to the library again. What if Sir Frederick was lying in wait for her? He'd kiss her again. She knew if he'd try to she'd be powerless to resist.

Rising, she wrapped a shawl about her shoulders and slipped her feet into warm slippers. Despite the balmy summer weather, it was cold within these stone walls. The windows let in very little light and the silence, when the heavy oak doors closed behind her as she stepped into the passage, was oppressive. How must Pernilla have felt, a prisoner of her father's, her desires irrelevant to him?

Picking up a sconce of candles from the wall, for they threw a much better light than her single candlestick, she headed for the tower. Yes, it was dangerous, the stairs crumbling, but Sir Frederick had helped the ladies navigate their way to the tower and that was exactly where Amelia was going now.

Was Pernilla becoming an obsession?

But if Pernilla was real, and so misunderstood, would it not be honoring the young woman to at least find out her real story? Yes, she had the letters that Lady Pendleton might dismiss as contrived or perhaps even written by someone else conducting a ghost or treasure hunt.

No, Amelia was certain there was something else to be discovered.

And if the three of them had made a general search of Pernilla's tower room, they certainly hadn't looked very hard. The moment they'd discovered the so-called letters—and it had been the fake letter written by Lady Pernilla—they had considered their job done.

But what if there was more? More that proved that William was indeed worthy, and that Lady Pendleton did her ancestor a grave disservice by dismissing her as a foolish and easily led young girl. Almost as if she deserved her premature end.

For some reason, the need to get to the truth was becoming an obsession.

So far, Amelia had discovered a treasure trove behind the loose brick Pernilla had used as a letter box. It was the perfect location because it was a general area where no one—not even William—would be questioned about accessing.

But could there be a loose brick in Pernilla's tower room where she kept more personal correspondence?

Pushing open the door, she stepped inside, placing the candle sconce in the bracket on the wall. With the large waxing moon, a surprising amount of light filled the room. Easily enough to begin a thorough search.

And with Amelia's mind so busy, she might as well turn her energies to something that would at least satisfy her curiosity, even if it didn't result in the bounty for which she might have hoped. That was the way of life. But if she didn't try, she'd regret it by the time it was time to go home.

Amelia was a methodical young lady. Therefore, she began at

the bottom of the brick wall and began to work her way around, her hands carefully feeling for any roughness that might indicate a cavity.

After an hour or so, her knees and hands were stiff and cold, and she'd found nothing.

Huffing out a sigh of frustration, she sat on the wooden kist at the end of the wooden four poster and surveyed the room. Could the drapery hold something? Unlikely, though she did rise and shake out the curtains, which yielded nothing except dust.

What about the kist? Had they thoroughly searched that? Leaning over once more, though her back ached, she raised the lid and stared into the darkness. She couldn't see anything, but she plunged her hand to the bottom and carefully felt for something like a letter on the base, beneath the fur-lined cloak that had been folded and kept there for what might be a hundred years.

In frustration, she tapped her fingernails as she tried to think where else she'd failed to look.

And then she had to tap them again, for that didn't feel right. With her ear to the wooden sides, she tested the sound.

Hollow?

She was sure of it.

With a fiercely beating heart, Amelia looked about for something she could use to prise up what she was sure was a false bottom.

SIR FREDERICK HAD spent a rather fraught afternoon between tempering Caroline's enthusiasm for phaeton-riding with unsuitable men and consulting the physician in town for a remedy for the insistent pain in his thigh occasioned by his war wound.

He was not going to bring attention to it by receiving a personal visit from the physician, so he'd made a rather clandestine trip into the village under the guise of riding into town to see the blacksmith.

Now, he was back in the conservatory, feeling slightly undone by Caroline's rather hysterical outburst that her brother was trying to ruin her life. Yes, he had been waiting at the end of the drive to halt the phaeton and inform Greene he did not give permission for Caroline to go bowling about the countryside, unchaperoned.

But what other caring brother would not have done the same thing?

He was just contemplating rising and going to his bedchamber to take the powders the physician had prescribed him when Miss Fairchild entered.

"There you are, Sir Frederick! I've been looking for you," she announced to his surprise, gliding over, her eyes alight with something he couldn't quite identify. The last time they'd parted, she'd seemed quite determined to ensure he got no ideas regarding the possibility of any romance between them.

So, he was therefore astonished when she added, in quite urgent tones, "Please, will you accompany me to St John's Church at your earliest convenience? To speak to the parson."

"I beg your pardon?"

Her excitement was so great that she didn't even register the irony in his tone.

"Lady Pernilla married her true love, William!" she went on. "I just don't know where, and I hope you'll come with me to ask the parson if there's a record in the parish register."

Sir Frederick sent her a fond look. "My dear Miss Fairchild, do you really suppose that her legal marriage would be registered in the local parish register when Lady Pendleton has told everyone her great-great aunt died when she fell to her death from the tower, because her father refused to sanction her love for a stable boy."

"Yes, that's what everyone was obviously told, but it's not the truth!"

Miss Fairchild took a seat opposite him, reaching into her reticule to withdraw a small book, which she opened.

"This is Lady Pernilla's diary," she said. "I found it in a false bottom of the kist that was in Lady Pernilla's tower room."

"The same place we found false letters written by Lady Pendleton to keep up the fun of the treasure hunt?" Sir Frederick tried to sound kind.

"Nearby. But this isn't false. It's not written by anyone pretending to play games." Miss Fairchild tapped the book before pushing it towards him. "Have a look at the entries which begin at the beginning of the year. Read a few of them until you're convinced they're not fabricated, and then read the last one."

Of course he had to humor her, even if he didn't for one moment believe this was really Lady Pernilla's diary from a hundred years earlier.

But what might have been a more cursory look through the small, leather-bound book packed with dense writing, difficult in places to decipher but generally quite readable, became a more drawn-out exercise.

And this was because Miss Fairchild, in her continued excitement, had drawn closer to him, her fragrant light brown hair almost touching his cheek, and causing such distraction it was hard to concentrate on the words he was supposed to read.

Fortunately, Miss Fairchild kept him to the task at hand with her frequent interjections.

"See, she states quite clearly here that though William is the son of a solicitor and had been acceptable at the start, William's father's bankruptcy and ensuing scandal meant William was no longer allowed to court Pernilla." She shook her head. "How could Lady Pendleton be so dismissive of poor William? Clearly, he was given a very damning accounting of in the annals of history which he did not deserve."

"How do you explain the letter which stated he was a stable lad?"

"Oh, now you are confusing Lady Pendleton's letters and

something written by William, wrongly interpreted." Miss Fairchild was clearly frustrated. "See what Pernilla writes here?" She tapped a page halfway through the book. "William had found work as a tutor, but his love of horses and his rare gift of soothing them had some of those in the area requesting his services. So, you can see how that would be blightingly referred to by Sir Pendleton if he wanted to force his daughter to marry a local landowner she didn't care for."

"Another of Lady Pendleton's falsehoods, I'm sure," Sir Frederick said in as bored a tone as he felt he could get away with, for he certainly enjoyed Miss Fairchild's darkling looks. How nice it was to get something other than a bland reaction which he'd expected when she'd decided it was safer to have nothing to do with him.

"No! See here!" Miss Fairchild turned a few more pages to nearly the end of the book, located a certain passage, then began to read:

"I fear Papa will pressure me to the point where I have no further means of resistance. William says that if I can hold them off—Papa and Sir Simon—for another five days, he'll have organized a special license, and we can elope."

She turned her wide-eyed gaze upon Sir Frederick. "Did you read that? William got a special license and he and Lady Pernilla eloped. I thought maybe the parson at St John's might be able to verify it because, as you can see, the diary ends several pages later when she's made plans to run away with William the following day." She shook her head. "Perhaps Pernilla forgot the diary. Or perhaps she had planned to take it with her but was unable to."

Sir Frederick didn't dismiss the idea that the diary was not real this time. There was something both real and compelling about the entries.

But now he shook his head as he said, "All this flies in the face of everything Lady Pendleton clearly believes about her ancestor. She says Lady Pernilla died here, at Pendleton Castle. If that's the case, her grave would be here."

"All right, let's find it." Miss Fairchild rose and took a few steps towards the door, turning to him in invitation.

"Do you mean right now?"

She nodded. "Of course," she said, as if there was nothing else that could be of any greater importance.

And despite the objections of Sir Frederick's painful leg, he found that he was more than happy to accompany Miss Fairchild on a visit to the family crypt.

Chapter Twenty-Five

AMELIA HAD GONE ahead while she waited for Sir Frederick to ask for the key to the Pendleton family crypt. The late afternoon sun cast long shadows across the manicured lawn, and a cool breeze stirred her skirts. She certainly didn't want to be seen in company with him more than she already had been, though her heart quickened at the thought of another private moment in his presence. As a majority of guests had gone on either a picnic or a ramble, leaving mostly the elderly to lounge about in the drawing room, Amelia felt beneath scrutiny.

Waiting by the large wooden door with its heavy iron studs, weathered by centuries of rain and wind, she observed Sir Frederick's approach. His limp, which hadn't been in evidence when he'd shepherded them around the castle, caught her attention. Despite it, he moved with a quiet dignity that she found herself admiring against her better judgment.

"A mishap during croquet, or were you practicing the waltz?" she asked with a smile, trying to mask her concern with light teasing.

"An old injury aggravated when I tried to follow my sister in Mr. Greene's phaeton," Sir Frederick said, raising an eyebrow as he closed the distance between them, holding up a large iron key. The way his eyes met hers held a warmth that made her chest tighten.

"Oh, dear, I wondered where you were when she was whisked away amid a group of admiring and envious lads and ladies." Amelia waited as he inserted the key, watching his capable hands work the ancient lock. "I don't think he's as serious as you might have feared earlier, though," she added softly. "I have seen him send other young ladies indications of his interest."

"Indeed. Ah, there we have it."

Screeching on old hinges, the door opened outwards, and Sir Frederick raised his lantern, its warm glow creating a golden sphere around them. He offered Amelia his arm with an old-world courtesy that touched her more than she cared to admit. She hooked her hand through his elbow, feeling the solid strength beneath his coat, and allowed him to lead the way along a row of effigies. The air grew cooler as they descended, heavy with the weight of centuries. These were the plaster casts of the more senior members of the family, their stern faces watching their progress in the flickering lamplight. The last one depicted Lady Pendleton's own parents, committed to the crypt during the last ten years.

"Here is Lady Pendleton's great grandfather, Sir William," murmured Sir Frederick, his voice pitched low in deference to their surroundings. "Pernilla could have inherited the viscountcy due to the special provision—the reason that the current Lady Pendleton was able to inherit—but Pernilla died childless. The title and estate went to her cousin, William, Lady Pendleton's great grandfather."

Sir Frederick stopped and his voice was hushed as he said, "See, and there is Pernilla's crypt." Pointing, he guided her towards a small crypt at the end of the row.

"Pernilla Pendleton. Born May 13, 1698. Died August 9, 1719."

"Poor Pernilla," Amelia murmured before gasping, "Why, she died the day after her last diary entry!" The chill of the crypt seemed to seep into her bones as the reality of the young woman's fate struck her.

"And we have no reason to doubt that what Lady Pendelton says is true: that her great-great aunt Pernilla died falling out of a window while trying to elope."

"Or jumping, as some others have said. It seems no one really knows the truth." Amelia sighed, aware of how close she stood to Sir Frederick, of how his presence seemed to ward off the crypt's gloom. "What a short life. And to be denied the happiness she writes about in her diary and letters with such hope."

"She did enjoy some happiness," Sir Frederick reminded her as they stepped outside, blinking in the sudden sunlight. His hand covered hers where it still rested on his arm, a gesture that felt both protective and intimate.

"Too little," Amelia responded, trying to ignore the warmth of his touch. "In her last diary entry, she imagined her life's dream was to be realized the following day."

"If that was indeed really her diary," Sir Frederick said mildly, though his eyes held a spark of challenge that made her breath catch.

"Do you not believe it? Do you truly think that could be another of Lady Pendleton's fabrications just for the entertainment of the guests?" Amelia challenged him, turning to face him fully. "Then why was it hidden in a false bottom of the chest? No one would go to the effort of writing a whole diary for a game."

Sir Frederick shrugged, a gesture that drew her attention to the breadth of his shoulders. "I can't answer that, but clearly Miss Pernilla did not live to marry." He indicated her crypt. "Not to William or to the man her father had lined up for her and which, I might remind you, did not make him especially tyrannical. A hundred years ago, a love match was not the common occurrence it is today."

Amelia sighed, feeling the weight of generations of arranged marriages pressing upon her. "I daresay the love would have died, besides. To fall in love is not to guarantee happiness in perpetuity, and the romantics who think that when they walk down the aisle are bound for disappointment."

Sir Frederick patted her hand, which still rested on his forearm as he moved her towards the iron door. The gesture felt more intimate than it should have, his touch lingering a moment longer than strictly necessary.

"As you do not speak from experience, I wonder how you can have formed such a dismal outlook on the institution."

Amelia sighed. "My mama was a renowned beauty when my father married her. He'd courted her, fought a duel over her, and said once he'd considered himself the luckiest man in the county when she'd consented to be his wife."

"And?" His voice was gentle, encouraging, holding none of the judgment she feared.

Amelia bit her lip, studying the weathered stone beneath their feet. It would be the height of disloyalty to say what she'd never said to a living soul. And to Sir Frederick, of all people.

Yet, perhaps he, of all people, needed to hear home truths like this one. Something about his steady presence made her want to confide in him, trust him with the tender places in her heart she usually kept guarded.

"He soon tired of her once her beauty began to fade. I loved my Papa. He was a good man, but he did not value my mama as he should have, God rest his soul."

Her voice trembled slightly on the last words. She certainly could not have imagined revealing such a thing to her Thomas, she realized with a start that made her question everything she thought she knew about her own heart.

"What else did she offer apart from her beauty? A lively mind like yours? Did you inherit your humor and curiosity from her?" His questions were probing but gentle, his gaze holding hers with an intensity that made her forget to breathe.

She thought it a strange response, but replied, "Oh, Mama did not have a sense of humor and no interest in book learning. That all came from Papa."

"Then do you not think that perhaps your papa might have hoped for more than a pretty face when he entered into a lifelong contract with your mama?" He stopped, growing serious as he looked at her on the threshold to the outdoors. The sunlight caught the silver threading through his dark hair, and his eyes held a warmth that made her heart flutter. "The lady I wed must have a keen intelligence as well as a pretty face for we all grow old and while our bodies age, our minds continue to offer diversion and entertainment. That has to be a reason for marrying, since I intend to remain true to the wife I choose."

Amelia shivered, and not from the crypt's lingering chill. She must not allow herself to be susceptible to his words, though they seemed to reach past all her carefully constructed defenses. He knew her just a little too well. No doubt this was carefully calculated to make her want to kiss him again, though the thought sent a thrill through her that she couldn't entirely suppress.

She glanced about her, suddenly aware of their solitude. The crypt was far away from the castle and there was no one about. It was, perhaps, not seemly that she should be alone with him, though she couldn't bring herself to regret it.

Slanting a nervous glance up at him, she was about to suggest they take a circuitous route back to the castle when a stranger's voice intruded.

"Sir, would 'ee like to hand over the key to the crypt and save yerself the trouble o' taking it back to her ladyship."

A gnarled and bent old man stood deferentially to one side as if he'd been waiting for a suitable moment to interrupt, his weathered face as much a part of the landscape as the ancient stones around them.

"Why, of course," Sir Frederick said affably, though Amelia thought she detected a note of regret in his voice as he handed over the heavy iron key. "You are one of Lady Pendleton's groundsmen?"

"We've just been to see Pernilla's grave," Amelia told him, grateful for the distraction from her turbulent thoughts. The old man looked almost ancient enough to have been alive in her time. On a whim, she asked, "Do you know the story of the young Lady Pernilla? The current Lady Pendleton's great-great aunt?"

"Aye, were a strange tale and not all will agree to the fate of the poor lassie," said the old man, his rheumy eyes holding a glimmer of something that made Amelia lean forward eagerly.

"We just saw her grave in the crypt," said Sir Frederick, his hand coming to rest protectively at the small of Amelia's back. "There's little doubt about her fate."

"Not according to the rumors from when I was a wee boy passed down to me by me da."

"And what were those rumors?" Amelia prompted, barely noticing how she'd shifted closer to Sir Frederick's warmth.

"Lady Pendleton says her great-great aunt fell to her death shortly after planning to elope with a man of whom her father disapproved." Sir Frederick raised an eyebrow. "And her grave is in the crypt, so I don't see there can be any rumors to discount that."

"Oh, there are rumors, to be sure," said the old man, a knowing look crossing his weathered features. "Rumors that when she ran away, her father chose to declare her dead." His hand closed over the key that Sir Frederick handed him.

"Is that what your father told you?" Sir Frederick asked and the old man nodded, his eyes taking on a distant look as if seeing into the past.

"The old Viscount Pendleton—Miss Pernilla's father—was a proud man and he would rather his daughter be dead than that he be publicly shamed by her defiance." He nodded. "That's what me own da told me, him wot were but a boy when it all happened and remembered it clear as daylight."

"And what else did your da tell you?" Amelia asked, feeling her excitement grow, her hand unconsciously finding Sir Frederick's arm again.

"That Lady Pernilla ran away with the man wot had been courting her and of whom her papa disapproved. Yes, ran away to start a new life while her da declared her dead."

Amelia jerked her head up and caught Sir Frederick's surprised glance. He smiled slightly, his eyes holding a spark of shared adventure that made her heart skip, then said, "Well, as it's hardly going to be possible to exhume Lady Pernilla's grave, perhaps, Miss Fairchild, you would like to accompany me to see the vicar. You did suggest earlier that a perusal of the Church Register could be informative, did you not?"

Chapter Twenty-Six

THE SHORT WALK to St. John's Church became considerably longer as Sir Frederick's limp grew more pronounced. Amelia, who had been striding ahead in her eagerness to reach the parish records, forced herself to moderate her pace.

"You need not wait for me," he said, correctly interpreting her sideways glances. "I assure you I shan't lose my way."

"Of course I won't walk on ahead," she said. The warmth in her voice surprised her, as did the smile he gave her in return.

Dark clouds had begun gathering on the horizon, but Amelia paid them little heed, her mind too full of possibilities.

Keeping pace with him, Amelia turned. "Oh, Sir Frederick! What if I'm right? What if we uncover proof of a marriage between Pernilla and her lover?"

Sir Frederick halted, maybe to consider the question though perhaps to ease the pressure on his leg, for Amelia darted a glance of concern at his thigh to which he'd pressed a hand, wincing briefly before he said, "Do you really suppose the crypt we saw belonging to Pernilla is a fabrication? Do you really think it possible she ran away one night, married her lover, and had a passel of children, one of whom would be the rightful owner of the Pendleton title and estate?"

Amelia squared her shoulders, her momentary sympathy for

her companion gone. "Then why are you accompanying me on this expedition if you think this whole idea is one fanciful notion of mine?"

He stared at her as if considering her question, then said, "It is true that I enjoy indulging your fancies—for your honest enthusiasm is more refreshing than anything I've encountered for a long time." Hesitating, he added, "I've never been a man who will discount a possibility merely because, on the balance of probabilities, it is almost certain to be proved wrong. No, Miss Fairchild, the truth is that I, in fact, owe my life to such a philosophy."

"That's very deep and mysterious," Amelia said, surprised when he laughed, and said, correctly interpreting her response, "You are suspicious that I am making up stories to appear less of the empty-hearted libertine you think me?"

"I think nothing of the sort!"

"Oh, you have done, and now you don't know what to think." Unexpectedly, he reached out a hand and gently touched her cheek, saying, "It's never particularly bothered me what people think but I will confess, Miss Fairchild, that, increasingly, I wish to be held in your high regard. Ah, now, here we are and, if my note has been delivered as requested, we will hopefully find the vicar is expecting us."

The church stood solid and imposing against the darkening sky, its ancient stones holding centuries of secrets. As they approached the heavy wooden door, the first fat drops of rain began to fall.

"The beadle did say we would find him here," Sir Frederick said, rapping sharply on the door. After a moment, he tried the handle. "Locked."

"We can't just give up. We leave the day after tomorrow." Amelia couldn't keep the frustration from her voice.

"Don't worry, my dear. I am not a man to give up so easily, though"—Sir Frederick glanced at the threatening sky—"I do think we should return to the castle before—"

A crack of thunder interrupted his words, and suddenly the heavens opened. Within seconds, they were both drenched.

"Quick!" Sir Frederick grabbed her hand, pulling her toward the church's side entrance. The small door, typically used by the vicar, opened to his touch. They stumbled inside just as another thunderclap shook the windows.

The vestry was dim and close, filled with the musty scent of old prayer books and well-worn cassocks. Amelia was acutely aware of Sir Frederick's presence beside her, of how his wet shirt clung to his shoulders, of the way water dripped from his dark hair.

"You're shivering," he said softly, shrugging out of his coat despite its dampness and draping it over her shoulders.

"I'm quite all right," she protested. "But your leg—you should sit."

He didn't argue, lowering himself onto a wooden bench with a barely suppressed grimace.

Amelia contemplated his pained expression. "Where did you say you received the injury?"

"I didn't."

"Oh." Amelia wrestled with her next question, then asked, "Bullet or sword?"

"Bayonet."

"Bayonet?" she asked, her voice sharp and high to her own ears. "But bayonets are only used during..."

She trailed off and he finished for her, "During war. Yes, it's an old war wound, and it troubles me particularly when the weather turns cold and damp."

"You fought in the war?" Amelia sat beside him, careful to maintain a proper distance despite the bench's narrow width. "But I thought—that is, Thomas said you spent the war years on the Continent, enjoying yourself."

Something flickered in his eyes. "Did he? And you believed him?"

"I—" Amelia stopped, suddenly uncertain. How much had

she accepted without question? "Where were you wounded?"

"In France." His voice was quiet.

The shock of this revelation left her momentarily speechless. Word was that Sir Frederick had gone carousing on the Continent far from the battlefield. "Thomas never mentioned—"

"No, I don't suppose he would have." Sir Frederick's smile held no humor. "My work was done behind enemy lines. I heard Thomas died bravely."

She stared at him, seeing him anew and thought of all her incorrect assumptions. The limp she'd attributed to some mishap during his supposedly dissolute years abroad. The shadows that sometimes crossed his face. The way he'd tensed when someone at dinner had made a careless joke about the war.

"Why did you never say anything?"

"Would you have believed me?" He met her gaze steadily. "You had formed your opinion of me long ago. The rakish baronet who fled to the Continent rather than serve his country. Who spent his time in pursuit of pleasure while better men died."

"I was wrong," she whispered. The admission cost her pride, but truth mattered more. "About so many things, it seems."

Thunder rolled again, but more distantly now. In the vestry's dim light, she could see raindrops clinging to his eyelashes.

"Not about everything," he said. "I did pursue pleasure on the Continent—after the war. I needed…something to drive away the memories. The nightmares." His hand moved as if to touch her face, then dropped. "But I am not that man anymore. Just as you are not the same girl who pledged her troth to Thomas."

"No," she agreed softly. "I'm not."

A shaft of watery sunlight suddenly pierced the vestry's high window, illuminating a row of leather-bound books on a nearby shelf. Amelia rose, drawn by their promise, and Sir Frederick followed more slowly.

"Parish records," she breathed, running her finger along the spines. "Dating back to… yes! Here's 1719."

Together they lifted down the heavy volume, laying it carefully on the vestry's small desk. The pages were yellowed but well-preserved, the clerk's careful handwriting still clearly legible. Amelia's heart beat faster as she turned to August's entries.

And there it was. Not in the book itself but written separately on a loose piece of paper.

"August 8th, 1719," she read aloud. "William Greene and Pernilla Pendleton, joined in holy matrimony." Her finger traced the line below. "Witnessed by…"

"The curate and his wife," Sir Frederick finished. "The very day before she supposedly died."

They stared at each other, the implications slowly sinking in.

"She didn't die," Amelia said. "She escaped. With William."

"And her father covered it up rather than face the scandal." Sir Frederick's voice held grudging admiration. "But why make this entry at all? Even if it isn't actually in the book? Surely that defeated the purpose?"

"Perhaps…" Amelia hesitated. "Perhaps someone wanted the truth to be known. Eventually."

His hand covered hers where it rested on the ancient page, and as he looked at her, his thumb traced small circles on her wrist, sending shivers up her arm that had nothing to do with her damp clothing.

"Sir Frederick—" she began.

But before she could continue, the vestry door opened, flooding the small room with light. They sprang apart as the vicar entered, full of apologies for his lateness.

"Ah, you found the records!" he said cheerfully, apparently oblivious to their flushed faces and damp clothing. "Fascinating reading, aren't they? All those old stories, waiting to be discovered."

Chapter Twenty-Seven

AMELIA AND SIR Frederick had barely made it back to the castle, their clothes still damp from their earlier soaking, when they heard Lady Pendleton's strident tones echoing down the corridor.

"Completely incompetent! I won't have it. Not in my house!"

Rounding the corner, they came upon a tableau that made Amelia's heart sink. A young maid kneeled on the floor, desperately trying to gather up the shards of what had clearly been an expensive Chinese vase, while Lady Pendleton loomed over her.

"Mama, please." The quiet voice was Lady Pendleton's son, Albert. He stood a few feet behind the young maid, his expression pained. "It was my fault entirely. I wasn't looking where I was going and bumped into Jenny as she was dusting."

"Nonsense, Albert!" Lady Pendleton rounded on her son. "You needn't cover for the girl's clumsiness. She'll be dismissed without a character, of course."

The maid's face went white. "Please, my lady, I beg you—my mother is ill, and my wages—"

"Enough!" Lady Pendleton's voice was quiet, but harsh.

"Mother," said Albert, his voice still gentle but now carrying an unmistakable note of authority, "I have already said it was my fault. I will, of course, replace the vase from my own allowance."

"But Albert—"

"And Jenny," he continued as if his mother hadn't spoken, "is one of our most conscientious servants. When Grand-papa was alive, he often remarked on her attention to detail, particularly in caring for the library's more delicate volumes."

At the mention of her late father, Lady Pendleton's expression flickered. Albert pressed his advantage.

"In fact, I was just coming to find you, Mama. I've been reviewing the estate accounts as you asked, and I have some questions about the tenant farmers' rents. Shall we discuss them in your sitting room?"

It was masterfully done, Amelia thought. In the space of a few sentences, he had reminded his mother of her father's values, demonstrated his own attention to estate matters, and offered her a graceful way to exit the situation without losing face.

Lady Pendleton drew herself up. "Very well. Though I still think—" She broke off, finally noticing their audience. "Sir Frederick! Miss Fairchild! I trust you haven't been caught in that dreadful downpour?"

"Only briefly," Sir Frederick replied smoothly. "Though long enough to appreciate the excellence of your roof repairs. The castle seems remarkably well-maintained."

Another masterstroke, Amelia realized. Lady Pendleton immediately launched into a detailed account of recent improvements to the estate, allowing Albert to help the maid to her feet and whisper something that made her grateful curtsey markedly less shaky.

As his mother swept down the corridor, Albert turned to them with a rueful smile. "I apologize if you witnessed any unpleasantness. My mother can be…passionate about the running of her household."

"It seems to me the household—and the estate—are fortunate in their future master," Sir Frederick remarked.

Albert's smile turned self-deprecating. "I try to live up to my grandfather's example. He always said that true nobility lay not in how we treat our equals, but in how we treat those who depend upon us." He glanced after his mother. "Though sometimes that requires a degree of…diplomatic skill."

"A skill you seem to have mastered admirably," Amelia said warmly.

He laughed. "Years of practice, I assure you. Though I'm still learning. There's so much to understand about running an estate of this size. The responsibilities to the tenants, the preservation of the house itself, the balance between tradition and necessary change…" He shook his head. "Sometimes I wonder if I'll ever be truly ready."

"Those who question their readiness are often the most prepared," Sir Frederick observed.

"That's kind of you to say." Albert glanced down the corridor where sounds of cleaning indicated the maid had returned with reinforcements. "If you'll excuse me, I should go review those accounts with my mother while she's receptive to discussion. I'm hoping to convince her to moderate this quarter's rents. The spring floods hit our tenants hard."

As he strode away, Amelia found herself exchanging glances with Sir Frederick. The weight of their recent discovery in the parish records seemed suddenly heavier.

"He'll make an excellent viscount," she said softly.

"Yes." Sir Frederick's voice was equally low. "One who clearly understands the true meaning of noblesse oblige."

IT WAS STILL a few hours before dinner, Amelia still had to dry her hair, the meager fire in the grate casting more shadow than warmth across the room.

Deciding the drying would happen faster outside, now that the sun had timidly emerged from behind slate-gray clouds, she gathered her shawl and headed back into the weak sunshine.

The gravel path crunched softly beneath her half-boots as she walked the path that led around the rose bushes, their late-season blooms hanging heavy with droplets from the earlier rain.

Rain threatened again, but for now the sun was winning the battle.

The battle.

Amelia gave a wry smile as she considered the various battles which she felt were playing about right now.

Caro and her battle of wills with her brother. Of course, the young girl was intelligent enough to understand, in her heart, that Mr. Greene was nothing but a fortune hunter. He'd already shown his colors by withdrawing his interest the moment he learned he'd have to wait several years for Caroline's fortune.

And then there was Amelia's own battle of the heart.

Why, oh why, did she keep thinking of Sir Frederick when she knew in *her* heart of hearts that relinquishing him to someone far more suitable was the only way to achieve long-term happiness?

Sir Frederick was not for her, and she was foolish if she thought otherwise.

If his smile grew warmer when he addressed her, and his tone held an edge of fondness that was absent when she heard him addressing other young ladies, wasn't that simply all in her imagination?

Besides, even if it wasn't, it was because he'd made a sport out of trying to get her to admit feelings for him.

Yes, that was it!

Her reflections were cut short when Henry hailed her from across the lawn, and he strode across to her side. "I'm so glad I've caught you alone, Miss Fairchild," he said, flicking a glance up at the fast-graying sky. As the distance between them closed, Amelia saw lines of concern etched around his eyes. His normally composed countenance was troubled, a muscle twitching almost imperceptibly at the corner of his jaw.

"Is Caroline in trouble again?" Amelia asked with a smile that did not quite reach her eyes, hoping to ease whatever burden weighed so heavily upon him. The smile was a practiced thing, designed to coax confidences from a reluctant source. "I think her brother will be very glad when she is back home and her foolish fancies have something else to focus on. Mr. Greene will not be allowed to call on her at home." She hesitated, the breeze lifting a wayward strand of hair across her cheek. "I presume it is Greene that is the source of your concern?"

Henry nodded, his gloved hand absently smoothing the lapel of his coat. "Yes, but not in relation to Caroline," he said. With a furtive glance that swept across the lawn—taking in the gardener pruning roses in the distant corner, the maid carrying linens to dry, the groundskeeper moving wheelbarrows near the kitchen gardens—he leaned slightly closer. "Would you be so kind as to come to the library with me? You see, I've found something, and I don't know what to do with the information."

Amelia hoped she stifled her gasp. Had he, too, realized that Pernilla and William had actually married?

But when they were back in the large, vaulted repository of books, Henry revealed that his discovery was of a different nature entirely.

"Let me show you," Henry said as the library doors closed behind them with a soft thud that seemed to seal them into another world. Here, the storm-washed afternoon light filtered through tall windows, catching dust motes that danced above the leather-bound volumes. The familiar scent of beeswax polish mingled with aged paper and ink—usually so comforting to Amelia, but now holding an edge of foreboding as Henry led her between the towering shelves.

"Do you recognize this handwriting?" asked Henry. His fingers, slightly ink-stained at the tips, pushed aside a precarious pile of volumes—leather-bound classics whose gilded spines caught what little light filtered through the heavy curtains.

Amelia did. She'd seen the correspondence in his hand—admittedly brief and lighthearted between Caroline and Mr.

Greene.

"I think someone interrupted Mr. Greene while he was writing a letter. He covered it with these volumes and obviously plans to return, though he clearly was unable to take the letter with him. But do you see what he has written? I certainly had no intention of prying into his personal affairs, but the letter was there to read the moment I picked up the volume of Virgil, which had interested me."

Amelia put her head closer to the paper, unwilling to disturb its position, and read that which had so disturbed Henry. The handwriting was unmistakably Mr. Greene's—the same flowing script she'd seen in his previous lighthearted correspondence with Caroline, now transformed into something far more consequential.

"Dearest Cousin," the letter read, *"Your research was correct. I believe I've found the proof we need linking the Greene family to Pernilla and William. Their marriage certificate provides all we need to prove our claim..."*

She turned to find Henry looking as shocked as she felt, the afternoon light casting long shadows across the library's intricate parquet floor.

"Mr. Greene believes he is the rightful claimant to Lady Pendleton's title and estate?" she whispered, the words barely disturbing the library's hushed atmosphere. "But why bring this to me?"

"Because you have a wise head on your shoulders," replied Henry. His voice was low, careful—the voice of a man who understood the delicate nature of the secrets that could destroy reputations. "If I told Sir Frederick, he'd have the man horsewhipped because he's already feeling such angst towards him with regard to Greene's blatant courting of his sister, Caroline. As for Lady Pendleton, well, I couldn't speak to her. I felt I needed to discuss what I'd found first with someone who had, perhaps, less at stake."

Amelia nodded, still looking at the letter. She'd taken care not to move it, conscious of the potential devastation such a document could unleash. It would be best, she felt, that Mr. Greene remain ignorant that his research had been uncovered.

"You did right not to take it to her or Albert, I think," she said, her tone measured and calm.

"Do you mean because you also think Mr. Greene is not a worthy inheritor of Pendleton Castle and all the rest of it?" Henry asked. He put his hand to his cravat as if it was too tight, a gesture that betrayed his inner turmoil. Then, in a lowered tone that seemed to invite conspiracy, he added, "Colonel Blackwood said he's heard whispers that if Greene's debts were called in tomorrow, the man would have to declare bankruptcy."

Amelia pressed her lips together as she frowned. Slowly she asked, her voice a mere thread of sound, "Do you think there might be some truth to this supposed connection between our Mr. Greene and Pernilla?"

"Lord, no!" Henry exclaimed, though he kept his voice low. "Pernilla is in the family crypt. Caro and I visited it with Greene only yesterday. Lady Pendleton said she died the night she tried to run away with her lover. I thought it was a story to add drama to her ghostly house party, but now I believe it. She certainly didn't disappear from her home, get married, and produce children, of which our Mr. Greene is the last in the line!"

But Amelia feared that was exactly the truth of it as her mind raced ahead to all the implications—not just for the Pendleton inheritance, but for Caroline, whose heart might be broken twice over when she discovered both Mr. Greene's duplicity and his true connection to her godmother's family history. Even Albert, who showed such promise as the future master of Pendleton Castle…

Chapter Twenty-Eight

"*T*HERE'S SOMETHING *I'D like to show you. Please meet me in the rotunda at 4 p.m.*"

Sir Frederick let the note flutter from his fingers to his writing desk beneath the window while inwardly he groaned.

He'd been watching Miss Fairchild through the window and had been on the verge of joining her when young Henry had spoiled his plans.

And now this note from Mrs. Perry had turned what could have been a pleasant afternoon into a potential nightmare. The paper felt heavy in his hands, weighted with implications he had no desire to face.

Mrs. Perry thought she had the measure of him and would be confidently reposing shortly in the trysting room within the rotunda, awaiting his arrival.

What a fool he was to have allowed his old, worn-out reputation to linger.

But it was his fault to have walked into temptation and embraced it with open arms in the first place.

Oh, that embarrassment with Lady Eldredge when he'd been only a greenhorn. He knew that those were the rumors that had fueled Miss Fairchild's distrust of him. She thought him a philanderer. A libertine.

Well, of course he enjoyed the company of beautiful, witty women. What red-blooded male would turn down the overtures of a lush beauty like Lady Eldredge, who had declared her marriage dead and who claimed her loneliness could only be assuaged by an evening with a dashing war hero like Sir Frederick?

Of course, she'd used other language. Sir Frederick was not a war hero. Well, he was in some circles, but it was not as if he'd been lauded for his heroics in the press so that the whole world knew what only a few within military and government circles knew.

But she'd couched her compliments in such a way that they'd gone completely to Sir Frederick's head, and he'd done what he knew very well at the time was rank stupidity.

Recently returned from war, in pain and licking his wounds—for he'd been unjustly maligned and it would be some months before he'd be exonerated—he'd needed tenderness and understanding.

That's what he'd mistakenly attributed to Barbara, Lady Eldredge. Tenderness and genuine admiration when, in fact, she wanted only to toy with a man she found, at that particular moment, attractive.

The scandal had been splashed throughout the broadsheets and in all the gossip sheets throughout the country once Lord Eldredge had got wind of his wife's infidelity.

Apparently, the marriage wasn't dead, and Lord Eldredge hadn't sanctioned his extramarital affairs while he dallied with his own mistress.

If Sir Frederick had been a few years older, perhaps he'd have been wise to it. But for a youth of barely twenty-three, with little previous experience of women, Sir Frederick had been ripe for the picking.

So excoriating was the experience that he'd thrown himself carelessly into another couple of liaisons, since nothing could damage his reputation any further, he'd thought at the time.

Now, Mrs. Perry was trading on the fact that he'd succumb to her lures.

She mightn't have been wrong a few years previously.

But she'd misread him this time.

Four o'clock in the rotunda.

Ought he go there just so he could explain to her that his interest lay elsewhere?

Or should he ignore her letter and run the risk of offending her? Sir Frederick knew that scorned women had a habit of finding an especially cutting vengeance for their targets.

But then, if he didn't try to make his case clear, when they were safely in private so that there was no risk of her being embarrassed, matters might progress from simply awkward to much worse.

Snatching up his hat, he strode to the door, not hesitating when, in truth, he had deep reservations about this assignation.

Best to nip in the bud any hopes she might have, he kept telling himself as he crossed the lawn, head down, shoulders hunched.

He did not want to go through with this. He suspected Mrs. Perry might have a temper to match her vivacity. She'd take his gentle let-down personally and then who knew what might ensure?

AMELIA AND HENRY had parted ways, stepping out of the library after she'd agreed to discuss the matter with someone trusted so as to help make a considered decision on the matter.

Sir Frederick? Henry had asked. Did she trust him?

And of course Amelia had nodded. Sir Frederick had been with her when they'd discovered the crypt, when they'd seen the register with its incriminating entry.

A crack of thunder in the far distance made her turn her head to look out of the window and she thought she glimpsed the figure of a gentleman heading towards the lake, but when she squinted, she could see no one.

Still damp from her earlier drenching outdoors, she was about to make for her room to change quickly when she saw Ladies Pendleton and Townsend approaching from the turn in the corridor.

"My dear Miss Fairchild! Have you been out in the rain?" Lady Townsend asked, her brow creased in concern.

Amelia put her hand to her bonnet and sent the ladies a rueful look. "I thought to dry my hair from the previous downpour when the sun showed its face. But I miscalculated, didn't I? Fortunately, my hair is dryer than the rest of me."

"Well, you just hurry along to your room so you'll have plenty of time to ready yourself for this evening," said Lady Townsend, adding slyly, "Aren't you the sensible one, coming straight back to the house instead of crossing the lawn to seek shelter in the rotunda which I've just seen some unwary soul do. You'd have been stuck, for I don't know how long since I do believe the rain has set in for the afternoon."

"Why, Lady Townsend, who could have been so foolish?" her friend asked, frowning out of the window. "Should you send a servant?"

"Oh, Sir Frederick perhaps wasn't so foolish after all and just wanted some privacy," said Lady Pendleton. "Half the ladies under this roof are chasing after him. The poor man can't turn around without Miss Playford asking his opinion on some inanity, or Mrs. Perry demanding admiration."

Lady Townsend looked a little startled before she said in a rush, "At least you, my dear Miss Fairchild, are someone with whom he can enjoy an intelligent conversation and whom he doesn't wish to run away from. Yes, that was in fact, the gist of his conversation with me only this morning."

"But he did also admire Mrs. Perry for her wit, so don't allow Miss Fairchild false hopes," Lady Pendleton cut in as she took her friend's arm and began to steer her away.

"I do think you should wear your blue gown, Miss Fairchild," said Lady Townsend over her shoulder, her voice cracking with concern. "Sir Frederick did mention how fine you looked in blue."

Her final words were lost as they rounded the corner, and Amelia felt herself rooted to the spot.

Sir Frederick was in the rotunda seeking respite from his female admirers, one of whom was Amelia?

No, that wasn't the tenor of their relationship and Amelia had no time to worry about niceties like whether it would be too forward to go on search of him.

Not when there was such a matter of urgency she needed to discuss with him.

Making sure that her hostess and Lady Townsend were far away, and that there was no one else to observe her, Amelia tied the ribbons of her bonnet, turned back the way she had come, and prepared to brave the rain once more.

The rain was still falling steadily as Amelia approached the rotunda. Its elegant columns looked almost sinister in the stormy light. Of course, she was here only because of Mr. Greene's letter.

It had nothing to do with the thought of Sir Frederick alone with Mrs. Perry in the rotunda's intimate inner chamber.

She was so caught up in her thoughts that she nearly collided with Sir Frederick himself as she entered.

"Miss Fairchild!" He steadied her with gentle hands. "What brings you out in such weather?"

"I…" The words stuck in her throat as she realized how close they were standing. "That is, Henry just showed me something—a letter—" Thunder crashed directly overhead, making her jump.

"Come inside before you're soaked through." He guided her into the inner room, his hand warm at the small of her back. "Though I confess, I'm glad of the interruption. I came early specifically to head off Mrs. Perry's advances."

"Oh?" Amelia tried to sound disinterested as she watched him close the heavy door against the storm. "I wouldn't wish to interrupt any… private meetings."

His laugh was unexpected. "The only private meeting I wish for is this one." He turned to face her, his eyes intense in the dim light. "Now, what's this about a letter? I thought we'd had enough excitement after this morning's visit to the church."

But before Amelia could respond, a gust of wind rattled the rotunda's windows, making the candle flames dance wildly in their sconces. The storm-darkened room felt suddenly intimate, almost too intimate, as Sir Frederick moved closer.

"Before you tell me anything, there's something I need to say." His voice was low, urgent. "I've been ruminating while waiting out the storm. I think it's fair to say that while you and I deal well together, you nevertheless keep me at a distance. And I know why. You alluded to it this morning, and you made clear that your Thomas was quick to attribute to me certain injustices. Others, I accept. You think me a libertine, Miss Fairchild, and perhaps once I was. But that affair with Lady Eldredge—it wasn't what you imagine."

Amelia's heart beat faster. "I don't need explanations—"

"But you do." His hand found hers in the dim light. "I was young, newly returned from war with wounds both visible and hidden. She offered comfort when I most needed it, though I discovered too late it was false comfort."

"I didn't follow every detail of the scandal…" Amelia looked away, glancing up when he laughed softly.

"Only some of them?" he asked. "You see, I had admired you greatly when we first met at the Bath Assembly Ball. I did not know you already had an admirer in Thomas Blackheath—"

"Nothing had been formalized," Amelia said. "I knew him only a little. And then we were introduced, and we spoke on so many shared matters of interest. I was greatly looking forward to seeing you at the Assembly Rooms but you weren't there—"

"I was called away." He shrugged. "On His Majesty's Business. At the time, the matter was of immense urgency. I spent a week in France, behind enemy lines, suffered an injury—" He indicated his thigh. "—and on my return, I met Lady Eldredge."

"Oh!"

Sir Frederick shook his head. "No, it's not what you think. We were introduced at Madame Belvoir's Salon and merely spoke. At the time, I couldn't wait to return to Bath to see you." He smiled. "It's the truth."

Amelia's eyes widened, and she put a hand to her lips. "When I didn't see you at the Assembly Rooms, Thomas claimed me for almost every dance, even though it wasn't respectable." She lowered her eyes. "He laughed as he recounted that he'd overheard you telling Lord Spade that while you'd enjoyed Miss Fairchild's company—as he phrased it—you'd never settle down with a bluestocking. That you were in the market for vivacious blondes who were up for a bit of fun rather than risking a potentially dangerous liaison with someone who intended anything more serious?"

Sir Frederick put both hands on her shoulders and his face closer to hers. "He said that?" he asked softly.

Amelia nodded.

"Then he lied."

Amelia swallowed, waiting for him to break the silence. But it seemed he was too caught up in his own thoughts, so she prompted, "And Lady Eldredge?"

Returning his attention to her, Sir Frederick's smile was rueful. "I rebounded into her arms after I found you so distant when I did finally return to the Assembly Rooms. By this stage, Thomas Blackheath had well and truly sunk his hooks into you, and before a few days were past, the pair of you were engaged." He shrugged. "I buried my disappointment and accepted I'd never see you again, while also deciding that, as my reputation couldn't sink lower, and I'd lost the woman I believed I could truly love, why try to salvage it? But I'm not that man anymore." His fingers tightened on hers.

"These past days with you—seeing how you value truth and

honor above all else—it's made me want to be worthy of your good opinion."

Amelia's carefully constructed defenses began to crumble while his words chased themselves around her head.

The woman I believed I could truly love…

He loved her? Then he'd surely kiss her now.

But wait. He was speaking again, and she hadn't responded. Maybe he'd been waiting for something from her which she'd failed to deliver.

He squeezed her shoulder. "But you came here to tell me something about a letter Henry had shown you."

Caught between frustration at the way he'd closed the door on her ability to tell him what was in her heart and the urgent need to pass on her disturbing news regarding Mr. Greene, Amelia said, "Henry showed me a letter written by Mr. Greene. It was in the library beneath a pile of books and clearly he'd been disturbed while writing it to his cousin. But he claims he can prove he's Pernilla's descendant. That she didn't die but married William and lived." Tensely, she watched his face. "I was fearful that was the truth of it. That Pernilla didn't die but instead married and had children. But if that is in fact the reason Mr. Greene is here at all—because he has proof that he's descended from Pernilla, then that changes everything. Lady Pendleton, Albert, the estate…"

"The man's a bounder and on the verge of bankruptcy," Sir Frederick said grimly. "Which makes me wonder—could Greene be manufacturing this claim? A man in his desperate financial straits might grasp at any chance."

"That's what troubles me." Amelia moved closer, drawn by his warmth, his steadiness, and the fact he didn't even seem to realize his arms were about her shoulders in a gesture far more intimate than warranted under the circumstances.

Or was it?

"The marriage record we found—it proves Pernilla and William wed. But her grave…"

"Do you really think we can have it exhumed? That could only be done under Lady Pendleton's authority, and she's hardly likely to do that."

Amelia nodded. "But if Mr. Greene has other pieces of evidence, she may be forced to. Oh, Sir Frederick..." She felt herself sagging under the weight of her distress. "Mr. Greene is the most unworthy of claimants. And to see the estate taken from Albert makes me want to weep."

"My dear Amelia." His free hand came up to cup her cheek. "Whatever the truth of this claim, only time and a court of law will untangle this knotty issue." He hesitated, then said, as if realizing that she was more than willing within his arms, "I want to return to what I was saying before. That my feelings for you are genuine. You've awakened something in me I thought long dead—the desire to be a better man."

The sound of her given name on his lips made her breath catch. "I...I would like to believe that," she whispered, though she didn't move away from his touch. "But I think I've underestimated you for a long time and I am ashamed. Ashamed of Thomas for speaking lies and at me for believing them so readily. But...you could have any woman you desire. Mrs. Perry—"

"Is exactly the kind of woman I once thought I wanted." His thumb traced her cheekbone. "Beautiful, vivacious, uncomplicated. But you, Amelia. You challenge me. You make me think. When we discovered Pernilla's story together—first during the treasure hunt and then afterwards when you were the one who believed there was more fact than fiction to the tale and you were determined to reveal the truth, I saw how your mind works, how deeply you care about honesty and justice."

Thunder rolled overhead, but Amelia barely heard it. "And yet I feel so conflicted about this truth. If Mr. Greene really is Pernilla's descendant, doesn't he have a right to claim his inheritance? But then I think of Albert, of all the good he could do..."

"That's precisely what I mean." Sir Frederick's voice was

husky. "Most women would simply choose the most advantageous side. But you wrestle with what's right." His other hand came up to frame her face. "Do you know how beautiful you are when you're pursuing a mystery? Your eyes spark with intelligence, your cheeks flush. Perhaps we should—"

But his suggestion was cut short by the unmistakable sound of footsteps on the rotunda's outer steps.

"Sir Frederick? Are you there?"

Mrs. Perry.

Chapter Twenty-Nine

THUNDER RUMBLED IN the distance as Amelia pressed herself against the cold stone wall, her heart hammering beneath her ribs. Through the heavy oak door, she could hear Mrs. Perry's delighted sigh echo in the rotunda's intimate chamber. The rain drummed steadily on the domed roof above, creating an oddly intimate atmosphere that only heightened Amelia's discomfort.

Sir Frederick had urged her to stay, his look intense as he'd whispered that Mrs. Perry needed to be disabused of any notions regarding his feelings.

But mortification had propelled Amelia through the hidden door behind the heavy velvet curtain beside the chaise longue, her slippers making no sound on the worn stone steps.

Now, despite her better judgment, she found herself frozen in place, the damp chill of the passage seeping through her thin muslin gown. Her curiosity—no, her need to understand— outweighed her natural inclination to flee.

But embarrassment had fueled Amelia's flight. She'd torn out of his embrace as the door had opened to admit Mrs. Perry— who'd been too forward to wait for an invitation—while Amelia had slipped out of the back entrance behind the curtain beside the chaise longue.

However, clearly her curiosity—no, nosiness—was even

greater than her embarrassment.

What did Mrs. Perry think she could claim from Sir Frederick when he claimed he'd given her no encouragement?

So, despite her best intentions, Amelia remained rooted to the spot.

Besides, she justified to herself, Sir Frederick had begged her to stay. And surely his earlier claim that he'd given the woman no encouragement ought to be tested if Amelia were to succumb to the lures he extended *her*?

"Oh, Sir Frederick, I knew you'd be here! And don't you look dashing?"

Amelia gritted her teeth to hear the plaintive delight and fawning in the other woman's tone.

How vulgar, Amelia thought, drawing her shawl more closely about her. What did she think she'd get from Sir Frederick? A marriage offer?

"Naturally, you understand I'm not interested in marriage—"

Amelia swallowed. It was, in fact, Mrs. Perry who said these words. And it wasn't a simple statement for Amelia to digest. What did a once-married woman want from a man like Sir Frederick if it wasn't a marriage offer? Did she want kisses and compliments like Sir Frederick had been in the process of delivering?

Or was there something more?

"My dear, perhaps this isn't the best place for us to discuss—"

"Oh, Sir Frederick, I'm not here to discuss!" Mrs. Perry delivered a throaty laugh. "You know exactly what I'm here for. It's what you and I both want."

"A scandal? I think not."

Amelia heard a surprised pause. "There'll be no scandal as long as we're both discreet. I cannot marry for another three years according to the terms of my late husband's will, so you know that I shan't hold you to a breach of promise. No, Sir Frederick, I'm merely here to follow up on what we started before."

Started before? Amelia didn't like the sound of that. She drew herself up indignantly, waiting for Sir Frederick to refute anything implied by the widow.

And was gratified when he said, "I'm truly sorry, Catherine, but I cannot."

A short pause truncated proceedings before Mrs. Perry's surprised, almost indignant, "You cannot? What do you mean, you cannot? You surely have not offered for that silly little Miss Playford? And even if you had, you'd have even more reason to want to enjoy the heady delights I'm offering. A silly little miss like that knows nothing about pleasuring a man of your discerning needs."

"Not Miss Playford." He paused. Maybe he was looking into her eyes to make her attend to him. Amelia hoped so. "It's Miss Fairchild who holds my heart."

"Miss Fairchild!"

The scorn in Mrs. Perry's tinkling laugh brought the blood to the surface of Amelia's skin. She felt herself burning with shame. What did Mrs. Perry feel for Amelia that caused such excoriation in her tone?

"Well, certainly if you're after moral-improving homilies, then Miss Fairchild is the young lady for you. Is that how you want to end your days? Dying of boredom?"

Amelia put her hand to her mouth to stifle her gasp. If Sir Frederick didn't defend her, she'd burst through that door.

But of course she wouldn't.

And of course Sir Frederick did.

He cleared his throat. "Catherine. There is no need for you to take this personally. Besides, Miss Fairchild is not in the habit of offering moral-improving homilies. Her conversation is delightful and entertaining—"

"Do spare me!" Mrs. Perry interrupted. "She's a shrinking violet. A frightened virgin. She knows nothing of what's needed to please a man like you."

The rustle of silk suggested movement within, followed by

what sounded like a struggle. Amelia's fingers clenched in the folds of her shawl as she pictured the scene. The widow's voice had taken on a desperate edge that made Amelia's cheeks flame with secondhand embarrassment.

Amelia was still trying to make sense of Mrs. Perry's words as she heard a muffled noise. As if Sir Frederick were trying to restrain the woman. What was Mrs. Perry doing?

"Please, Catherine—This is not what I intended. It's not the reason I am here to meet you. Put on your pelisse—"

"I'm beautiful! Touch my breasts and tell me I'm beautiful." Her voice sounded ragged. "Would your Miss Fairchild offer you this? And with no strings attached. I don't think so. She'll lie on her back and stare at the ceiling, thinking of England while you try to have your pleasure. But how can a man enjoy pleasure from a woman who believes sex is purely for making babies, and who squeaks and holds her breath rather than responding and touching you as a man like you would—"

"Enough, Catherine! Put on your cloak. I had no idea you came here with nothing underneath. Your slander has only determined me more that following my heart means dealing honorably with Miss Fairchild. You know nothing about her and how she—"

"How she would respond to you and your overtures? Nor do you but you're willing to take a chance that she's not the frigid virgin I believe she is? You're willing to be saddled with a wife for the rest of your life without knowing—"

"Enough, Catherine!"

Shivering with emotion, Amelia heard the exchange from within the room. She should go. Perhaps Mrs. Perry did speak the truth. What truth? She was referring to matters that no unmarried young woman could know about.

Certainly, Amelia had felt stirrings when she'd been kissed by Thomas. She'd felt far more stirrings when she'd been kissed by Sir Frederick, but how could she find the language to explain how her body tingled and tendrils of desire curled through her loins?

But this was a whole other unknown world about which Mrs. Perry spoke.

And was Amelia really up to satisfying a man like Sir Frederick when she had no idea what a husband truly needed?

Wanted.

Amelia pressed her burning cheeks against the cool stone wall, her mind reeling. The storm outside matched the tumult in her thoughts. Mrs. Perry's words had opened a door to knowledge Amelia wasn't sure she was ready to face. Yet something deeper than curiosity stirred within her. A need to understand this aspect of marriage that no one had ever dared discuss with her.

The sound of Mrs. Perry's angry departure echoed through the rotunda, followed by silence broken only by the steady drumming of rain. Amelia's fingers traced the rough stone of the wall as she wrestled with her decision. Should she leave now, retreat to the safety of her room and the familiar world of books and propriety? Or should she step through that door and demand answers to questions she barely knew how to frame?

Her hand trembled as it found the doorknob.

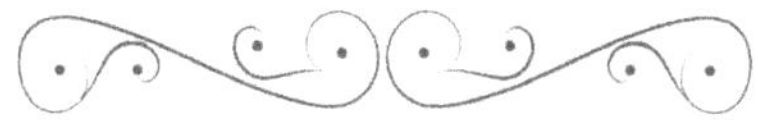

Chapter Thirty

AMELIA STEPPED BACK into the rotunda's inner chamber, her heart thundering against her ribs. Sir Frederick stood by the window, his broad shoulders tense, one hand braced against the rain-streaked glass. He turned at her entrance, relief flooding his features.

"I wasn't sure you'd come back," he said softly.

"I wasn't sure I would either." Amelia clasped her hands together to stop their trembling. "I heard things I should never have heard. And I have so many… questions."

He straightened, wariness replacing relief. "Amelia—"

"No, please hear me out." She took a steadying breath, forcing herself to maintain eye contact despite the heat suffusing her cheeks. "Mrs. Perry spoke of things about which I am admittedly ignorant." She hesitated, biting her lip before she went on softly. "Do I really hold your heart?"

He nodded, and she felt her heart hitch and a strange roiling in the pit of her stomach, the like of which she'd never felt before.

"And you, Miss Fairchild? Could I truly hope that you hold me in at least a little higher esteem than you have hitherto led me to believe?"

Amelia felt her whole body relax as she smiled. Slowly, she nodded.

"And this game we've been playing?" he asked. "Where one minute you laugh at my witticisms and happily kiss me, but the next, you disdain me? These are all symptoms of a disordered heart which needs only me to reassure you that—surprisingly, Miss Fairchild—I can't seem to get thoughts of you out of my mind?"

Amelia felt herself sag even more within his embrace.

But Mrs. Perry's words resonated.

"I couldn't help but overhear," she confessed. "And some of what I heard I found confusing." She hesitated. "If you truly harbor feelings for me, as you claimed earlier, do I not deserve to understand what... what would be expected? As Mrs. Perry said?"

Sir Frederick ran a hand through his hair, clearly uncomfortable. "This is hardly a suitable conversation."

"When would it be suitable? After I disappointed you with my... inadequacies?" The words tumbled out before she could stop them. "Wasn't that the word the widow used?"

His expression softened as he crossed to her, taking her cold hands in his warm ones. "My dear girl, nothing about you could disappoint me."

"Mrs. Perry seemed quite certain otherwise." Amelia tried to withdraw her hands, but he held firm. "She said I would lie there thinking of England while you—"

"Catherine Perry," he interrupted with surprising vehemence, "speaks from a place of wounded pride and excessive worldliness. The intimacies between husband and wife are meant to be discovered together, with tenderness and patience."

"But how am I to know if I'm even capable of... of responding as I should?" The question emerged barely above a whisper, and it shocked her, for the implications were enormous. She'd all but insinuated that this was the prelude to a marriage offer, yet he'd made no such undertaking.

Perhaps her foolish innocence had mistaken the matter altogether and he'd soon be crowing over his success at his latest dalliance.

Sir Frederick's thumb traced gentle circles on her palm, sending unexpected shivers up her arm. "Do you recall how you felt when I kissed you by the elm tree?"

The memory made her breath catch. "Yes."

"Did your body not respond of its own accord? Did you not feel something stir within you that had nothing to do with duty or obligation?"

"I…" Amelia swallowed hard, distracted by the continued motion of his thumb. "Yes, but that was just a kiss."

A smile tugged at his mouth. "Just a kiss? Shall we test that theory?"

Before she could respond, he had drawn her closer, one hand sliding to the small of her back while the other cupped her cheek. This kiss was different from their previous encounters. Slower, more deliberate. As if he were proving a point.

When he finally drew back, Amelia had to grip his lapels to stay upright.

"You see?" he murmured against her temple. "Your body knows what it wants, even if your mind hasn't caught up yet."

"But that's precisely what frightens me," she admitted. "These… feelings. They're so overwhelming. How does one maintain any sense of decorum when—" She broke off as his chest rumbled with suppressed laughter.

"My dearest love, marriage beds have no need of decorum." His expression grew serious. "But they do require trust. Do you trust me, Amelia?"

She studied his face, the warmth in his eyes, the gentle set of his mouth. "Yes," she whispered. "God help me, but I do."

"Then trust that I will guide you through each discovery with as much care as I promise to take in helping you unravel the mystery of Pernilla's fate." His fingers traced the line of her jaw. "Though I confess, watching you pursue knowledge with such determination does make it difficult to maintain my own decorum."

Amelia felt a smile tug at her lips despite her lingering uncertainty. "Are you saying my intellectual curiosity affects you physically?"

"Powerfully." He pressed a kiss to her palm. "When you bite your lip while puzzling over a clue, or when your eyes light up upon making a discovery…it's intoxicating."

"More intoxicating than Mrs. Perry's… direct approach?"

"Infinitely more." He drew her closer, his breath warm against her ear. "Seduction without wit is like… a meal without flavor."

The intimate timbre of his voice sent a shiver down her spine. "I believe," she managed, "that was a rather poetic way of saying you prefer a woman with a brain."

"I prefer you," he corrected. "With your questioning mind, your fierce determination to uncover truth, and yes, your occasionally maddening tendency to overthink everything."

"I do not overthink—" She broke off as he raised an eyebrow. "Very well, perhaps I do."

His laugh was rich and warm. "Now, shall we return to the castle before your reputation is thoroughly compromised?"

The rain had eased to a gentle patter, casting shifting patterns through the glass dome above. Amelia knew they should leave, yet she lingered, reluctant to break this fragile moment of understanding between them.

"One more question," she said, her fingers still resting against his lapel. "When you speak of trust and discovery… does that mean you aren't as experienced as your reputation suggests? Have I done you a grave injustice by believing everything the gossip sheets, and the rumor mongers, say about you?"

His hand stilled where it had been tracing patterns on her palm. "My reputation," he said carefully, "is both better and worse than reality. Yes, there have been…indiscretions. But true intimacy? The kind that comes from genuine love and trust?" He shook his head. "That I have yet to discover."

Lightning flickered in the distance, illuminating his face as he bent to kiss her once more. This time, Amelia let herself melt into the embrace, trusting both his words and the answering warmth that bloomed within her.

When they finally parted, his voice was husky. "Now we really must return to the castle."

"We must indeed, for we have a mystery to solve before we leave here."

"Ah yes, our ghostly romance." He offered his arm. "Though I must say, helping uncover Pernilla's story has led to some rather fortunate developments."

Chapter Thirty-One

"SIR FREDERICK AND Miss Fairchild look like they're smelling of April and May."

Lady Pendleton adjusted her lorgnette as she leaned forward in her chair within the cozy alcove where she and Eugenia sat.

And Eugenia couldn't help noticing there was a hint of disdain in her tone. As if she couldn't abide the notion that Eugenia might just win her wager.

So for a few seconds, Eugenia worked on her response, tempering the hurt that might have risen to the surface in earlier times. Lady Pendleton seemed to become more animated if she suspected she'd hit a nerve.

"And don't they make just the perfect couple?" Eugenia said with a smile, leaning back in satisfaction as she regarded the handsome couple on the dance floor. "See how she's smiling up at him? And look! He's laughing at some remark she's just made. Doesn't he look—" She leaned forward, frowning. For now she was not just trying to bolster her case, for what she was seeing was quite extraordinary. "Why, he looks quite smitten! Oh!" She couldn't help it, but she actually squealed. "He touched his finger to her cheek as she laughed. Very discreetly, but so intimate! Oh, Lady Pendleton, I do believe the pair are in love."

"Nonsense!" snapped Lady Pendleton, her mouth now down-turned so that she looked as if she'd just eaten a sour apple. "It could not possibly have happened in such a short time. You're imagining it!"

"Imagining what?"

As ever, Eugenia's heartbeat ratcheted up just a little more as Lord Thornton joined them, offering a sardonic smile as he glanced in the direction both ladies were looking, before taking a seat.

"My, my, Eugenia, perhaps you have more of a nose for romance than I gave you credit for." He frowned, then added, "But Sir Frederick is a renowned rake. And Miss Fairchild is clearly susceptible to flattery. She's hardly dressed to attract attention, but it appears that she likes it. Hmm."

Eugenia wasn't sure how to interpret his remark. Was this grudging acknowledgement that she might be on the path to winning their wager? Or was his added caveat really throwing cold water on any premature notions of success she might be having?

"Eugenia, my dear, won't you find Albert for me and tell him his mama wants him?" Lady Pendleton waved a languid arm in the direction of the supper table.

Eugenia blinked. Of course, she was in the habit of doing Lady Pendleton's bidding, but this evening she felt strangely obstructionist. Perhaps it was because her old friend was clearly so reluctant to accord Eugenia any credit that she might be right for once.

What did it matter to her that Sir Frederick and Miss Fairchild might make a match? She had nothing to win or lose. Did she really hate the notion of Eugenia enjoying her wish of a flight in a hot-air balloon over London with Lord Thornton? Was she really motivated more by churlishness?

"Perhaps Pendleton is nearby and can find him," Eugenia suggested with uncharacteristic obfuscation.

"Oh Pendleton!" Lady Pendleton's tone made no secret of her disdain for her husband. "He went to bed hours ago. Said he couldn't hear a word anyone said to him. He certainly never hears a word *I* say." She glanced at Thornton. "You surely are not going to give up so easily and sacrifice your Persephone to instead take Eugenia over London in a hot-air balloon, are you? I never heard such an outlandish, unladylike proposal." She slanted a glance at him over her ivory-tipped fan that first encompassed Eugenia with a moment of acid.

"Are you suggesting I'm a man who doesn't honor a wager?"

"I'm suggesting no such thing!" Lady Pendleton looked highly offended. "You are a gentleman of honor and integrity. You're not the one lacking refinement." She glanced at Eugenia before waving her hand once more, saying, "For goodness' sake, Eugenia, what's wrong with you? I asked if you would find Albert and send him to me."

Eugenia rose. What else could she do? Pushing back her shoulders to maintain as much of the dignity that her friend had been at such pains to shred, she stepped out of their cozy alcove and into the crowd.

The magnificent ballroom with its crystal chandeliers and ornate frescos was like so many others where she'd danced and flirted.

Or had she never flirted, she wondered as she thought of Lord Thornton. Had she been so shy and self-conscious that even a glance in his direction had felt like she was branding herself a harlot? Or, at least, wearing her heart on her sleeve in the shameless manner Lady Pendleton now attributed to her wager.

Lady Pendleton.

Her friend's barely veiled barbs were growing sharper each year.

As she made her way across the floor, a flash of green and a girlish giggle made her turn.

Miss Fairchild? It wasn't a sound that usually came out of that restrained miss's mouth. No, Miss Fairchild was far too self-contained for that.

Yet now, having obviously finished dancing the last dance,

she and Sir Frederick remained in close conversation, their heads bent together in a way that spoke of intimacy rather than mere flirtation. There was something pure about their growing attachment—nothing like the calculated maneuverings she so often witnessed at gatherings like this. Sir Frederick's reputation might suggest otherwise, but as Eugenia studied his expression, she was sure it wasn't just her imagination that there was something more genuine than blandly charming. Could Miss Fairchild's influence really have been responsible for channeling his natural charm into something more genuine?

Or was she being a mawkish, sentimental old woman, as Lady Pendleton would surely say.

A burst of artificial laughter drew her attention to where Mrs. Perry stood with Mr. Greene, her fan working overtime as she touched his arm with careful casualness. The widow's eyes, however, kept darting to Sir Frederick, their expression shifting between—

Eugenia tried to work it out. She wasn't of a particularly imaginative nature… No, that was not true. She was immensely imaginative, but still, was that wounded pride and calculation?

Hesitating, Eugenia took in the scene, ostensibly to locate Albert, however it wasn't Mrs. Perry's look that was of most concern, she decided as she encompassed Mr. Greene in her perusal, but rather the way Mr. Greene's gaze fixed on Caroline across the room; and as, with a smoothness that spoke of practice, he drew the young girl into their orbit.

Something about the tableau made Eugenia's skin prickle. Mrs. Perry's smile held an edge she recognized all too well—the look of a woman planning… revenge.

But of course! Mrs. Perry had sent a lure to Sir Frederick and now he was throwing it back in her face. Or rather, that's how she interpreted it, clearly.

Eugenia knew such nuances of the facial features well, and what came from the heart was not well disguised when someone had no idea they were being observed.

Having been on the receiving end of Lady Pendleton's subtle vengeance more times than she cared to count, Eugenia knew the signs.

She found Albert in the card room, his tall frame bent over a game of whist. Unlike his mother, he rose immediately upon seeing her approach, his manners as impeccable as always.

"Lady Townsend, what a pleasure. I trust you're enjoying the evening?"

"Your mother has asked for you," Eugenia said, already anticipating his response.

"Ah." He glanced at his cards, then at his companions. "Please convey my apologies to Mama, but I'm rather in the middle of something important. Lord Rutherford and I—" He shrugged, adding, "It's not important to Mama who has no interest in such matters, but I would prefer not to abandon some illuminating discussion." He lowered his voice. "She'll likely just want me to fetch her shawl or rearrange her cushions. Jenkins can see to that."

Eugenia couldn't help but smile at his understanding of his mother's ways. "Of course. I'll let her know you're occupied with estate business."

"And that's exactly what it is," said Lord Rutherford. "Improving tenant's conditions might seem like an unnecessary expenditure, but I assure you that loyalty and gratitude bring dividends. I wish more landlords understood this."

Returning to the alcove, Eugenia slowed her steps as she heard Lady Pendleton's voice, pitched low but clear.

Again, the note of dissatisfaction was nothing new and so would not have deterred Eugenia from resuming her seat. However, it was the way she heard her mention Sir Frederick and Miss Fairchild in the same sentence that made her halt before she'd rounded the swathe of curtain and made her presence known.

"Really, Thornton, it's hardly as if Sir Frederick and Miss Fairchild are two souls pre-destined for one another," Lady

Pendleton said with a sniff. "They met each other for the first time under this roof and obviously Eugenia has been doing all sorts of meddling to bring them together purely so she can win her wager." Her friend's voice became wheedling. "I know how much you covet that Persephone. It can so easily be yours. And thus without you suffering an undignified loss."

Lord Thornton cleared his throat. "I don't know, Lady Pendleton. What you're suggesting—" He broke off, glancing over his shoulder as if he was somehow aware that Eugenia was close by.

And his smile was affable and not at all cagey or resentful, as Lady Pendleton's was when Thornton said, "Welcome back into the fold, Eugenia. But I see you're missing something."

"Albert," said Lady Pendleton.

"Some refreshment was what I really meant," said Lord Thornton.

Chapter Thirty-Two

HAVING ESCAPED THE stuffiness of the drawing room, Amelia was grateful for the fresh air and solitude. Her mind was still wrestling with the implications of Mr. Greene's possible claim to the estate when voices from the rose garden caught her attention.

"But surely you can see how impossible it is?" Caroline's voice carried clearly on the autumn breeze. "Frederick would never agree."

"Your brother's approval is not required, my dear." Mr. Greene's silky tones made Amelia halt mid-step. "You're of age to make your own decisions."

Amelia eased behind a tall hedge, her heart pounding. She knew she ought not eavesdrop, but the memory of that half-written letter in the library steeled her resolve.

"I'm not quite of age," Caroline replied, a note of uncertainty creeping into her usually confident voice. "And Frederick says—"

"Frederick says, Frederick thinks, Frederick decides." Mr. Greene's voice took on an edge of frustration before smoothing out again. "My dearest, sweetest girl, don't you see? Your brother means well, but he cannot understand the depth of feeling between us. He sees only what society expects him to see—the differences in our ages, our circumstances."

"He says you're a fortune hunter." The words burst from Caroline like water from a dam.

There was a pause, during which Amelia scarcely dared breathe. Then Mr. Greene laughed, a rich, warm sound that even Amelia had to admit was appealing.

"A fortune hunter? I, who stand to inherit—" He broke off abruptly. "My dear girl, if I were after a fortune, I assure you there are easier targets than a young lady whose inheritance is years away. No, what draws me to you is something far more precious."

"What?" Caroline's voice had dropped to barely more than a whisper.

"Your spirit. Your fire. The way your eyes dance when you laugh. The way you see the world as full of possibilities rather than constraints." Each phrase was delivered with careful precision, like individual arrows finding their mark. "You remind me of someone I once knew—a young lady who also dared to follow her heart, despite what society dictated."

Amelia's fingers dug into the hedge. Was he referring to Pernilla? Did he dare use that connection to further his aims with Caroline?

"Who?" Caroline asked, clearly captivated.

"A lady who lived long ago. She too was told whom she could and couldn't love. But she had the courage to defy convention, to reach for happiness despite the odds." Mr. Greene's voice dropped lower, compelling Caroline to lean closer to hear him. "The question is, my dear, do you possess such courage?"

"I—I think so," Caroline stammered. "But surely there's no need for such dramatic measures. If we simply wait—"

"Wait?" The word cracked like a whip. "Wait while your brother arranges a more 'suitable' match? Wait while society whispers and schemes? No, my love. Sometimes one must act decisively to secure one's happiness."

Amelia shifted slightly, trying to see around the hedge without revealing herself. The scene before her made her chest tight: Caroline, looking young and vulnerable in her white muslin, while Mr. Greene towered over her, one hand resting possessively on her shoulder.

"What are you suggesting?" Caroline's voice trembled.

"Meet me tonight, after the household is asleep. At the park gates. I'll have a carriage waiting." His voice grew urgent. "We can be in Scotland before anyone realizes we're gone. Once we're married, even Frederick will have to accept it."

"Scotland?" Caroline's voice rose sharply before Mr. Greene shushed her.

"Keep your voice down, my dear. Yes, Scotland. Where we can be married without banns or licenses. Where no one can prevent us from following our hearts."

Amelia's mind raced. She had to stop this, but how? If she revealed herself now, Mr. Greene would simply find another opportunity to press his suit. If she ran to tell Sir Frederick, Caroline might feel cornered and more likely to rebel.

"I don't know…" Caroline sounded torn. "It seems so drastic."

"Love is drastic, my dear. It burns away all conventional considerations, leaving only truth behind." Mr. Greene's voice grew tender. "I know it frightens you. But think—by this time tomorrow, we could be man and wife, free to love as we choose. No more disapproving brothers, no more society's rules."

"But Freddy would be so hurt…"

"He'll forgive you once he sees how happy you are. How could he not?" Mr. Greene pressed his advantage. "The only question is whether you trust your heart enough to follow it."

Amelia had heard enough. Gathering her skirts, she stepped out from behind the hedge, deliberately crunching the gravel beneath her feet.

"Miss Caroline! What a lovely surprise. I was just looking for you—Lady Pendleton has been asking after you. Something about the musical entertainment planned for this evening?"

Caroline jumped guiltily, her cheeks flaming. Mr. Greene's expression darkened for just a moment before smoothing into its usual bland charm.

"Miss Fairchild. How…fortunate we are to encounter you." His tone suggested quite the opposite.

"Indeed." Amelia smiled pleasantly while hooking her arm through Caroline's. "Shall we return to the house? The evening air is growing quite chill."

Caroline allowed herself to be led away, though Amelia noticed how she glanced back at Mr. Greene. His face, when Amelia dared a quick look, was thunderous.

She'd prevented the immediate danger, but Amelia knew this was far from over. Mr. Greene was not a man to give up easily, especially not with so much potentially at stake. As they walked back to the house, she squeezed Caroline's arm gently.

"You know," she said carefully, "I once knew a young lady who was tempted to make a hasty decision regarding marriage. She very nearly threw away everything—her family's trust, her reputation, her future happiness—all because a gentleman convinced her that dramatic gestures were proof of love."

"What happened to her?" Caroline asked, her voice small.

"She was fortunate enough to have friends who helped her see that true love isn't proved by grand gestures or secret meetings. It's proved by patience, by respect for those who care about us, by willingness to face obstacles together openly rather than skulking about in shadows."

Caroline was quiet for several steps. Then, "Did she regret not running away?"

"No," Amelia said firmly. "Because she realized that any man who truly loved her would want to protect her reputation, not compromise it. Would want to face her family proudly, not skulk about like a thief in the night."

They had reached the house. Caroline paused at the door, her young face troubled. "Miss Fairchild?"

"Yes?"

"Thank you. For… for coming to find me."

Amelia squeezed her arm again before releasing it. "That's what friends are for, my dear. Now, shall we see what Lady Pendleton has planned for the evening's entertainment?"

As they entered the house, Amelia's mind was already racing ahead. She needed to find Sir Frederick. Between them, they would find a way to protect Caroline from Mr. Greene's machinations without pushing the headstrong girl further into his arms. It would require delicacy, tact, and above all, patience.

She only hoped Caroline was not as headstrong as she had proved in the past.

Chapter Thirty-Three

However, it was Henry she met first, coming upon him in the library. Shafts of late afternoon sunlight pierced the tall windows, catching dust motes that danced above the leather-bound volumes and casting long shadows across the Persian carpet. He rose from his chair at the desk, his look furtive and guilty before it relaxed into a smile as Amelia pressed upon him to sit.

"Well, Miss Fairchild, you are the very person I hoped to see," he said, running a hand through his already tousled ginger hair. "Have you spoken to Sir Frederick about the letter I showed you?"

"I have," Amelia said slowly, coming into the room and closing the door gently behind her. It was thick, studded oak and they'd not be overheard. The library held that peculiar hush that seemed to absorb all sound.

"And what does he say?"

Amelia cast her mind over their discussions which, while certainly concerned by the threat Mr. Greene posed, had primarily revolved around their gilded future. Her heart quickened at the memory of certain moments that had nothing to do with the current crisis.

"Miss Fairchild, are you all right?" Henry's concerned voice broke through her reverie. Amelia realized she was smiling, her thoughts far away and centered on herself. She drew herself up and adopted a more sober expression, smoothing her skirts with slightly trembling fingers.

"Sir Frederick is deeply concerned, as you would imagine. But what proof does Mr. Greene have? We know nothing of his evidence. Just that proving his claim would take time and no doubt be costly as it was dragged through the courts."

"But the marriage is recorded." Henry's fingers drummed nervously on the polished desktop.

"Perhaps…though it was on a separate sheet within the register. It was very odd. However, there is no record of any children born to Pernilla. And her crypt is concrete evidence. I doubt Lady Pendleton would either agree to have it exhumed—or could be made to do so." Amelia thought a moment, pacing before the desk. "Sir Frederick said that if her father was as wily as we're led to believe, he may well have placed the body of some other unfortunate in her grave, just so there was no evidence pointing to anything other than that his own daughter had died on the night he claimed she had."

Henry's shoulders sagged. "You're right. And that's what I am so worried about. I just think Albert is a capital fellow and I cannot bear to see him usurped by Mr. Greene."

Amelia moved to the side of the desk, her shadow falling across the scattered papers. "Of course, he has removed his letter, has he not?"

"Of course," said Henry. "He knows how to cover his tracks."

"He may not have been so clever at that this afternoon," said Amelia, before recounting what she had overheard. The memory of Mr. Greene's silky persuasion made her shiver. "I was hoping to find Sir Frederick here to tell him."

She noticed Henry had gone rather green, his freckles standing out starkly against his pallor. "Do you really suppose he might go through with an elopement, even after he suspects you may have overheard?"

"I think the man is desperate enough for anything. Colonel Blackwood says the creditors are baying at his heels. And even if he is the rightful heir to the Pendleton estate, he's not going to have that proved in time for a financial bailout."

"Bailout!" Henry sneered. "He'll suck every penny from this place and see Albert and his mother and father destitute. A good thing his sister married well," he added.

"You are a kind man," said Amelia. "You always think of others. Caroline would do well to find a man of your caliber. But she's young and too susceptible to compliments."

She was struck suddenly by how easily her youthful self had been swayed by her own Thomas's words. He'd been cunning the way he'd made her his by speaking ill of Sir Frederick and somehow turning Sir Frederick's easy charm into something to be denigrated.

Yes, young girls were far too easily swayed by the honeyed— or barbed—words of men whose intentions were to use them, and their susceptibility, for their own ends.

How much wiser Amelia had grown in the past few years.

"Oh, goodness, I'm too young to be looking for a wife," Henry mumbled. "And Caro's more like a sister."

Still, the way his face flamed and he couldn't meet Amelia's eye told its own story.

"But I can't let Greene ruin her life if you think she really could be swayed." He hesitated, his young face creased with concern. "Caro's more sensible than that, surely?"

Amelia bit her lip. "Sometimes a sensible young lady can be led astray through no fault of her own." Thinking, she tapped her fingers on the edge of the table. "To be honest, I think we should be on our guard. I don't think we should let Caroline out of our sights, for I truly suspect that Mr. Greene might be emboldened to take even the gravest risks to make her his wife. He needs leverage over Sir Frederick and if he succeeds in spiriting Caroline away, it might be too late to wind back the damage done…if you know what I mean." Amelia cleared her throat and Henry's face flamed anew.

"By God, I won't let that happen!" he said, slamming his fist upon the table and rising. "In fact, it wouldn't be too bad a thing if Greene does go ahead and do his worst!" He stopped suddenly, his embarrassment growing, as he amended, "I don't mean 'do his worst' but rather if he goes ahead with hiring a chaise and four to take Caroline to the border."

"I see you know how it all works, then, Henry. That's good," Amelia said with a smile. "I've read enough romance novels—and there are incidents aplenty in the news sheets. It's not such a rare thing as we might suppose. And it so often is not the lady's fault."

"I know what exactly to do." Henry took a few steps towards the door, then turned. "I shall take a trip into the village now and visit all the coaching inns and posting houses to put out the alert. And I shall go farther afield in case Greene has been more cunning than to make his request local."

"Which he probably has." Amelia sighed. "What I worry about, though, is that there's nothing like thwarted love to make a young girl more inclined to follow what she thinks is following her heart when she's really just incensed that her brother or friend, in this case, has decided what is best for her."

Henry nodded slowly. "You're right, of course. That is so very like Caro. The moment you tell her she can't do something is the very moment she decides that is the thing she wants most in the world to do."

"If that is her nature, then this will be a particularly delicate operation."

Henry nodded. "It will, and so I have just come upon a plan."

"You have?"

A sly grin spread over his face. "Yes," he said with a short laugh. "If Greene does go ahead and order a postchaise and four, and if Caro is foolish enough to be persuaded, well, then let him spirit her away."

Amelia frowned. "I'm afraid I don't quite understand how that can be of any help, Henry," she said.

Henry chuckled, his face transformed by a boyish enthusiasm that reminded Amelia how young he really was.

"It will if one of the postilions is actually me dressed up in livery and sitting on the back, where she won't see me until they've arrived at the first inn along the way. If I know Caro like I think I do, she'll have arrived at the conclusion that her hotheadedness has once again plunged her into hot water. And she'll be fearful and full of remorse and despair, thinking that for once, I'm not there to rescue her. Again."

His grin grew broader and, making a fist, he beat his chest three times as he drew himself up to his full height before gripping the doorknob to let himself out into the passage. The late afternoon light caught his profile, and for a moment Amelia saw not the boy who'd grown up following Caroline about like a loyal puppy, but a young man capable of protecting what he held dear.

Turning, he said over his shoulder, his voice full of quiet determination that spoke more of love than he perhaps realized, "But I will!"

Chapter Thirty-Four

TONIGHT WAS A night for pearls. Amelia didn't possess pearls, but she had a velvet ribbon to weave through her dark hair, and an evening such as she anticipated most definitely warranted the extra care and attention on her appearance.

A knock on her bedchamber door and the appearance of her brother made it clear that her efforts were not in vain.

"Why, Amelia, don't you look quite up to the mark!" he declared, hooking his thumbs into his waistcoat and slowly pacing around her like an art critic at an exhibition. "One would almost imagine you were about to be let loose husband-hunting." He cleared his throat. "It's on that point that I'm here. Yes, my dear, I have come to reassure you that although this be the final night, I am quite assured of success in ensuring that your future rusticating away alone in a quaint and cozy cottage is assured."

Amelia was so startled she dropped the pearl drop earring she'd been in the process of hooking through her earlobe. It bounced once on the Turkish carpet before rolling under the dresser.

"But Edward—"

"No buts about it," he said, grinning, as he headed back towards the door, closing it behind him despite her calls to bring him back.

Amelia sighed. She should have gone after him, but for once, she wanted to spend more time in front of the mirror. The blue silk of her gown—her finest—caught the light as she turned, showing hints of silver thread in its weave.

This evening she would dance again with Sir Frederick. It was a balmy evening, and the moon was full, so she also had every expectation that he would lead her out into the garden.

And he would kiss her.

Her heart sang at the thought, a warm glow suffusing her chest that had nothing to do with the temperature of the room.

Marriage was where they were headed, though he'd not yet spoken in such overt terms. She was sure that her responses to him were sufficiently encouraging that it would be a natural conversation they would have before they left Pendleton Castle.

And what joy the future did hold.

Yes, she should have acquainted Edward with the fact that his wager was now null and void. Sir Frederick would not be hustling any vivacious blonde to the altar because…

He'd be marrying Amelia. And she couldn't be more joyful about it.

Another knock at the door interrupted her happy reverie. "Come in," she called, expecting Edward's return.

Instead, Jenny the maid bobbed a curtsy. "Begging your pardon, miss, but this just came for you. The messenger said it was most urgent."

Amelia took the folded paper, noting the fine quality and the familiar seal. Her heart quickened—a note from Sir Frederick? But as she broke the seal and unfolded the paper, her smile faded.

My dear Miss Fairchild,

I find myself compelled to write what I fear may cause you pain, but honesty demands no less. While I have enjoyed our intellectual diversions these past days, I find myself increasingly aware of the unsuitability of any deeper attachment between us.

Your serious nature and scholarly pursuits, while admira-

ble in their way, would prove stifling to a man of my temperament. Indeed, I fear your outdated modes of dress and somewhat provincial manners would make you an object of ridicule in the circles I frequent.

Moreover, a lady of your years requires a more staid companion, one who would better appreciate your improving conversation and moral rectitude. I myself require someone more… accomplished in the ways of society.

I trust you will understand this gentle correction of any misconceptions you may have formed.

Yours sincerely, Frederick

The paper trembled in Amelia's hands. Each word seemed to strike like a physical blow, targeting every insecurity she'd tried so hard to overcome. Her knees weakened, and she sank onto the edge of her bed.

Could this truly be from Sir Frederick? The hand resembled his, yet…She read it again, tears blurring her vision.

Of course it was not!

But even if this letter was not genuine, did it not speak the truth? Was she not indeed serious, scholarly, unfashionable? Did she not lack the vivacity and sophistication that a man like Sir Frederick deserved?

The moon had risen fully now, casting long shadows across her chamber floor. Somewhere in the house, a clock chimed the quarter hour. The ball would be beginning soon.

Rising on unsteady feet, she crossed to her dressing table and stared at her reflection. The velvet ribbon suddenly seemed a poor substitute for pearls, her careful coiffure provincial rather than elegant. Everything Mrs. Perry had ever implied with her cutting glances now seemed confirmed in black and white.

Turning abruptly, Amelia snatched her shawl from its hook on the back of the door, changed her slippers for her sturdiest—the ones ruined the night of the treasure hunt—and made for the outdoors.

At times of great emotional distress, she could not be confined within the four walls of what always felt like a prison. Nature and fresh air calmed her.

And right now, she needed to be calmed.

She wanted to breathe in the fresh late afternoon air, and gaze at the cloud-filled sky…

And be alone.

Because she'd never felt more alone.

How much more painful it was to have the world turn dark when so recently she'd thought joy and mutual regard were her future.

"Miss Fairchild!"

Oh, she did not want to have to make polite conversation with Lady Townsend right now.

Steeling herself, she turned, forcing her trembling mouth into submission while she crumpled the paper in her fist.

"Miss Fairchild… is everything all right?"

Lady Townsend was not yet in her evening wear as Amelia was. And, glancing down at her blue silk gown, which was obviously what she'd be wearing to the ball, she realized she'd be a curiosity. Not that she'd given that much thought as she'd rushed out of the castle.

Amelia opened her mouth to respond, then, realizing she couldn't trust her voice, she just nodded.

"Very good. It's a lovely evening for a walk, isn't it?" the older lady remarked. "Do you mind if I accompany you? Just a short turn about the rose bushes and then I must get ready for this evening. I see the great outdoors beckoned while you were part way through dressing. That's a very lovely gown. The shade of blue reflects your eyes. I saw Sir Frederick appeared very taken with it when you wore it last."

"I've worn it three times. He must wonder if I possess anything else in my wardrobe," Amelia said, knowing she must sound as forlorn as she felt but unable to think of anything else to say.

"Oh, I don't think Sir Frederick worries about such matters. He's a man who admires a lady's intellect more than her dress."

"I hope he does."

A surprised pause greeted this pronouncement before Lady Townsend took Amelia's arm as she steered her around an elm tree and headed towards the lake. "Now, why should you question that? I've been quite struck by how interested that gentleman appears in everything you say. Why, these past two days, he hangs on your every word, Miss Fairchild." She cleared her throat. "If I may be allowed to speak my mind from an observer's point of view, I would say that you are the lady he prefers above all others here. And there are some charming young ladies—and not so young—who clearly favor the gentleman."

"You mean, like Mrs. Perry?"

"Exactly! But while he joins in the kind of mindless banter she clearly enjoys, it's you in whom he's interested."

Amelia shook her head. "I am convenient. And here only until tomorrow." Despite herself, Amelia unfisted her right hand and proffered the letter she'd recently received.

Lady Townsend frowned. "What is this?"

"I received it a few minutes ago. While I was preparing for this evening, in fact. It's the reason I couldn't continue in front of the looking glass." She closed her eyes briefly, the pain washing over her again while Lady Townsend quickly scanned the missive.

"You know he didn't write this, don't you?"

Amelia raised her head to look at the older woman, then shrugged. "Even if it's not what he thinks, it's what a great many other people do."

"But you surely don't think Sir Frederick actually penned that letter."

Amelia sighed, bit her lip, then looked at the ground. "To be perfectly honest, I think Mrs. Perry wrote that letter. Sir Frederick would never be so cruel. Not after everything he's said."

"Then why are you so downcast?"

"Because this letter reveals the truth of what I am. I'm past my first flush of youth, I'm dowdy, I'm too interested in book learning."

"It's your mind that must first excite a man. Why, that is the very first consideration, Miss Fairchild. A pretty face is almost as essential, and indeed, you have that. So, you have both. All this letter suggests is that you have a deficiency in modish attire. And how easily that can be rectified. My dear, I think it is nonsense that you're taking to heart a missive forged by a rival. Why, this is exactly what Mrs. Perry is hoping for: that you will meekly concede defeat so she can launch herself into the playing field. Or, whoever did write that letter—if it *wasn't* Mrs. Perry—knows that you are a young lady of character and discernment, but perhaps a little less robust in personal confidence. Please, Miss Fairchild, do not allow the evil perpetrator of this poisonous missive to win the day."

"I know I should not." Amelia exhaled in frustration. "But now that I know the true caliber of a man I once considered a libertine, I wonder if it won't be long before he realizes that the supposedly learned woman he admired falls far short of his expectations."

Chapter Thirty-Five

EUGENIA MARCHED THROUGH the corridors of Pendleton Castle. Portraits of stern-faced Pendleton ancestors seemed to watch her progress with disapproving eyes.

It was rare that she marched anywhere.

In fact, her usual mode of travel was languid and ladylike, but it was rare that she was fueled by such indignation.

No, rage. That would be a better word for it. The emotion burned in her chest, heating her cheeks and making her normally steady hands tremble.

She found Lord Thornton reading a news sheet in the depths of a leather wing chair in one of the two drawing rooms. The familiar scent of beeswax polish and leather bindings filled the air, and a fire crackled softly in the marble fireplace despite the mild weather. A couple of guests were chatting a little distance away near the pianoforte, their tone convivial, their words mercifully muffled by the thick Turkish carpet.

Glancing about her to ensure that they were sufficiently private and distant not to be overheard, Eugenia sank down onto a straight-backed chair opposite and huffed out a breath. The chair's rigid posture matched her own.

Slowly dropping the news sheet, Lord Thornton raised his head and sent her an enquiring smile. The afternoon light caught the silver at his temples, reminding her painfully of all the years they'd known each other.

"Eugenia, my dear… Shouldn't you be getting ready for the ball? Instead, you look strangely ready to do battle. Why, I have never seen you in such high dudgeon since that morning at Almack's when young Lord Rutherford spilled punch on your new silk gown."

The reference to their shared past only fueled her anger. Eugenia clasped her hands in her lap to stop them trembling and said with a low hiss, "I have always considered you an honorable man, Lord Thornton. Indeed, I have always admired you highly. I've wished for *your* high esteem and that is the reason I proposed the wager." Each word felt like it was being torn from her throat.

Pursing his lips, he studied her with interest, his keen eyes missing nothing of her distress. The newspaper crinkled as he set it aside. "I almost think I'm about to hear that you believe me guilty of committing some egregious crime that has caused me to fall from this lofty pedestal upon which you once placed me."

"To so cruelly play with the hearts of decent, honorable young people purely so you can claim my Persephone is beneath you, Lord Thornton. That is what I wished to say." She rose, lancing him with a final look of disgust as she prepared to depart, her skirts rustling with the force of her movement.

"I really have no idea what you are talking about, Eugenia," he protested, and despite herself, she halted as she was about to walk away. The genuine bewilderment in his tone gave her pause, but she could not let him have the last word.

"You know very well, for if you did not write that note to Miss Fairchild, then you set someone up to do the job. Mrs. Perry, perhaps?" She heard the sarcasm that dripped from her tone and didn't care that the couple at the far end of the room had ceased their conversation to look at her, their teacups frozen halfway to their lips.

"I know nothing about any letter," said Lord Thornton carefully. His usual easy manner had vanished, replaced by a gravity that might have given her pause had she not been so caught up in her own righteous anger.

Eugenia tried to control her breathing, conscious of the tight band of emotion constricting her chest.

"I do believe I am owed an explanation, Eugenia," he said, mildly. "What is this letter of which you speak?"

"Miss Fairchild received a letter purportedly from Sir Frederick that cut her to the quick. She showed it to me in the gardens just a few minutes ago. He derides her outmoded clothes, denigrates her mind, and makes it clear that he has no wish to be associated with her. Do you think this is the kind of letter she was expecting after we'd observed the closeness of the pair of them these past couple of nights?"

"No, but love does not spring up overnight. He may well have decided the kindest course was to ensure she was disabused of any expectations." A muscle twitched in his jaw as he spoke.

"Sir Frederick would not have couched such a let down in such cruel terms." The certainty in her voice surprised even her.

"Then surely Miss Fairchild knew it was not from him." Lord Thornton drew himself up, his shoulders squaring beneath his perfectly tailored coat as he added, clearly offended, "And it certainly was not from me."

Eugenia wrinkled her brow, studying the face she'd known for so many years. He did seem to be sincere. But of course he would be embarrassed.

"Lady Pendleton set you up to it, did she not? For some reason, she does not wish me to win my wager. I think she would go to any lengths to stop it, from what I know of my old friend."

"Then take your accusations to her, not me, Eugenia." Lord Thornton picked up the news sheet he had set down and looked at her over the top of it. The paper trembled slightly in his usually steady hands. "Frankly, I am offended. I thought you knew me better than you obviously do. I thought you knew that I would never resort to such underhand dealings. Of course I want to win your Persephone, but I am not a cheat. And what you have called me by your insinuations is tantamount to being a cheat."

The hurt in his voice struck deeper than anger would have done. For the first time since entering the room, Eugenia felt the first stirrings of doubt.

"IF YOU COULD raise your arms a little higher so I might put on your shirt—" Sir Frederick's valet began before halting in embarrassment, his eyes fixed on the lattice of scars visible in the mirror's reflection. After a moment, he added, "I beg your pardon, sir. Your injury—"

"Why, I had quite forgotten my injury, Dombey." Sir Frederick smiled, remembering the gentle concern in Amelia's eyes when she'd noticed his discomfort. "Miss Fairchild suggested a salve made by one of the servants here—your sister, perhaps? It has been quite helpful."

Indeed, the scars on his back had almost been forgotten when prior, they had pained him each time he stretched.

As for his leg, the pain came and went, but he looked forward to many pleasant evenings when Miss Fairchild—Amelia—would perhaps use her hands to massage the pain away. The thought brought warmth to his chest that had nothing to do with his injuries.

When she was his wife, that was.

"I'm very glad to hear it, sir. Miss Fairchild is a very amenable young lady," said Dombey, carefully adjusting the fall of the shirt. "Why, it turns out we even share a birthday. She said she'd remember me when the 21st came around in three weeks' time."

"Indeed?" Sir Frederick turned so quickly Dombey nearly dropped the brush he'd been about to use on his master's coat.

Dombey looked embarrassed, his face reddening as he busied himself with brushing invisible specks from the coat's shoulder. When he didn't respond, Sir Frederick pressed him. "And how did this joyful exchange come to pass? When did the pair of you discuss birthdays?"

"My sister, Jenny, is lady's maid to Miss Fairchild while the visitors are here, and I had to speak a word to her just outside the door when Miss Fairchild was having her hair brushed." Dombey's accent grew broader with his nervousness. "She must'a overheard Jenny saying that our ma 'oped we'd both have an afternoon off to eat a cake for coming into my majority—as you gentry call it—and I heard her tellin' me Jenny that she came into her majority the same day."

"Oh. September 21, did you say?" Sir Frederick was glad he'd gleaned the date from what sounded like an innocent exchange. Three weeks' time. He felt something expand in his chest. Enough time to plan a wedding. It would be a fitting date for a double celebration.

"Yes, sir." Dombey hesitated, then added in a lower voice, "Me sister told me later that when I'd gone, Miss Fairchild put her head in her hands and looked like she were cryin' and when Jenny asked what were wrong, she said she were set to lose everythin' on September 21."

"Good lord, she said that?" Sir Frederick's reflection showed his shock.

Dombey nodded, clearly wishing he hadn't spoken.

With his coat smoothed nicely and his cravat tied to perfection, Sir Frederick was about to head into the reception rooms in the hopes of seeking out Miss Fairchild when there was a short rap upon the door. A few seconds later Dombey returned bearing a note addressed to him on a silver salver.

The paper was expensive, scented with lavender, and sealed with an ornate 'P'. Breaking the seal, Sir Frederick unfolded the missive:

My dearest Sir Frederick,

I write in haste, my heart heavy with concern for your future happiness. While I have held my tongue these past days, I can no longer stand silent while watching you be ensnared by one who is so clearly unsuited to a man of your vitality and charm.

Miss Fairchild may present herself as a paragon of virtue and intelligence, but I have it on good authority that her "scholarly pursuits" mask a calculating nature. Even now she plots to secure you before her fast-approaching majority, when (as I have learned) she stands to lose what little independence she possesses.

Would you truly wish to shackle yourself to such dreary respectability? To spend your evenings listening to improving lectures while society laughs behind their fans at your dowdy bluestocking wife?

If you would know more, meet me in the library at midnight. I have evidence that will open your eyes to certain truths about your "proper" Miss Fairchild.

Your sincere friend, Catherine Perry

P.S. I have procured that volume of Byron you expressed interest in. The one containing certain... passionate verses. Perhaps we might read them together?

Sir Frederick's lip curled as he crumpled the note in his fist. The paper's cloying scent suddenly seemed sickly sweet, like decay masked by perfume. But the timing of this letter, combined with Dombey's revelation about Amelia's September deadline, made him pause.

What skullduggery was Catherine Perry planning?

HE FOUND MISS Fairchild speaking with her brother, Edward, in one of the large reception rooms. Sir Frederick had had few exchanges with the young man who was of a very different mold from his sister.

His nervous energy was palpable, and he had a mischievous smile that made him appear younger than the twenty-one years

Frederick had learned was his age.

For a moment, Sir Frederick watched the pair of them before advancing.

"I tell you, sis, all is not lost," the young man was saying. "Time is not quite on our side, but my motto is to never give up. If this plan doesn't work—"

He broke off when he glanced up to see Sir Frederick standing by, mumbled something in embarrassment, and hurried off.

Feeling increasingly disconcerted, especially by the deep flush that rose to Miss Fairchild's cheeks, Sir Frederick closed the distance to stand by her side.

"You look very lovely this evening," he complimented her. And she really did. The deep blue of her gown matched her eyes, which had never looked so intense. In fact, there was an intensity to her whole manner that was as palpable as her brother's embarrassment had been earlier.

"You're very kind, Sir Frederick," she responded, but he noticed that the easy manner she'd adopted towards him the past few days was absent. Her brow was furrowed, and she couldn't look him in the eyes as she added, "Lady Pendleton very kindly lent me something of her daughter's. She said we were of similar build and that she couldn't bear to see me appear so outmodish."

There was a twist to her lips as she finished, this time slanting a look at him. "Unfortunately, that is what I am. Outmodish, bookish..." She shrugged. "Most gentlemen like a woman who has...more style than I do."

Sir Frederick's first instinct was to put his hand on her shoulder and say something bolstering. But there was something pricklish about her today. And her brother's parting words returned to trouble him.

Mrs. Perry's letter was malicious, but had she really discovered something that Sir Frederick didn't know?

Carefully, he said, "But you're beautiful. And you can dress as fashionably as you choose, surely, when you come into your inheritance?"

His words seemed to startle her, for she jerked her head back up to look at him, before a sad smile settled upon her lips. "I have no inheritance to look forward to, Sir Frederick," she said. "I've battled with myself the past few days as to how truthful I should be with you." With a sigh, she went on, "But that is how it is, and it's better you should know now."

For a moment, Sir Frederick wasn't sure how to respond. While the size of her inheritance was immaterial when it came to spending the rest of his life with a woman he thought would entertain and amuse him with her wit and her mind, he was certain she was putting a different slant on matters than when they'd first become acquainted.

"I hope you are not recalling an earlier conversation during which the size of a lady's dowry was discussed, Miss Fairchild," he said. "You do know that I consider a lady's mind more important. The amount to which one is provisioned is nothing to be embarrassed about." He frowned, trying to broach the matter delicately. "I recall you did mention that you looked forward to retiring quietly to the country when you came into your inheritance in a few weeks."

What *did* she really want? What did he really want? And why was he suddenly so concerned as to her answer?

"I no longer have an inheritance to look forward to," she said, squaring her shoulders and looking suddenly defiant while he tried to hide his shock.

Turning on her heel, she added over her shoulder, "I gambled it all away."

EDWARD HAD NEVER felt so troubled.

Being troubled was not a state of mind that generally afflicted him. Every problem could be easily solved, he had always thought, studying the patterns made by the setting sun on the polished parquet floor. And that had been the case every time.

Until now.

Leaving his sister's side as he caught a glimpse of Sir Frederick, he was deeply conflicted. The buzz of conversation and tinkling of glasses from nearby guests only heightened his sense of unease.

No, not conflicted. There was nothing to be conflicted about because the matter required a simple outcome.

The trouble was that the outcome he'd imagined would be so simple to effect had proved a monumental conundrum.

None of the blonde vivacious debutantes whom he'd thought would be just what Sir Frederick would find irresistible had managed to win from him a second glance. The carefully arranged "accidental" meetings in the rose garden, the strategic placements at dinner—all had come to naught.

And Edward had been ever on his guard to gauge what Sir Frederick might find alluring, studying the gentleman's reactions from behind potted palms and through the reflections in gilt-framed mirrors.

At first, Edward had been convinced that he was right on the money when Miss Playford had emerged as a likely contender during the treasure hunt.

But while there'd been lots of playful banter and giggling, there'd also been nothing more serious. In fact, Sir Frederick hadn't even danced a single dance with Miss Playford, despite Edward's careful maneuvering to place them together at every opportunity.

Not like he had with Mrs. Perry, whom Edward had quickly seen as an aspirant to his affections. The widow certainly knew how to command attention, her silvery laugh drawing eyes whenever she entered a room.

Except that the moment she was out of his orbit, Sir Frederick reverted to his usual self: impossible to read. More often than not, he was with his sister, which Edward thought proved Amelia was pretty clever. She obviously wanted to know exactly the kind of young lady Sir Frederick preferred, so she could push the right contender his way.

Except that nothing seemed to come of anything.

"Oh, Edward! Did I spill my drink on you? I'm so sorry?"

In the midst of his reverie, he turned to find Miss Playford smiling happily at him, her golden curls catching the candlelight. She really was a diamond of the first water, if Edward said so himself, and the fact that Sir Frederick didn't think she was wife material was quite astonishing.

"Oh, Edward! I did, didn't I? Otherwise you'd not look so downcast!" the young lady exclaimed, running her gaze the length and breadth of him which he found he really rather liked. Her genuine concern warmed something in his chest that he forced himself to ignore.

He had more important things to worry about.

His sister was depending upon him and Miss Playford had, from the beginning, been a potential solution. Though looking at her now, with her eyes sparkling with mischief and kindness, he felt an unexpected pang of guilt at seeing her merely as a means to an end.

"Do you think Sir Frederick dashing?" he asked abruptly.

She blinked in surprise, then answered with another of her happy smiles, "Oh, he's quite the most dashing gentleman I think I've ever met."

"And I'm sure he must think you the most charming and beautiful of all the debutantes here. Has he danced with you?"

Miss Playford blinked. "Really, Mr. Fairchild! What a question? He thinks I'm all those things, but he thinks I'm a child and should have stayed another year in the schoolroom. Yes, that's what he said!"

"Oh, good heavens, he said that?" Edward asked, and he must have looked so downcast that Miss Playford looked quite concerned.

"I say, I can't imagine why you are looking like that. What is it to you whether Sir Frederick admires me? I'm sure he admires a great many other young ladies in this room."

"Any blonde ones?' Edward asked quickly.

"Blonde ones? What an odd question. I daresay he admires plenty of blonde ones. And dark-haired young ladies, too."

"But I only want to know if you've noticed him admiring any blonde ladies."

"Well, there's Mrs. Perry. Does she count?" Miss Playford tapped him playfully on the arm with her fan. "What is going on here, Edward? Why are you asking all these questions? You almost look as if your life depends upon it."

"Well, not my life, but my sister's future." Edward sighed.

"Tell me more."

"I can't else everything will be exposed and the game will be up and my sister will have nothing and it'll all be my fault."

"Goodness! What will be your fault?"

"The fact that I made a wager about Sir Frederick walking down the aisle with a vivacious blonde before six weeks was up. And I bet my sister's inheritance upon it, I was so sure he was already about to get leg-shackled. There! I shouldn't have told you. The game is up. Truth is, I don't know what to do. Poor Amelia doesn't deserve this. And it's all my fault."

After a short silence, Edward realized Miss Playford was looking at him with great sympathy rather than the derision he'd expected. "Well, you obviously were only trying to help her."

"Yes, but her inheritance should have been sacrosanct. I don't know what I was thinking except that, yes, I wanted to double it for her. Now Sir Edward is going to eschew ladies—blonde or otherwise—beyond the next six weeks. Or at least, he's not going to marry any of them."

Edward was by now feeling so wretched, and was about to make his excuses when Miss Playford said, "What, exactly, was the wager? That he marry a vivacious blonde? Or that he just walk down the aisle with one within the next six weeks." She giggled suddenly. "Because if it's the latter, I'm sure he'd walk down the aisle with me if I asked him nicely. As long as he knew I wasn't about to leg-shackle him."

Chapter Thirty-Six

AMELIA WATCHED SIR Frederick disappear into the crowded saloon, his broad shoulders vanishing amid the press of silk-clad figures. The feeling of witnessing her last chance at love slip away settled in her chest like a physical ache.

Three days ago, she'd have scoffed at the idea that this was love. If her heart had been in any way stimulated at the sight of the gentleman in question, surely it was merely due to the challenge of achieving her goal.

Well, her several goals, for getting to the bottom of Pernilla's fate had assumed similar importance to seeing Sir Frederick allied to a young lady of the right stature and hair color who would secure Amelia's future. The schemes had seemed so sensible then, so necessary.

Until they hadn't.

Perhaps she hadn't realized the tender feelings she'd developed for Sir Frederick until she watched him now walk away from her, his every step across the polished floor echoing her mounting regret. The murmur of conversation and tinkling of crystal seemed to mock her folly.

She should have told Sir Frederick about her concerns regarding his sister. Henry had told her just five minutes earlier that he'd learned that Mr. Greene had ordered a postchaise and four from a posting inn in the next village.

So, Miss Caroline had succumbed.

And yet Amelia had chosen to keep that information from him. If the plan went wrong, she'd be guilty of ruining his sister's life, which would quite rightly fuel his ire far more than Amelia's knowledge that she'd ruined her own life through stupidity.

For, if Amelia hadn't gambled away her future in quite the overt way Edward had, she was as complicit in exploring underhand ways to lay claim to that future she'd thought she wanted above all others.

So, what now?

She had no inheritance to look forward to. And she had lost her chance at love—if she were foolish and vain enough to think she ever had it.

Blinking away the dampness that suddenly weighed down her lashes, she ran her gloved hands down the lustrous folds of her dress and gazed once more upon the throng.

Never more had she felt such an outsider. She did not belong in an environment like this. She was a country rustic at heart. Didn't she know that?

What a foolish young woman she was for having dreams above her station.

WITH A SENSE of disorientation, Sir Frederick circled the populated saloon. The scent of beeswax candles and ladies' perfume did nothing to clear his head.

Lord Pendleton waylaid him with talk on a matter Sir Frederick could barely take in—something about horse breeding or perhaps it was crop rotation—and then instantly forgot.

Miss Playford smiled at him as she passed, her golden curls bouncing with each step, before stopping to speak to young Edward Fairchild. Miss Fairchild's brother.

Amelia. The very thought of her name caused his chest to tighten.

The woman he loved had just frozen him out by revealing something so damning about her and her situation that he still couldn't quite comprehend. Her eyes, usually so warm and direct, had been unable to meet his, and that perhaps had hurt more than anything.

She had a secret. Well, didn't everyone? But clearly hers was dark, and she wanted to hold it close to her. She'd tried to deceive Sir Frederick.

That's what she'd inferred before she'd walked away.

And then Henry crossed his line of vision and without remembering quite why he needed him, he hailed the young man with a short command, which he knew sounded terse.

But he wasn't very happy about anything much this evening.

"Sir Frederick? I beg your pardon, but I'm in rather a hurry." The young man cast a furtive look about him and then at the door, before saying, "My apologies, Sir Frederick, but something rather urgent has come to pass that I must attend to."

Sir Frederick didn't feel very sympathetic towards anyone else's so-called emergency. His own was far more important.

"I need your help with a delicate matter—"

"A delicate matter?" Henry repeated, looking—Sir Frederick thought—remarkably alarmed.

"Yes. A woman." Sir Frederick scowled at the thought of her. Bold, brash Mrs. Perry who'd be waiting for him in the library tonight to tell him, no doubt, more of why Miss Fairchild was so patently unsuitable and what she, instead, could offer him.

"What woman?" Henry asked, shifting from foot to foot as if he was itching to get away.

Sir Henry lowered his voice. "The widow. She wants me to meet her and I fear she plans to entrap me." He hesitated. "I thought you might accompany me. You could ensure propriety was maintained. In fact, if you hid yourself, she could speak freely and then it would be proved what she was about. Would you do that for me?"

Sir Frederick had known Henry his whole life. The lad had always been too happy to accede to Sir Frederick's requests, so he was taken aback when Henry shook his head saying sorrowfully, "I must leave urgently, Sir Frederick. A… a message has just been handed to me and I'm afraid I'm required to attend a matter that really demands my attention immediately." Casting about with an air of desperation, young Henry's gaze suddenly alighted upon Edward who was in earnest conversion with Miss Playford, before he called him over.

"Fairchild! Perhaps you could assist Sir Frederick with a request that I am unable to fulfill," he said. "You're an amenable chap."

And then Henry was gone and Sir Frederick was in the rather embarrassing situation of having young Edward gaping up at him.

Except that before either Sir Frederick or Edward actually said anything, Miss Playford suddenly unleashed her delightfully candid smile and said, "Sir Frederick, I know this is frightfully bold of me but Edward has just been discussing a very great conundrum with me that I know could be so easily fixed with such very little trouble on your part but that would ensure the future of a very deserving young woman who is about to lose it through no fault of her own."

"Good Lord, Miss Playford! There's no need to spill everything!" young Fairchild protested before Sir Frederick had a chance to respond. Which was just as well, because the truth was that Sir Frederick was considerably taken aback by her pronouncement.

"What is this? I'm the answer to safeguarding a young woman's future? One she is about to lose? A little cryptic, don't you think?" He knew he sounded ill tempered. But the truth was, what was more important than the fact Mrs. Perry had set alarm bells ringing—compounded by Amelia's own cagey behavior—and that the widow planned to use all her wiles to entrap him?

If not tonight, then at some stage. Why, he was concerned enough that he might find her insinuated in his bed this evening, such was her tenacity.

And then Miss Fairchild really would have reason to have nothing more to do with him. She'd already tried to insert a wedge between them with her strange talk of having a gambling habit she'd not mentioned before.

That certainly did not make sense.

And now young Edward Fairchild and Miss Playford were speaking in riddles; and just looking at Edward with his eyes so like his sister's was painful because Sir Frederick had got a double dose of disappointment.

Was it really not going to work out with Miss Amelia Fairchild?

For whatever reason, there were obstacles of which he had a horrible inkling but which now appeared frighteningly insurmountable. Why else would she have greeted him with such reserve before revealing the extent of her wrongdoing?

And how did Sir Frederick feel? Confused? Conflicted? Yes, all of these things.

Now her brother was wanting something from him and he felt highly disinclined.

Frowning, Miss Playford sent him a more piercing look, then repeated, more slowly, as if Sir Frederick were an imbecile, "Edward very foolishly wagered his sister's inheritance upon something that you can easily fix."

"Really, Miss Playford—" Edward demurred, but she turned to him with a frown, asking, "And how else would you phrase it, Edward? Oh, I know you were only trying to help. I know you said you were so fond of your sister and were sure you'd be able to double her income by wagering it on a sure bet so that she could retire to the country in much greater comfort, but the truth is that you made a very foolish wager, thinking that Sir Frederick's sister was Sir Frederick's potential bride, and really dropping Miss Fairchild right in the middle of it."

"What?" Now she had Sir Frederick's full attention. "What was this wager? And what has Miss Fairchild to do with it all?"

"Go on, Edward, you tell him if you think I'm not telling it properly. It's time to come clean, as I've heard the expression." Miss Playford suddenly looked a little more combative.

Edward hung his head, shuffled his shoes, then, with a big sigh, looked up at Sir Frederick.

"Truth is, that I always thought my sister was more suited to high jinks than moldering in the country. That is, before she met that curmudgeon, Thomas Blackheath. And then he went and died, making himself a hero and a martyr in her eyes, so finally she persuaded me she'd turned recluse and her only path to happiness was a cottage in the country to which she'd retire when she gained control of her inheritance at the age of twenty-five which is in a few weeks. Well, not so long ago, I overheard you mention the word marriage while talking to a very lovely blonde young lady and, being a little in my cups, I accepted a wager when needled into it. As you can imagine, my sister was not happy—"

"You heard *me* speak of marriage? And what *was* this wager?" Sir Frederick asked, growing increasingly impatient. "So you say your sister had nothing to do with the wager? She didn't gamble away her own inheritance?"

"Amelia? Gamble?" Edward laughed. "My sister has a very dim view of wagers and gambling, which is why she was understandably furious when I told her what I'd done." With a sigh, he went on, "Having heard you mention the word marriage while speaking to an attractive young blonde, the wager was dependent upon you walking a vivacious young blonde down the aisle within six weeks. I stood to double my sister's inheritance, and it seemed a sure thing at the time."

"Except that what you observed was Sir Frederick talking to his sister," Miss Playford interjected, "and no doubt the word 'marriage' you heard was not said meaning at all what you thought he meant."

"Indeed, not!" Sir Frederick said with some ire. "Good lord, lad, what were you thinking? And what right had you to do that to your sister?"

"I was trying to help her," Edward defended himself, his face flaming. "And quite rightly, she was incensed. And then, when we were invited here, we thought that if we could encourage your acquaintance with some suitably blonde and vivacious contenders, that I would, in fact, win my wager, and all would be well."

Sir Frederick suspected he looked as thunderous as he felt. "You…and Miss Fairchild…tried to ally me with—" He stopped, his mind suddenly going over all the blonde and vivacious young ladies who had crossed his path these past few days.

His gaze rested on Miss Playford, and she glanced away before looking up, embarrassed. "I had no idea about this wager when we went on the treasure hunt, Sir Frederick. I certainly wasn't trying to help Edward win his wager." She hesitated. "But I *can* help him—and so you can—without anything more than simply *walking* together down the aisle of a church. You see, the wager was written into White's Betting book by two young men in their cups who apparently used language that didn't at all stipulate that a wedding had to have occurred. A simple wander with some witnesses should ensure that Edward wins his wager, and his sister can in fact substantially increase her inheritance so she can enjoy much greater comfort when she retires to the country in a few weeks' time."

Chapter Thirty-Seven

AROUND HER, DOZENS of beautifully garbed women of all ages seemed to talk and laugh with ease, their fashionable clothes making the room appear like a mass of butterflies to Amelia's eyes. She wished she could be like them. She wished she belonged, but Mrs. Perry's spiteful letter just reminded Amelia that she had never belonged in places like this.

"Miss Fairchild, you look particularly charming this evening."

Amelia glanced up to see Lady Townsend bearing down on her, a gleam in her eye. "And I see you were just talking to Sir Frederick. What a charming gentleman he is."

Amelia had no answer. Lady Townsend had always had a strange preoccupation with Sir Frederick. And Amelia had once felt a thrill whenever the lady had coupled the pair of them in a sentence.

Right now, though, her words evoked the opposite.

"Indeed," Amelia agreed, her answer sufficiently lackluster that Lady Townsend raised her eyebrows and was about to answer when a slight disturbance near the doorway caused them to glance in that direction.

"Why, it's Caroline," Lady Townsend murmured as the crowd parted and Caroline made her way through the room, hurrying in such an unladylike fashion that many turned in curiosity. She seemed oblivious, her gaze roaming the room as if she were looking for someone. When Amelia stepped in front of her, the young girl gasped, then asked, still looking about her, "Where's Henry? Oh, Miss Fairchild, the most terrible thing happened. Mr. Greene…"

"He hasn't hurt you, has he?" Amelia asked before she could stop herself, for Caroline appeared highly agitated.

"No! I mean—Please, I need to find Henry!"

Amelia's disquiet escalated. "Henry's not here, Caroline. He…he went after you!"

"Why?!"

Amelia swallowed, then lowered her voice so that the interested group of guests nearby who'd stopped talking would not hear. "He was afraid you'd do something…rash. He went to stop you."

"Stop her?"

Sir Frederick's deep tones cut into the conversation and, gasping, Caroline turned, her anxiety metamorphosing into near panic. She stepped back suddenly, almost stepping on Amelia's foot.

"Frederick! I… I didn't expect to see you here," she said as if she didn't know what else to say.

"I don't know where else I would be," her brother said drily. "Please tell me why you appear so discomposed and why you are so anxious to see Henry, who left rather abruptly about half an hour ago." He appeared to gather himself, taking a step closer to his sister after ascertaining that they were not under public scrutiny, and asking, "What are you not telling me, Caroline?"

Caroline's large blue eyes appeared to well with tears and Amelia took her hand to comfort her, murmuring, "Sir Frederick, this is not the place."

This seemed to calm him, but while he did not persist with his questioning, his eyes darkened and the furrow between his brows deepened.

And then a young male voice intruded, and Amelia stepped

back to let in the newcomer as Henry said with clear relief, "Caroline! Here you are! I can't tell you how relieved I am to see you! I thought—"

"Yes, I know what you thought, which is exactly what my brother thought," added Caroline, with a baleful look at Sir Frederick, before she rushed on, "Which isn't very flattering to me, is it? Do you truly think I would be so *foolish?*"

"Would someone tell me what is going on?" Sir Frederick asked, looking between Amelia, Henry, and his sister. "Or should I take you elsewhere for a severe talking-to, Caroline, because you clearly have taken leave of any notion of propriety—"

"No, Sir Frederick, you cannot speak to her like that!" Amelia interjected, indignation welling up in her breast. "It's because she has a good, sound head on her shoulders that no damage was done, I suspect. Isn't that right, Caroline?"

Caroline nodded, wiping her eyes with the back of her hand before taking a step closer to Amelia and Henry, away from her brother.

Henry put a comforting hand on her shoulder. "I was going to save you, Caro. I wouldn't have let him take you. Not while I had breath in my body."

Cognizance seemed to dawn for Sir Frederick. Finally. "Caro really was about to elope with Mr. Greene? This time the threat was real?" Again he looked between the three of the young people before him, then added, "And no one thought to tell me? Why, I'd have had the man horsewhipped out of town if I'd known—"

"Yes, and that's why we didn't tell you, Sir Frederick," began Henry before Amelia cut in, "Because if you had put up such opposition it would have been highly likely that Caroline would have jumped into the postchaise and four he had waiting by the park gates right now and in which Henry was about to stow away so he could aid Caro as soon as she came to her senses."

Sir Frederick blinked rapidly before his pride appeared to return. "If I had been told when I should have been told, Mr.

Greene would not be waiting by the park gates in a postchaise and four."

"And your sister would have just waited until the next opportunity to defy authority in the name of true love before she realized the extent of her greatest, un-doable mistake," said Amelia, not hiding her exasperation. "Isn't that right, Caroline?"

Looking like the child she so recently had been, Caroline nodded her head and her brother's mouth dropped open.

"That's why Amelia and I decided not to say anything to you," said Henry. "We weren't sure if Caro would be so foolish, but after I'd investigated and found that Greene had hired a getaway carriage from a nearby village, I had to make sure I was hidden away on it before Caro climbed in and was whisked away." His voice grew more tender as he went on, "But it sounds like Caro came to her senses in time."

Caroline sent a grateful look at him, then said, "But he's there now, expecting me," she said. "I told him I'd forgotten something I couldn't live without and then hurried back here. And now I don't know what to do." She took a trembling breath. "He's so very insistent and I did rather give him the impression that I'd sacrifice my life to be with him."

"What?" expostulated both men. "Why did you do that?"

"Because it put him in such great humor so that he let me leave." She took a trembling breath. "But now I don't know what to do, for I fear he'll never let me go."

Sir Frederick nodded slowly as he met his sister's frightened gaze. Then he said, "I think I know exactly how to ensure Mr. Greene leaves you alone. Henry?"

"Yes, sir?"

"I asked you earlier if you would assist me with a certain delicate matter in the library. Now that you no longer are on pressing business on account of my sister, I wonder if you would oblige me. I assure you that not only would those acting skills that were untested just now be put to good use, but both Caroline and I would be most grateful."

Chapter Thirty-Eight

"EUGENIA, AS SOMEONE whose ability to sniff out the nuances of delicate situations, I defer to you. Kindly tell me what skullduggery or scandals are afoot or about to be averted."

Eugenia, who'd remained rooted to the spot as she watched Sir Frederick Weston and young Henry Ashworth head towards the library, turned at Lord Thornton's urbane tones.

For a moment, she considered how truthful she could afford to be. A great deal hung in the balance, and the least of it was how much she could use this opportunity to impress Lord Thornton. Her whole life had centered on impressing Lord Thornton, but now she just said, "Please fetch me a lemonade while I order my thoughts and decide if—or how much—I can tell you all."

When he returned, his curiosity clearly piqued, he said, "Sir Frederick is out of charity with Miss Fairchild. That I could not help but notice. And with his sister. What have they done?"

"What have they done?" Eugenia repeated. "Must it always be concluded that the lady is to blame? Usually it is not, and in this case it certainly is not." She took a sip of her drink and frowned. "That disreputable rogue, Mr. Greene, is waiting to spirit Miss Caroline away, having thought she was ripe for abduction."

"And she has run in seeking help?" He hesitated, then said, "With all due respect, the young lady certainly did signal her interest in Mr. Greene. I thought, however, that the fact she does not come into her inheritance for three years—and that her brother would certainly not sanction a match, so offer no dowry—would have watered down Mr. Greene's interest."

"Mr. Greene is desperate. You've heard the rumors. The creditors are baying at his heels. He needs money fast and is wagering that if he were successful in eloping with Miss Caroline, then Sir Frederick would relent and release her inheritance earlier in order to make her life easier."

"And our lovely Miss Fairchild? Why, I grow more admiring of her by the day. I admired her intelligence but, dressed to compete with the other young ladies here, I see she is a beauty." Lord Thornton's eyes narrowed. "But Sir Frederick is not rushing to make her his bride, is he? The Persephone hangs dangerously in the balance."

Eugenia saw that his eyes were now twinkling. He really was charming with his salt and pepper side whiskers and his physique still trim and sprightly.

"Sir Frederick has other matters on his mind and was piqued that Miss Fairchild and Henry concocted a plan to rescue Caroline without telling him."

"That is awfully underhand, not to mention quite praiseworthy. As is the fact you know so much. So, Sir Frederick does not like it when he is not the most important man in the room?"

"I don't think it was that. He was worried about Caroline and possibly hurt she felt she couldn't confide in him."

"And so now the Greene threat has been neutralized?"

"Not at all. He's still waiting in the carriage by the gates, I believe. I daresay Sir Frederick will confront him." Eugenia nibbled at her lower lip. "Lord Thornton, there are several things I wish to say. The first is to apologize. I realize that I attributed to you a letter Miss Fairchild received—purportedly from Sir

Frederick telling her that her dowdiness and love of learning were not ladylike attributes he sought in a future wife. Or, if not directly from you, that you prevailed upon Mrs. Perry to write it. But I suspect, now, the letter came directly from Mrs. Perry. The widow has, I believe, set her sights on Sir Frederick."

The force of Lord Thornton's outburst was far greater than Eugenia had expected.

"You truly thought I would stoop to such depths? I would never impugn a lady, much less one of such virtues and kindness as Miss Fairchild. And I certainly would never do such a thing to win a wager. You truly thought I could be so underhand?"

Eugenia shook her head. "I didn't, really. But I was confused and out of sorts. And then there was the other troubling matter Miss Fairchild confided to me, which has been niggling at me ever since and which concerns Mr. Greene. You see, he does not pose a threat only to Miss Caroline."

Lord Thornton raised his eyebrows in enquiry.

"No, Mr. Greene is not here for the sole purpose of enjoying a week in the country and eloping with a future heiress."

"There's more?"

Eugenia nodded. Perhaps it was unwise to reveal everything. She always had been too free with her disclosures.

But while Lord Thornton was someone she'd always sought to impress, he also had a wise head on his shoulders. It was one of the reasons, among so many—not least being his dashing salt and pepper side whiskers—that she admired him.

Glancing about her to ensure they were not overheard, she whispered, "You've heard Miss Fairchild's claims that Lady Pernilla did not in fact die the night she supposedly fell to her death while attempting to elope with a lowly groom?"

Lord Thornton nodded.

"Apparently, Mr. Greene has proof that this is true. Not only that, but that Lady Pernilla had a family." Eugenia took a sustaining breath for Miss Fairchild's claims that there was more to Pernilla's story than Lady Pendleton would allow, had begun to sound increasingly credible. She looked Lord Thornton in the eye and said, "And Mr. Greene claims he is the last in that line. Meaning," she added, "that he is the rightful Sir Pendleton."

"And you clearly believe there is truth in that?"

Eugenia nodded.

"My dear Eugenia," said Lord Thornton, "I have just thought of something." He took her arm and began to lead her through the throng.

"Where are you taking me?" she asked.

"To the library," he said. "There is something there that I've just thought of that might have some bearing on all of this."

Chapter Thirty-Nine

WITH HENRY AT his heels, Sir Frederick strode purposefully towards the library. The events of the evening had left him in turmoil.

First there had been the shock of Miss Fairchild's cool manner towards him followed by her strange confession about gambling. Then there was Caroline's near-elopement.

And now he was forced to respond to this summons from Mrs. Perry. The widow's note, scented with that cloying lavender, burned in his pocket like a brand.

His leg ached, but he ignored it. He'd endured far worse pain in battle.

Oh, he'd not been hailed a hero like Amelia's former fiancé for the full extent of his involvement was more in the nature of diplomacy.

He'd hoped to talk to her of those dangerous, heady days.

Now he wondered what the future held with the women he loved. Everything seemed to have shifted on its axis.

But right now, with the backup he needed, he was suddenly full of resolve. And ire.

So Mrs. Perry had written that cruel letter denigrating his Amelia? The memory of Miss Fairchild's hurt expression when she'd confessed to "gambling away" her inheritance made his blood boil. He understood now. She'd been protecting her brother, taking the blame for Edward's foolish wager. Just as she'd protected Caroline by keeping the near-elopement secret.

He would make Mrs. Perry pay for her perfidy.

Just as Mr. Greene would pay for his schemes—both against Caroline and, if the rumors were true, against the entire Pendleton estate with his outrageous claims about being a direct descendant of Lady Pernilla.

Sir Frederick was not usually one for vengeance. He'd experienced the brutality of war and but knew that the diplomacy of negotiation was a far better antidote to conflict.

Nevertheless, he was on the warpath.

Mrs. Perry had conducted an act of war by trying to separate him from Amelia.

Mr. Greene had initiated an act of war by targeting his sister.

They deserved each other, and each would pay.

"Stay!" he commanded Henry, turning abruptly at the door so that the lad nearly bumped into him. The library's leather-and-paper scent wafted out as he adjusted his cravat. "I shall enter the usual way. But you… You need to take up position from the French doors leading into the garden. I believe they are unlocked on a balmy evening such as this. I need you to ensure that you hear, and witness, all that takes place between Mrs. Perry and myself."

It did not need putting into words what Mrs. Perry intended. Sir Frederick's very future depended upon ensuring that the scheming woman failed in the clear goal she had tonight.

Miss Fairchild's very future depended upon it too. And that was more important to safeguard than anything.

"Sir Frederick." The temptress's voice was a purr in the dimly lit library, and as his eyes adjusted to the gloom, he saw her rise from the depths of an armchair and take a step towards him. The candlelight caught the diamonds at her throat and the calculating gleam in her eyes. "I wasn't sure if you'd come."

"And what do you suppose that my answering your summons tonight signifies, Mrs. Perry?" He kept his voice cold, remembering Amelia's forthright gaze, so different from this woman's practiced seduction.

"Call me Catherine, please." Her voice was warm honey, but the desire burning in her eyes was terrifying in its naked ambition. She moved closer, her expensive French perfume threatening to overwhelm him. "What does your presence here signify to me? I hoped you'd ask that question, Sir Frederick. Because I want to tell you honestly what burns in my heart."

"I doubt honest is the word I would choose for anything about this encounter, madam." He took a deliberate step back, noting how her eyes narrowed at the rejection. "Just as I doubt the honesty of certain letters that have been circulating."

She froze for just a moment—a telling pause—before letting out a silvery laugh. "Letters? My dear Sir Frederick, I'm sure I don't know what you mean. I'm here only to save you from making a terrible mistake." She moved to the desk, trailing her fingers along its polished surface. "That bluestocking Miss Fairchild... surely you can see she's completely unsuitable? A woman who values dusty books over social graces, who can't even dress properly without borrowing from others..."

Sir Frederick clenched his jaw. Every word she spoke only confirmed his suspicions about the letter's author. But more than that, every criticism she leveled at Amelia only served to highlight what he truly valued in Miss Fairchild—her intelligence, her integrity, her complete lack of artifice.

"I find Miss Fairchild's qualities exactly to my taste," he said coldly. "Her love of learning shows a lively mind. Her concern for others reveals a generous heart. And her choice of dress reflects a sensible nature unconcerned with frivolous display."

Mrs. Perry's perfect features twisted into something ugly for just a moment before she smoothed them back into a practiced smile. "Oh, but my dear sir, you can't really mean to saddle yourself with such a... limited creature. When you could have someone who truly understands the pleasures life has to offer."

She moved closer, her intentions clear in every languid movement. Sir Frederick thought of Amelia's blush when he'd kissed her, the genuine passion that had flared between them, so different from this calculated seduction.

"Someone who knows how to please a man of the world," Mrs. Perry continued, her voice dropping to a whisper as she reached for his cravat. "Someone who won't bore you with improving lectures or expect you to spend your evenings discussing dusty philosophers…"

Sir Frederick caught her wrist before she could touch him, his grip firm but controlled. "Madam, you go too far."

A sound from the direction of the French doors made Mrs. Perry whirl around, her composure cracking. "Someone's there!"

"Indeed." Sir Frederick's voice was cold. "Just as someone was there to vet that malicious letter you wrote attempting to malign Miss Fairchild's character. Did you think I wouldn't recognize your hand? Your particular turn of phrase?"

Her face transformed, the mask of seduction falling away to reveal raw calculation. "That prim little bluestocking doesn't deserve you. And she has nothing to offer—no fortune, no connections worth mentioning. Why, I heard her brother gambled away what little she had…"

"How interesting that you should know that," came a new voice from the doorway. "When it was meant to be a private wager recorded only at White's."

Mr. Greene stood in the library entrance, his handsome features twisted in a sneer. "Really, Catherine, my dear, you're making a mess of things. Sir Frederick wasn't supposed to be here at all—you were meant to keep him occupied while I secured my own interests."

"Your interests?" Sir Frederick's voice was deadly quiet. "You mean my sister? Or perhaps your fraudulent claim to the Pendleton estate?"

Greene's face went pale, then reddened. "I dislike the charge of fraud, but I knew that's how it would be. It's why I thought an insurance policy to shore things up while my claim was proved would be in order. But yes, I have proof that Pernilla lived and bore children after her supposed death. And I am the last in the direct line. Once that's established, this estate and title will be mine, as they should have been all along!"

"So, that's why you needed my sister? To force my cooperation and keep you in funds while your claim was challenged in the courts?"

"It would have simplified matters," Greene admitted with a shrug that made Sir Frederick's blood boil. "A marriage to your sister would have given me leverage, made the transition smoother. But now…" He reached into his coat.

"I wouldn't," came Henry's voice from the French doors as he stepped into view, a pistol trained steadily on Greene. "Sir Frederick thought we might need this precaution. And I've heard every word about your scheme."

"As have we," said Lord Thornton, appearing in the main doorway with Lady Townsend and Miss Fairchild. "Most illuminating. Though I believe we have something that might interest you regarding Pernilla's true fate…"

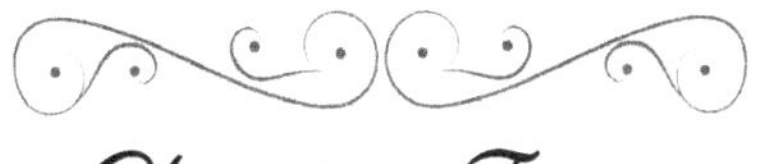

Chapter Forty

I T WAS IN the small hours of the morning, when the guests had departed to their beds for their final slumber before getting into their carriages and rumbling home in the last promised good weather before a spate of rain was predicted. The library held that peculiar hush that comes in the deepest part of the night, when even the ancient house's settling creaks had stilled. Moonlight spilled through the tall windows, catching the gilt lettering on countless spines, making them gleam like stars brought down to earth.

Two of the guests had already departed.

Prematurely and in disgrace, Amelia reflected, still smiling as she turned to Sir Frederick, her hand upon a book on the bookshelf. The events of the evening seemed almost dreamlike now—Mrs. Perry and Mr. Greene's hasty departure in the same post-chaise he'd intended for Caroline, their mortification complete when Lord Thornton had produced Pernilla's true diary. How fitting that the library itself had yielded up the final truth, proving both Greene's claims false and vindicating Pernilla's romance, even if it had ended in tragedy.

"What is there to smile about, my love?" Sir Frederick asked, and the endearment was so unexpected that Amelia's hand dislodged the book at hand, which went crashing to the floor.

The sound echoed in the quiet room like a gunshot.

Instantly, Sir Frederick was at her side, raising the volume to read the title, his eyes widening for a moment before he replaced it and snatched another, which he presented to her with a flourish.

Amelia's heart squeezed at the tenderness in his expression.

"*Pride and Prejudice* has a lot more to tell us about love and happiness than the Marquis de Sade," he said, his eyes twinkling. "And that is what I would gift to you had I the command of this library." He hesitated, took a step closer, and put his hands on her shoulders. Through the fine silk of her gown, his touch felt tender and precious. "And if we had our own library, we could fill it with all the wonderful books we chose. I'd consider that a worthy goal, would you not, Amelia, dearest?"

Amelia felt her heart swell and the breath catch in her throat as she waited for what was to come. All thoughts of retiring alone to the country seemed impossibly distant now, like a story she'd once read but no longer quite believed. Pliantly, and so full of love, she inched closer, her look inquiring. "A library?" she murmured. "I could think of nothing more I would like than a library."

She nearly repeated that it would be one they could fill with books together, but he had not yet said the magical words. The air between them felt charged with possibility, like the moment before lightning strikes.

"Now that Mrs. Perry and Mr. Greene have been equally condemned and have departed in their postchaise, and Lord Thornton has produced the Bible that records the birth and death of Pernilla's only child, thus disproving Greene's claims to the estate, I think it's now time for us to concentrate on all that is left to make our futures the happiest we can." His voice grew husky. "Henry and Caroline have shown they are so much more than the children I thought them. And your brother's wager..." He smiled. "Miss Playford's clever solution of walking down the church aisle with me on Sunday will satisfy the exact wording while preserving your independence."

Suddenly he was on bended knee, *Pride and Prejudice* clasped to his breast. The moonlight caught his face, showing a vulnerability she'd never seen before. "I've made so many mistakes, my darling, despite having the benefit of Miss Austen's good advice. But one learns from one's mistakes and I would hope that is only to the betterment of one's hopes and dreams and of achieving the greatest fulfillment. Amelia, my darling, clever one. I would be so deeply honored if you would be my wife."

Gently taking *Pride and Prejudice* from his hands and replacing it carefully on the bookshelf, Amelia dipped her face, so that she was but an inch from his. Her heart felt full enough to burst, yet somehow lighter than air.

"I will," she said, kissing him gently on the lips.

And as she registered his gentle sigh of relief, she felt that suddenly the world that had to date only opened up to her through books was about to take on an entirely wonderful new dimension. His arms came around her, drawing her closer as the kiss deepened. When they finally parted, his eyes held both tenderness and passion.

"My bluestocking bride," he murmured against her hair. "How fortunate that I learned to value substance over show, and real passion over mere pleasure."

"And I learned that not all charm masks insincerity," she replied softly.

From somewhere in the house, a clock chimed four. Morning would come soon enough, bringing with it the bustle of departures, the exchange of directions for correspondence, and all the delightful chaos of new beginnings. But for now, in the library's moonlit quiet, two people who had found their way to each other through misconceptions and mysteries, through pride and prejudice of their own, simply held each other close among the books that had helped bring them together.

THE END

About the Author

Beverley Oakley is an Australian author of more than 30 Regency romps, and Victorian and Georgian-set romances laced with mystery and intrigue.

Under her other pen names—Beverley Eikli and B.G. Nettelton—she writes Africa-set romantic suspense and Women's Fiction.

Born in the African mountain kingdom of Lesotho, Beverley married the handsome Norwegian bush pilot she met in Botswana's beautiful Okavango Delta while managing a safari lodge.

She began her writing career as a journalist, but it was during long aerial survey contracts around the world—typically as the sole woman among the crew—that she in effect launched her romance novels, finding in them an escape from the isolation.

Beverley also adores making historical costumes, knitting, and travelling, usually to Norway to visit her older daughter.

She lives just north of Melbourne with the same wonderful husband she whisked away from Botswana thirty years ago, together with their youngest daughter, and a gorgeous, dopey Rhodesian Ridgeback who weighs more than she does.

When she's not writing, she runs a bed & breakfast & Farm-stay business (called *Wuthering Heights*) in South Australia's beautiful wine growing Clare Valley with her two sisters.

You can visit her websites at:
www.beverleyoakley.com or www.beverleysbooks.com

You can also find her at:
facebook.com/AuthorBeverleyOakley
instagram.com/Beverley.Oakley
TikTok: @beverleyoakley